BROTHER and the DANCER

ABOUT THE JAMES D. HOUSTON AWARD

Known as a masterful writer in both fiction and nonfiction genres, James D. Houston was also a dedicated teacher and passionate promoter of emerging authors. Friends and family have established a fund to honor his memory and further his legacy. The James D. Houston Award supports publication of books by writers who reflect Jim's humane values, his thoughtful engagement with life, and his literary exploration of California, Hawai'i, and the West.

BROTHER
and the DANCER

———— a novel ——

KEENAN NORRIS

Heyday, Berkeley, California

© 2013 by Keenan Norris

Library of Congress Cataloging-in-Publication Data

Norris, Keenan.
Brother and the dancer : a novel / Keenan Norris.
pages cm
ISBN 978-1-59714-245-8 (pbk. : alk. paper) —
ISBN 978-1-59714-244-1 (hardcover : alk. paper) —
ISBN (invalid) 978-1-59714-254-0 (google e-book) —
ISBN 978-1-59714-253-3 (apple e-book) —
ISBN 978-1-59714-255-7 (amazon kindle e-book)
1. Brothers and sisters—Fiction.
2. African-Americans—Fiction.
3. College students—Fiction. I. Title.
PS3614.O7687B76 2013
813'.6—dc23
2013005026

Cover Design: Lorraine Rath
Interior Design/Typesetting: Joe Lops
Printing and Binding: Thomson-Shore, Dexter, MI

Orders, inquiries, and correspondence
should be addressed to:
Heyday
P.O. Box 9145, Berkeley, CA 94709
(510) 549-3564, Fax (510) 549-1889
www.heydaybooks.com

10 9 8 7 6 5 4 3 2 1

This book is dedicated to my mother and father,
Hiawatha Gwendolyn Norris and Calvin Preston Norris.
Love. Honor. Peace.

This dedication extends to both family lines,
those here still and all who have passed on.
From our families come my stories.

Contents

I

Creation Myth

———

Touissant remembered a better world. Christmas candles set upon shelves and mantels, the spirals of wax melting away the green and red decorations, the little gold of the chandeliers, all of it shining so lovely. The small, low-ceilinged house of narrow snaking halls, of little rooms and crowded tension. Golden and shaded luster, nostalgic light, magical in his memory.

He could see the light in the steam and smoke that filtered from the kitchen, smell it burning behind the door like an unattended ache. People's images misted over and their voices slowed and thickened with the hot old air. It was Christmas night, it was the family house, he was six years old and yet this beautiful world already seemed dark and distant to him.

"They did him dirty," his gramps proclaimed, remembering his own dad, who was Touissant's great-granddad, who had been dead the boy had no idea how long. "They did him dirty!"

"He was a criminal, how you expect he get done?" Granny's gummy voice rose up in tired opposition. Touissant had heard the story once for every Christmas in his life; how many times had she heard it? Hundreds, probably. She might even know its words by heart.

"They did him dirty jus due to he wadn't tryina fight in no World War they made like he hated his government, chased him across the South to put him on the chain gang. It didn't have nothin to do with no government, it had to do with he wadn't tryina die in Timbuktu. So one day he woke his woman up, said, 'Tain't happenin. This is one man won't take it lyin down. You keep still now, girl, get yo rest. Don't fret. I'm free 'n plannin to stay that way.' Then he left.

"He left his life in Lou'siana, which he couldn't keep no-way, then never looked back. If he had, all he'd 'a seen woulda been them dogs 'n federal agents on his tail. He tol me how he evaded them slave catchers, 'cause that's what they called 'em, slave catchers, by hookin on with travel crews, then have hisself the time 'a his fugitive life. Ain't matter, white, black or green, them crews courted his services 'cause too many they boys was gone overseas 'n not enough was comin back. So he'd get a train ticket for work in the next county, freight over there wit whatever work-crew, then sell the ticket for somethin 'n get a new one so's to keep hustlin. Always snuck away first chance he got, them chasers on his tail. Seen the whole entire South that way. Womens e'rywhere, he tol me. So many husbands, boyfriends, lovers gone, they womens was lonely onto restlessness.

"So one night he was stopped in Jackson, had got down to business with this *beau-ti-ful* Coke bottle bird, 'n right while he's obligin her, his ears commences hearin this rustle-noise outside the house. Gets to thinkin it's them dogs 'n federal agents. He untangles from her, jumps out the bed, jumps out the window two-three stories down, 'n what do you know, on the backside 'a that broad's house she been tendin her a graveyard! Her old man must had been a coffin-maker 'cause there's all these empty coffins just a-sittin out brand new, all 'n whatnot. So he scared as hell, you gotta understand. He jumps hisself down in one 'a them there coffins, closes the lid, 'cause, what'd he always tell me, 'Ain't no Freeman dyin in no *Si-beria,* or wherever it was they fought that mother.'

"So he waits out the night, falls asleep in that coffin, 'n when he wake up all's there is, is darkness. But he knowin it's gots to be light outside. Then he remembers the girl. He wonders what it is she do with the coffins. He tries to open the thing, but he cain't. It won't open near as easy as it closed. So he starts to flustration. It's bad times now. He feels hisself gettin borne up 'n there's voices, old tired patty-rolled voices talkin, hollerin, 'n after a while they commences to singin them ol' field songs. He thinks, *they done took me back to slave times, oh Death.* But then he gets a-hold 'a his composure, realizes that he bein borne along by the chain gang. He can hear they chains a-rattlin, he can hear they voices a-singin, 'n he can feel where it is he headed. So he musters all his strength, 'n he wadn't no small man now, 'n straight pushes that coffin-top clean off. Breaks it off like it were a feather or somethin. Now he in the open air 'n the mens jus lookin at him like he Christ returned. Don't nobody touch him, not even the authorities. He jus walk off nice as you please. He come back next day, finds the girl whose daddy had him such a lucrative business, 'n he tells her how he done lived through death. She laughs at his story, tells him the *real news:* e'rybody who had managed not to die had lived through the end-time, the Great War was over, it was safe to come out into the light again. So then he proposed to her, fell to his knees."

"And then he divorced her. Moved on some more, to Alabama, where he finally married your great granny, settled hisself down. Crazy nigger," Granny said.

"Language."

Granny sniffed, then started back in: "Your gramps a natural storyteller, he know what to put in, what not to. But me, I done forgot my manners."

"How did you forget your manners, Granny?" Kia asked.

"Got old. Got smart," Granny said.

"Isn't Gramps older than you?" Dea wondered, in her delicate voice.

"Yes and no," Granny said, "Yes and no."

"Why yes?" Kia asked. She twisted her beatific face into an expression of sheer beatific puzzlement.

"Because he was born in '27 whereas I's born in '32," Granny answered with thinning patience.

"Why no?" the twins asked in one voice.

"Because he ain't made use of the head-start God given him." She closed her eyes halfway and leaned back in her chair: "Don't try to reason it out." Her half-closed eyes were big and warm and sad, and golden-brown in the kitchen half-light. The skin around those eyes was wrinkled, worn slack, like God had patched her face of crumpled brown-paper bags. The twins counted the decades and the years on their hands and both came to the silent conclusion that their granny shouldn't look so old at fifty-seven.

Touissant had already sneaked out of the living room. He was such a quiet, to-himself child that he could come and go and people would rarely notice his presence or absence. They only became aware when they wanted him for something. Since he was six years old they only wanted him around to give him gifts and since poor people could only give each other so many gifts their awareness of him fluctuated with their income. He drifted in and out of the lives of his grandparents and aunts and uncles, and even his sisters, without much notice: they hardly knew him, not that there was much to know just yet, and he hardly knew them. He thought of these people like fogged and sporadically illumined ghosts of an intense dazzling dream: they spoke fast and elaborate, retelling tales too old for him to comprehend; they sang and danced and showed-out; and they gave him what they had, their money, their food, their love. He loved them back in the uncritical way that people love when they are young and the world is given to them, before they grow up and look backward and measure their memories against their scars.

So he didn't see the wrinkles around his granny's eyes, he didn't hear the weariness in her voice. Instead, he explored the house. Its construction was that of a slithering country snake, its head wide and densely packed, its body a slim, tortuous tunnel of fine skin, small pores and cuticles open and closed, locked and unlocked: these doors led into rooms that were the site of his exploration. Some rooms were too uninviting even for his curious mind. A makeshift tool shed that he was afraid to enter for fear that he would bump into something and his gramps's vast store of tools and supplies would come raining down on his forehead—aside from the physical pain, how would he explain it when they heard the crash and came running? There was a room across the way from the tool shed that was equally ominous, though he chanced entrance here. The room had no lights so far as he could see and he had to stumble around inside it to find its treasures. Old dismantled rifles, a baseball bat with an incomprehensible signature scrawled across it, black mote-crusted books that looked too ugly to open; magazines with sleek naked women splayed along their worn-thin pages. Then, the grandparents' room: a low bed and bedstand; a picture above the bedstand of them looking fine on their wedding day; a stained and tattered Bible opened to its first page where birth and death dates of Freemans familiar and unfamiliar to his eyes were scrawled in confusing combinations, and relations that may have made good common sense a long, long time ago now seemed as disordered as a dream to his young eyes. He looked until he found his father's family line and name.

Sabine married R.W. Freeman 1833—New Orleans
Bore R.L. 1833
R.L. married Landine 1853—Slidell
Bore Diamond 1853 Crystal 1855 Quannis 1857 Alfonse 1858
   Toussaint 1859
Immacula 1861
Quannis married Melva 1880—Slidell
Bore Hill 1879
Hill married Estrella 1917—New Orleans married Fern 1918—
   Jackson
married Celie 1919 —Tuscaloosa
Bore L.A. 1917

L.A. married Ruth 1941—Tuscaloosa
Bore Hilda 1946 LaLa 1948 Ferna 1950 Celia 1951 Bobby A.
  1954

He knew something was not quite right about the dates, numbers, names and places. Something was mixed up, wrong, but he didn't know quite what. He felt that the dates, numbers and names were the vestiges of some older truth he would never be able to touch, never be able to know.

Placing the book back where he'd found it, he went exploring further. There were rooms and more rooms stretching off seemingly without end. He wondered if the house was really built invisibly up into the sky or down beneath the earth because looking at it from the outside it seemed so small and limited to him; he didn't know how except by magic what seemed so little on the outside could be so vast on the inside. And behind all the rooms, back at the very end of the snaking house, there stood a screen door and then the yard. In the nights, the backyard looked haunted, the leaves of its trees over-wrapping it, branches splaying out like arms and hands arranged all crazy, grass grown high and too wild to tame. There were animals living in that wild garden whose night sounds he could hear, sounds like songs, a singing that broke out of the darkness, a strange night music. His senses were overwhelmed with it. He reached up and began to unlatch the door. Unoiled, the knob gave out a metallic creak as he turned it. Then he heard his mother calling for him: "Touissant. Touissant! *Touissant!*"

Her voice was an unwanted sunshine blinding him from premonition.

Later, in the dark, he could hear Dea and Kia's riffing, one voice dancing light along the heavy, fragrant air. It was never hard to get away from them when they were concentrated on their singing:

neither cared to look after him to begin with and they came up with every excuse they could think of to escape that chore. He was still too young to appreciate them, too young to see them as sisters and not restrictive roads forcing him back to his mother and the table and dinnertime.

He expected to hear his mother's voice sheer across the darkness any time now, but it never came, and the night stretched on. He could hear a new record playing and the sounds of voices and feet moving in time. Apparently, they'd forgotten him this time and his solitude would be his to own. He tucked himself away in the unlit unadorned room with the open Bible with the names and dates in it. He lay on the sheets of his grandparents' old, creak-ridden bed and tuned the small portable radio that sat near the nightstand.

There were men talking about Jesus on the first station he found. Jesus had not been a wealthy man. He had not prized wealth. Jesus, who was God's Son, was without wealth. The conversation circled around itself and he wondered if this was what people meant when they said that God's wonders were mysterious to men. But if he twisted the knob a little to the left he could hear mariachis singing. And if he twisted it to the right he could hear a brave new sound with singers who didn't even sing, just spoke over the beat as fast and clever as his gramps entertaining the table at dinnertime. He wondered again at the story that to him was the beginning of the world: his great-granddad running from the War, pursued by the government, loving and marrying women as he went, and finally beginning a family in Alabama. Or was it Mississippi? And which woman had it been, Estrella or Fern or Celie, that gave him his son? Where had he gone to, this old man? The beginning of the family world was as mysterious as God, as mysterious as God's wonders.

Touissant fell asleep and only woke when he felt his granny tapping her fingers against his stomach. Her hands were rough and reminded him of his mother's touch, so infrequent that he wasn't even sure if she meant to comfort or reprimand, the feeling was so mixed. He wanted her to explain to him what he should feel, but she was whispering to him in a register below hearing. He heard his gramps's loud voice from down the hall, not his words, only the voice itself, deep and loose. Now he felt her fingers squeeze him a little tighter and now he felt her climb into bed beside him.

"That old boy," she said, "that old boy. Think he got all the stories in the world, don't he now?"

Touissant didn't realize that that was a question and didn't answer.

"See, Two-saint," she went on, "we all got our stories, e'ry life got its story, but only some be yellin our business in the street, you see what I'm sayin? Yo' grandaddy, he gotta tell the world." Her fingers had stopped on his shoulder. "But it ain't who shout the loudest. That's why I like you, Two-saint. Not too many people be quiet like you."

She paused and he could hear a quick wind beat its reproachful Godhand upon the low roof. He grew aware of the outside world, the night-darkened valley.

"You gon' have yo' own, baby, if you keep that quietness and don't feel like you ain't got you somethin important just 'cause you ain't loud, carryin on." Over the low and sagging sound of her voice he could hear the twins riffing away again. He wondered if his mother, who reminded him so much of Granny, could sing; and if Granny herself could sing. "E'rybody got theirs," Granny said again. "E'rybody got stories. His old man was a nationalist runnin from his government; my daddy, on the other hand, he was good people, honest to the last degree, worked hisself to death out in them Alabama fields. I still remember his mule carryin him home . . ."

Erycha was six years old. Erycha was six years old and a girl. Erycha was six years old and a black girl. Erycha was a little six-year-old black girl. Erycha was a little six-year-old black girl living in a poor, cramped under-lit little apartment on the other side of town. Erycha was a little six-year-old black girl living in a poor, cramped under-lit little apartment on the other side of town with her unmarried and impoverished parents: her father, who drifted in and out of the apartment and in and out of her life; her mother, who enabled him in his transience and unreliability with her forgiveness and by paying the bills on time and on her own. Their daughter, being only six years old, took things as they came.

Erycha was a poor little six-year-old black girl living in a poor, cramped under-lit little apartment on the other side of town whose distracted mother would occasionally pay her surprising affection, would buy her a book about ballet or let go an hour in first-grade gossip, rubbing her feet. Erycha was a poor little six-year-old black girl living in a poor, cramped under-lit little apartment on the other side of town whose changeable father, though unreliable and often unemployed, never was away from home for more than a few hours at a time, never truly absent. Erycha was a poor little six-year-old black girl living in a poor, cramped under-lit little apartment on the other side of town who took advantage of her parents' distracted ways, escaping the cramped under-lit little apartment house by

walking out the apartment, down the stairwell, across the walk and
over the gates. Standing there, on the empty Avenue, she could see
where her Del Rosa Gardens apartment complex ended and the
empty street stretched on indefinitely. Erycha was a poor little six-
year-old black girl living in a poor, cramped under-lit little apartment on the other side of a beautiful new town called Highland.
And she was learning.

"Fresh food," her mother would say. "*Or-ganic.* What's so hard to
understand about that word?"

"Best I could do."

"O'viously. If you actually payin me attention an' still cain't buy *the
expensive ones that say organic on the label.*"

"Those the only two options. Either I'm stupid or I ain't payin
you mind, huh? I'm tryin to save you some money. That's the way I
think, practical. I'm not no boojie gentleman like you want me to be,
Evelyn. Jus a roughneck, I suppose."

"Really, now?"

"I'm jus sayin."

"I'm just askin, why not help me out, make some damn money so's
we don't gotta go buyin this low-grade unhealthy shit?"

"I been explained this: Messicans take e'ry damn job where they
ain't gotta show papers, which is e'rything but security, an' you know
my paperwork won't stand up to that background check."

"Mexicans mess up *your* papers? Mexicans the reason you gotta
mark 'yes' where they ask if you been to jail? I never had to trouble
over that question, Mexicans or no Mexicans."

Erycha would hear her father's heavy steps nearing the apartment
door, then the slow apprehensive opening of that door, and finally its
close and lock. Then her mother's voice would again scorch the air
with questions. It was always this way, a known protocol: even when
he was working and there were no issues around government assis-

tance or staying away when the welfare woman came, even when he was bringing checks home regularly, there'd still be a fight if he brought the wrong groceries, or did something else that could be judged unreliable. Erycha hated it but she was used to it, too, how her dad would come back home after however long away and walk slowly in, sit himself down with that pain in his slouch, and commence to look down darkness. And how her mom would come from her kitchen with suspicion in her voice.

"Takes you this long to get groceries?"

"Stepped out."

"Been steppin three hours now. Long time to shop. Short time to go to the casino with my paycheck money, though."

"Wudn't at the casino. I just don't like shoppin in the daytime is all. A man shouldn't go shoppin while it's light out, all them girls at the stores, makes him feel unemployed. But you wadn't even home three hours back so how you think you know how long I been gone?"

"Right, of course. I was at work. But Erycha said you left while it was still light out." She nodded at the child.

"Babygirl." Her father shook his head. "Dime-dropper."

"Don't bother her. She playin."

"Solidarity, babygirl. We locked down together."

"You think you're funny."

"I'm truthful."

"Truthfully broke."

"Warden."

"Con-vict."

Erycha remembered her father actually had been a convict at least one time in his life so she knew the joke was a joke with cutting power. The way his story went, he hadn't infringed on the law in a felonious manner, he just lost control a little bit and ended up with his car in somebody else's front lawn, a small Cupid statue severed at the loins. Early '80s East Oakland was apparently so insane and calamitous with drugs and gunfire that drunk joyriding and minor vandalism wasn't worth much police attention, let alone jail time. But when he was unable to pay his fine he ended up in the county pen. As this was not the first time that they had looked up and found him in County, his loved ones used up all his phone time counseling him bout how he needed to find a higher purpose in life. Religion. Or something like that.

He said that this time he spent his first free Sunday at Allen Temple Baptist Church trying to find that higher purpose. But instead he found the mechanics of praise and worship boring as the Good Book itself. All the gospel music in the world couldn't hold a candle to a good Ant Banks record burning up a club past midnight, the most animated preacher's sermon had nothing on the three in the a.m. testament of a girl moaning something that sounded like his name. The only worthwhile thing about church, he decided, was that there were so many fine young ladies there. Of course he knew these were morning, not night, women, but he found them irresistible nonetheless. So he spent each Sunday morning getting dressed as sharp as possible and showed up on the church steps just as the worshippers were filing out. He would pad at his face with his fingertips, whistle loud like the spirit was just too down deep inside him and would generally pretend that he, too, had come from the House of God weary with worshipping. Then, he said, he would go about meeting the righteous sisters with the blessed backsides. Maybe at eighteen, and impressionable, Erycha's mother had been too naive to realize that he had worn more orange jumpsuits than church clothes. But seven years had smartened her.

"*Con–vict* . . . You know what, Morris? I love you. I love you, I love Erycha, 'n that right there's my problem. That's my one sole problem in this whole world. If I could just escape that, go off, do my own thing, be my own person, not have to worry bout, bout, all this. Just escape."

"That food's still fresh, warden."

"I, I know, I know it is."

Erycha knew this dance, knew its rhythms. She'd studied its intricacies of condemnation, forgiveness and eventual seduction and she knew its every last step. So even though she'd yet to learn the difference between a relevé and a Chevrolet, she could already sense the music and move out of her parents' way, out the door, down the stairwell, across the walk. Up over the apartment gate, past the corner boys who posted like sentinels or statues along Del Rosa Avenue, across that street and into the scrub forest that lay in the narrow little gully there. Maybe after years of education and refinement, professors and critics would praise her for the naturalness of this art. But she was only six years old and for now the world was blind to her talents. Her parents had closed a door between them and her. The statues and sentinels remained blind, too. Only the small scrub forest hidden from the street seemed to know that she even existed, but it welcomed her as its child. Maybe because the forest was as unseen as she was, it became her private comfort, a shaded grove for imaginative play where the figures indifferent and dangerous that composed her usual life became dream-things. Where rude corner boys became goblins and her parents the comic jesters of the court, and she, of course, the queen.

Who knows. But Erycha conducted this shadow symphony from one thicket of scrub to the next. Piles of vegetation that to outside eyes would look like dead heaps turned into something more once she knelt down and gazed into their intricate work of dry brown branches and leaves. Then she saw the unique tangles and secrets in each. The most secret of all was the thicket where she found the white pagoda and its bullfrog: here, shadowed by a mound of abandoned construction work, piles of gravel, broken boards and such, she had chanced upon the pagoda. Gazing at it, looking it over absorbed her completely. Now she didn't even need to use her imagination: the pagoda was about a foot high. Its white paint had begun to chip away in flecks, exposing the grayed wood from which it had been sculpted. She had seen pagodas before, in pictures in books, and always admired their spiraling design, the dragon twisted around the twisting tree, and the open house completing it. The only difference was that this one was painted white instead of black, and a bullfrog lived within its open house. Sometimes it would shade itself inside during the days and she would see it then. Other times she would have to stay awake till long after her parents and everyone else in Del Rosa Gardens, even the corner boys, had gone to bed, and then she would listen as its weird croak filled the silence. The sound mushroomed out and out, a gentle explosion. She imagined the way its head and gills had to fill up with air to make that sound. In the days when she found it stooping in the open house she would run her fingers carefully across its notched dry skin trying to learn its secrets.

The bullfrog never liked her touching him, though, and he'd bluster if she kept at it too long; then his body would expand, his eyes would get big and bright like she imagined them in the dark. But the croak never came except at night and from far away.

One night, he didn't come home for a long, long time.

Her mother cooked dinner. They ate and waited. They took showers. Talked to Miss Simms on the telephone. Knelt and prayed for his eternal soul and ephemeral body, for their own souls and bodies, and waited for him.

About the time Erycha was used to hearing the bullfrog croak, instead she heard a different sound waking her from what had only been a light sleep. It was her mother. "Uphold Momma in somethin, OK, sweetie?" the sweetness-tinged voice asked from across the couch. "OK, Erycha?"

Her mother was a thin woman but her face was girlish with baby-fat and tenderness sometimes. But looking at her across the space of couch where they'd fallen asleep, it was like God had painted her in blacks and blues: her looks had hardened and chilled with the night.

Erycha wasn't sure what it meant to uphold a person in something and she didn't want to ask. It was best not to ask about adults, just do as they said. She didn't even ask what needed upholding. She followed her mother into the bedroom—the apartment's only true bedroom, her own being an improvisation consisting of a makeshift curtain, some bedsheets, two pillows and an inflatable mattress— and let her eyes do the asking.

In the dark room she could make out a pile of her father's things. They sat out like so much unbagged trash. Socks and shoes, two pairs of jeans, several pair of slacks, shirts and vests and thin coats; hats, a beret, a fluffy white Kangol, an open jar of Sulfur 8, a necklace and silver-colored promise ring. His car and girl magazines, his few, age-damaged albums. His manly supplies: cases of beer, a bottle of cologne. And maybe even his smell, she imagined.

His things lay heaped. It was strange that a man as big and impressive-looking as her daddy could get reduced so fast, to so little.

"Let's gather this mess." Her mother nodded at her. "As much things as he's put me through."

Erycha took a load of his things in her arms. She tucked the awkward objects in the crook of her arm like a great big football and tottered out to the center room.

She heard her mother's voice behind her, over her shoulder. Keep it movin, girl. Keep movin. She noticed that the front door was open. The winter wind escaped inside, its quick jets stinging her skin. Her nostrils filled with the smell of freshly frozen air. She shuffled across the apartment and out onto the porch, where she waited for her mother again. She saw the boxes rowed one after the next leading down the steps and the miscellany of objects contained in them: now she caught on and understood what would come next. She didn't want to put him out, not like this. She just stayed there, staring at each different-marked box.

"As much things as he's put me through. Since the beginning, I had his back, Lord knows why. Cut my roots for this nigga. Didn't judge him. Didn't play him short. Not once. Not even when I's eighteen an' stupid an' I's cuttin from my roots, leavin home for a nigga in prison." Her mother stopped and glanced fast at Erycha, like she was trying to judge something about her girl. Erycha was so confused now, she was half-ready for the world to end. She didn't know why her mother was looking at her like this, or why she was putting her man out, or why winter was the beautiful season where she lived. Everything from plain little words to the turning earth was a mystery.

They started down the stairs, packing first the Salvation Army box, then the Goodwill box, then another Salvation Army box. They had scavenged so many clothes and things from Goodwill and the Salvation Army that now they had plenty of moving boxes, enough boxes to travel across the country and back.

As she went back up the stairs, Erycha heard a faint rustling just above her head, like the flutter of birds. But it was nighttime and no birds were out, only the moon and the stars. The sky and the street below and everything seemed wrapped in the same silence and emptiness, and she remembered again that she should have heard the bullfrog by now. She wondered when he would come back.

Re-entering the apartment, she asked, "Why idn't he back yet?"

Her mother bobbed her braided head as she bent down to gather up the last of his things. "It's what he gets for leavin the civilized labor force," which didn't answer the question.

"But why cain't he come back?" Erycha wanted to know.

"Ask him."

How could she ask him if he wasn't home? How could she ever ask him if he never came home? Erycha wanted to know. But she could tell by her mother's hardening face that she probably shouldn't ask. It was such a tired, frustrated face. Erycha watched the face and the woman with it struggle out through the open door and down the stair-steps one careful one at a time and decided against any and all questions. She figured her father couldn't stay away forever. He'd get hungry or cold eventually, just like the bullfrog would eventually return to the pagoda: as many times as he had left, he had come back home. She looked up into her mother's eyes as she returned through the open door and closed it behind her, pushing back the frozen night.

By the time he returned, the bullfrog was croaking again. Erycha was listening for the occasional croaks and she almost didn't hear her father's small, resigned knock-knock noise on the apartment door. Then she heard it only faintly. But as she listened closer, she heard her mother rolling over in bed. How she made that old contraption creak and wail in ways that no inflatable air mattress ever could. She listened to her father's retreating steps down the staircase and onto the cement walkway, where in the silence he fumbled clumsily through the cardboard boxes. But she didn't hear him leave. She didn't hear his brogans go down that walkway any further. The sound of his shoes told her where he stood and where he walked, and for now they made no sound and no stand at all, as if he had simply stopped.

She heard the bullfrog croaking.

She reached her head over the bedsheets and looked around. It was safe to come back into the world, she decided. When she pulled out of the sheets, the mixture of silence and sound felt strange in her ears: it was easing her through sleep and calling her out into the world all at once.

Excitement thrilled through her as she slipped out of the bedroom that was not a bedroom and past her mother's closed door, out the apartment and down to where her father lay sleeping in amongst his scattered life. This was another new dance she'd made for herself, except now she had a partner to hold her in his arms.

Then, dawn. The boxes were looking down at them from the staircase when they came awake in each other's arms. She noticed that some had been turned on their sides, their contents spilled along the steps. But despite all that, her father started in thanking God and Stevie Wonder and Raphael Saadiq: he made it seem like a miracle that he got to wake up with his stuff all put out of doors just as long as no one had robbed or cut him and his daughter up. "Thank you," he mumbled. "Thank you. For not lettin these niggas do nothin. For not lettin none of these heartless-ass people take us out. Thank you."

Erycha had never been afraid of her neighbors or her neighborhood day or night. It was her neighborhood, her home, after all. So it surprised her to see her big strong dad getting all thankful for divine protection when all that had happened was that they went to sleep and woke up. What was there to be frightened of? she wondered. Scanning their quiet, familiar surroundings she didn't see anything new or exciting or scary. "Why you scared?" she asked, looking into his dancing eyes. "What's wrong?"

He shook his head real slow. "Because." She waited for more, but he didn't elaborate.

Because. It was the kind of answer Erycha heard all the time in her classes and on the playground. It didn't seem appropriate for any adult to be saying it and plain wrong for a dad-adult. Her teachers told her not to begin sentences with that word, and he told her to listen to her teachers, so why didn't he have to, too?

"Because what?" she challenged him.

He looked at her with surprise and hurt. "Babygirl," he said, his lips parting in the silence, his boyishly handsome face dropping as if suddenly loaded over with responsibility, "Babygirl."

She stared back at him in frustration.

"Don' turn into one 'a them type women. Please. For my sanity sake."

It was only morning, but she already noticed his mood darkening over like a lowering sky: she could see the future as he saw it, not one but two women berating him. Telling him when to come and when to be gone, when to speak and when to elaborate even though he felt like he had already said enough. She was coming into intuition like into a bad cloud: her dad would never really leave. She realized that. He was too scared of something out there in the world to leave, and he was not enough of whatever it was her mother wanted him to be to make peace at home. He would always be somewhere between staying and going. Her poor daddy. He was about to go back up those stair steps, pick up the boxes and return to whatever waited for him inside.

She felt him stir and then stand up, raising her off the ground with him. He held her there for a second, like a jewel, his and not his.

"OK, Erycha, I'ma drop you. We bout to go back up the stairs, K? Ladies first."

"K." She nodded. She seemed to have all the answers and he all the questions. "OK."

She squirmed in his grasp, a signal to let her go. But he didn't, not right away. She had the sense that he didn't want his hands empty. She squirmed some more, but he kept her tucked in his arms. After her, there would only be boxes for him to hold and at that point he might as well be empty-handed. She wondered if her mother was waiting on them right now and listened for her call. She thought of the pagoda and the bullfrog, wondered if he was still in his little chamber, waiting for her too. It was nice to think that people and things thought of her and waited for and wanted her. Many years later, after she had become a college student and left her mother's home for the last time, Erycha would buy a baby iguana that ate the rose petals from off the walls of her apartment building. The iguana would eventually grow to six feet in length counting its tail, and every day when she woke and left her room the iguana would see her and whack the thin wall with its thunderous tail, making the apartment shudder just a little. It was, she figured, its unique way of saying good morning and breaking the loneliness that was her life, just like the bullfrog of her girlhood had kept her company at night with its own reptilian kindness.

Orientation

B allet slippers might as well be glass slippers; matter-fact, might's well be glass ceilings, Erycha thought. The ballet slippers she could buy, but it was all the expenses that purchasing the slippers entailed that became the problem. The slippers were an investment, followed by one expense after the next, so much money down the rabbit hole that her dancing life had become. There was no way to justify spending all that money, but once those slippers were on her feet again Erycha knew how hard it would be not to take the next step. Her whole body went tense at the thought of those slippers, like a noose drawn tight. The boy sitting next to her in the bleachers must have felt it, too, because he flinched a little and gave her a quick, concerned glance.

Erycha looked back at him. Couldn't take her eyes off him now. She hadn't had but two hours of sleep and figured the Kool-Aid red veins around her pupils probably made her look crazy. She noticed how the boy was leaning away from her and into his mother as he frowned back in her direction. He even lowered his gaze. But she couldn't take her eyes off him.

Erycha didn't know what college would be like. Already she was having trouble concentrating on what the student speaker wearing a gray U.S. Army T-shirt was preaching from his pulpit of a podium at the basketball gym's center court. Her attention had run off and hid and no matter what the man said, he couldn't call it back.

Sitting next to her but leaning away and into his mom, Touissant Robert Freeman wasn't interested in ethnic diversity or a more perfect university culture or anything else that the student speaker had to say. The speaker was from the military, which meant that he probably knew a lot about the mercenaries and losers that populated college campuses. A speech along those lines, or to do with the coked-up Christian college kid who earlier that year went wilding like an act of God and burned down the neighborhood Buddhist temple, *now that* would make for an interesting speech. Touissant thought about the brand new mega church, its cement foundation snuffing out smoldering embers. The best stories never got told, or people long after the fact and far from the source mixed things up and got it all wrong.

He listened to the speaker firing off automatic rounds of platitudes, but his attention drifted to the girl sitting next to him: just a second prior she'd leaned into him out of carelessness or suggestion and he'd noticed the momentary friction of her skin on his. She was the color of chocolate and wood, her body small and light so that it only slightly moved him when she leaned in. Her eyes were fierce, charged with an intensity not of her environment. He didn't try to meet her gaze.

The second phase of orientation involved ushering the parents away with suggestions of fine dining in city restaurants and the refettering of the students based on their intended majors. Touissant kept his eye on the girl from the bleachers as she made her way out of the gym. He decided he would major in whatever she had decided to do with her life.

He followed the girl underneath a placard reading Dance. She had a long striding walk, elegant for such a short and shapely girl.

And she moved *slow* too, slow enough that he walked up too close behind her and ticked her foot, which caused her to lose her footing and tremble in her heels.

"Hey there, what's your name?" he asked opportunistically. He came shoulder-to-shoulder with her.

She cut her eyes his way. "Erycha Evans."

Erycha gave him her hand.

He was already looking at her, appraising her. She judged him and his appraising eyes right back, a full-on stare. Like so many boys, he had eyelashes that she would kill for; even once-a-week trips to Miss Simms's beauty parlor couldn't lengthen her lashes that long. Ironic, she thought, how pretty a boy could be. She thought about the beauty parlor back home, the sweet smells, the sour talk, the divas coming and going and prettying her up. She didn't have money enough to go there and get fine right now. She knew she was half as pretty as she could be, wondered why he was even interested.

"Where you from?" she asked.

He blinked at her like the question was unusual somehow even though it was the first question everyone asked where she was from. "Highland," he said after a second.

"You are?"

He nodded.

"Me too," she stuttered, "I'm from there, too."

She had never seen him before. He had never seen her.

"You are?"

"Yeah."

"Highland isn't big enough to hide people." He laughed. "I live over by where the Buddhist temple used to be."

She laughed. "I'm a lot closer to Central City Mission than that Buddhism place."

The mystery was solved. "Oh," they said in unison.

"You're from the Westside." He laughed.

"You from *East* Highland." She smiled, letting her teeth show
this time. "But it's all good: we still from the same city."

"The same suburb." He corrected her.

"Nah, where I'm at, it's city."

Like the city that had birthed and nurtured it, the university was
vast but uncrowded and serene, a hot and windless plain of scattered
trees and infrequent buildings and wandering students who came
and went in ones and twos. The campus's long deserted pathways
seemed to reach out into the sky or over the edge of the world they
ran so long and so deserted. The pathways ran into and out of the
school and because of the lack of trees and buildings the new students had a view onto the city that would soon be their home, a non-
descript industrial sprawl of shopping centers and apartment houses
and motels and tire and brake shops and supermercados. This wasn't
San Diego or San Francisco, Santa Cruz or Santa Barbara; there was
nothing picturesque or even vivid in these polluted skies. "When
the smog recedes in the evening, we have the loveliest sunsets," their
tour guide told them.

"On your left," he continued, "is the Science Library: it's newly
renovated with beautiful new carpeting, couches for study groups
and individual desks for individual students. We've installed a
temperature control panel. And to your right, you'll notice two
towering smokestacks in the sky. Those constitute the mathematics hall . . .

"Now here's our English Library. Constructed in 1964, it is the
oldest building on the campus, and what it lacks technologically it
makes up for in charm and dignity. Though the air conditioning is
only a feature of the first and third floors, the second and fourth
floors have been equipped with large electric fans . . . "

The tour lived and died like this, a long string of introductions to
various inanimate objects.

The sun shone overhead, a cruel brilliance of heat and light.

"We the only two," Erycha said, peering up at him to catch his expression. She still didn't know his name. "Did you notice that, we the only two?"

"The only two from Highland?"

"Yeah. And the only two *black* people from there or from anywhere else. At least we the only two with this major that I'm seein. You seen somethin different? Nahright. You see what I see. What you think about that?"

"I think it's not true." He pointed at one black boy here, one mixed girl there. "There's, like, several."

But in fact the black boy and mixed girl weren't even freshmen. The boy, Erycha remembered from the student speaker's opening address, was an editor for the school newspaper. And the girl was the chief coordinator for the ASU, Asian Student Union, and MSU, Minority Student Union (the BSU having been dissolved into this more embracing exclusivity).

Erycha explained these facts and watched him think it over for a second before nodding, conceding. "A'ight, now you know to trust me." She smiled. "So, what you think about that?"

"About us being the only two?" Touissant weighed his options, his fabrications: he didn't want to tell her that his choice of major was passing, false and solely contingent on her presence, but on the other hand telling the truth would require less thought. "I think you make up for the scarceness," he finally said.

Erycha narrowed her eyes into slits and shook her head: "You still gotta mack, huh?"

"I'm just saying."

"Well I'm just *askin*. Seriously."

The newspaper editor visited them where they sat on the stone bench along the spacious walkway beneath the sunlight and heat. He informed them that it was 2001 the Year of the Lord and yet in the state of California, at one of its premiere universities, he was still the only field Negro on the staff of the college's supposedly representative newspaper. His voice echoed down the empty walkway like down a funnel. And as he preached on, his red, black and green beads clinked like dice against his neck.

Touissant listened and thought what it would be like to write for or edit the school newspaper. His goals hovered vaguely round the possibilities of writing books, speeches, closing arguments. Writing for the paper would be a great way to find his literary voice. But for now he was a dance major. He shook his head, no.

The editor looked to Erycha, his beads rattling like a gambler's last chance. "What's your black gift, sister?"

"Ballet."

The mixed girl had hazel eyes and mocha-colored skin. Erycha looked at her and saw the earth rotating, fucking and birthing. The girl smiled and waved and approached. She was wearing a clingy, tie-dyed dress that sort of lilted right over her breasts in the attractive way that only a garment made with individual care could. Intricate lace-stitching, clearly hand-done, ran along its sides, fringing each moment of her form.

Erycha could tell that the girl wasn't going to leave her alone until she said whatever it was she had to say.

"Heyyy," Erycha drawled, not sure what to make of the girl but figuring it was probably best to speak first.

"Hi! Hi there!" The girl's voice was a chime struck by a champagne glass. Defiant of the slow summer day, she broke quickly into an introduction. "My name's Kai Jefferson. I coordinate the MSU, Minority Student Union. The Union motto, Teach, Educate, *Organiiiize."* Her

voice broke over the word. "Just so *exciiited*, sorry. It's my personal slogan, too: Teach, Educate, Organize. You probably already know that this is a majority-minority school and a majority-minority state, California, so we are an important institution on campus and in our many diverse communities. Although the minority population is increasing, our population as African-Americans on campus is shrinking. Dropout rates for African-American students are increasing, 35% now. GPAs and other academic indicators are trending distressingly. I'm one-eighth, Granddaddy is St. Lucian, or whatever you call it, so I know the intimidation, the real isolation of the black experience at the university. But that's where MSU comes in and saves academic lives."

"Coo'," Erycha said, cutting Kai off.

"Ballet?" Touissant asked.

"Yeaaah," Erycha sighed, "Yeaaah. What about you?"

"You're a ballerina," he said, evading the question. "Tell me more."

She didn't seem to notice his dodge. "Ballet," she began, then paused self-consciously, as if choosing her words more carefully than she knew she should. "I'm tryin. Tryina get on pointe, so it's all about the shoes right, the ballet shoes. Cain't be on pointe without 'em. But they cost."

"But you need them, so you'll get them."

"Hopefully you'll be correct. But they cost." She looked away at the sun or something. "And somebody went an' stole my old pair so it's not like I can just be payin for the same thing twice, na'mean?" Her fierce eyes came back to him. "What about your struggles, though, that's what I wanna hear about."

Right then, a white kid who Touissant recognized from the guided tour appeared in their view. His shadow fell across the stone bench and rippled along the heat waves above the concrete like risen black water. "What's up, you guys." He smiled.

"Hey."

"Heyyy."

"I hope I'm not interrupting something."

"Nah." Erycha shook her head. She tucked her arms in against herself and smiled up at him: "What's up?"

"Yeah. Um, I think they're about to get into the next thing, whatever it's gonna be. Anyway, you guys were way over here, and I didn't think you'd hear so . . ."

"Thanks." Touissant nodded. He tapped Erycha's knee and stood.

She stood slowly, unfurling herself in elegant little sections. She moves with real grace, he thought, like every dancer I know.

They started back toward the center of campus. The white kid was talking, making background vocals to Touissant's thoughts. The white kid said that he had noticed how the MSU girl and the guy with the red, black and green beads had both so rudely interrupted Touissant and Erycha's conversation and how people could really get on your nerves when they did shit like that. Terrible, truly. Especially agenda people, people with gender and racial agendas. As far as the white kid was concerned, there should be no unions or alliances or fraternities or sororities or group identities whatsoever. He was an individual, he said, and individuals didn't conform. All organizations and groups were formed by conformist minds, he told them, especially the organizations and groups founded on college campuses.

These were the kinds of things a white kid would say, Touissant thought. The kind of things whiteboys had been telling him for years. Probably why he had never had a white male friend. His mind wandered to the late lunch he was supposed to have with his parents and with his sisters, who attended USC and were in town only briefly. There was no getting around the commitment. He would either need to take his chances on running into Erycha later, or interrupt the whiteboy and invite her to lunch right then.

———

Erycha's hands opened and closed upon an imaginary razorblade. Her weapon was back at home, where she left it whenever she went to colleges and other safe places. Now she wished she hadn't taken Touissant's invitation. His family's refined voices scared her more than any thug: listening to his mother and father and twin sisters speak with all the smooth and intellectual grace of the world, she knew that she wasn't close to ready for college. It was too much of a leap, too much of a change. Her body didn't bend quite right when she danced, her words didn't sound sophisticated when she spoke.

"Do you like the campus?" the first sister asked.

"Yeah."

"Did you consider any private universities?" the second sister wanted to know.

Erycha noted the USC sweatshirts that both twins sported. Their enviable chests made each letter stand out as if embossed upon the fabric. They had both highlighted their hair Trojan red, which more than hinted at their preference in the private vs. public question. She had seen both these girls before, locally, though she couldn't fix a time and place to the twins. She figured they were dancers like herself, probably better dancers than herself. Maybe she had seen them dance, maybe wished she could hold a position the way they held themselves and wished she could move as they moved.

"I was always wantin to be here," she answered, neglecting to mention that Riverside was the only university that pledged to pay her way for four full years. "Ever since I was lil," she added. "Little."

"Where are you from?" The mother asked, light and sharp at the same time.

Erycha answered that she was from Highland and thought she noticed the woman's expression brighten a little.

"We live over by the new church. Where's your parents' house?" the lady asked.

"Round there," Erycha lied. "We live nearby," she said more properly. "East Highland's so small, right?"

The lady laughed and nodded.

Erycha stole a quick glance at Touissant. He looked stunned, or hurt, as if it mattered that she had lied to his momma. She knew that lying went contrary to every book of rules from the Bible to the Student Catalog handed out during orientation and was obviously wrong before God, but doubted that it mattered before Mrs. Freeman. Better to just tell the lady what she wanted to hear. That she had two caring parents, that her life was good and getting better.

She kept on lying to Mrs. Freeman and her husband all lunch long: yes, she'd always loved all forms of dance, especially ballet. She had never lost faith in her talent, had always been supported by her folks, had always made a way out of no-way, like black folk know how to do, she quipped. She played her black card in just the way she knew boojie black people like their black cards to be played, displaying it in order to describe her pride, determination and success, but never her poverty, anger or loneliness in a world full of black folk who never gave a damn about her unless she was braiding their hair or spreading her legs. She even loved writing about dance, she told the Freemans. She was so committed to it, she might get a PhD in the field one day.

Mr. and Mrs. Freeman seemed to like all this. The twin sisters smiled at Erycha with twin precious approving gazes. Touissant just seemed bewildered by everything he was hearing; his fork stayed in his mouth the whole meal.

Erycha started to realize just how good a liar she could be. So good she didn't have to think about the lies before she said them. All she had to do, in fact, was say anything that she wasn't actually thinking. Her true thoughts were a little too strange for public disclosure. All lunch long, she stayed thinking about Josephine Baker. Queen Josephine, the baddest lil black girl dead or alive. What would Josephine do if she were ever tricked into lunch with a bunch of boojie black folk? Would she figure a way to gloriously devastate the ceremony and expose the class struggle beneath the bed of lies being told? Would she manipulate the young man who was trying so hard for her? Or would she be the nice girl, smile, do right, say right, and save the real talk for another time? Josephine might do just about anything. After all, Erycha had read where the woman once walked her cheetah along the Champs-Elysées. A black girl controlling a big dangerous cat. Everybody staring her way. Erycha knew that it would take some doing before she could bend nature and folks to her will like *that*.

She kept on with the pretty lies about a different world.

When lunch was done, the twins went one way and the parents and Touissant another.

Erycha followed after the parents and Touissant, so as not to end up at an expensive private school. She got in the backseat next to Touissant. As the engine revved, she felt him lean into her the way she had leaned into him at orientation. "Were you lying to me or to them?" He whispered very quietly, almost too faint to hear.

Erycha was surprised by the question but took it in her stride. She was still impressed by just how easy it was to lie. She dug in her purse, found a pen and a large business card for a hair salon. The card had nothing written on the back.

to them

She handed over the card and looked at him, straight at his dishonest eyes.

He took the pen along with the card. *Why?*

they wanted the lie you wanted the lie

He looked into the blood spider explosions that were her eyes. *That makes no sense.*

yes it does

How?

you wouldnt understand.

Is your name even Erica?

erycha evans are you really a dancer?

Touissant knew she already knew the answer to that question. If she hadn't figured him out at orientation, she surely had at lunch, when his parents went on and on about his goals in the fields of political science and later law school and local and state government. None of what he had going for him had anything to do with dance. And he had planned to tell her the truth anyway, sometime before the dancing started. Really, Touissant just didn't understand why his not being a dancer would make her want to retaliate in kind. He had lied, but for a good cause. He was just trying to get closer to her.

No.

Erycha kept thinking about Josephine and her cat and that incredible walk she took. She imagined herself in that beautiful body. She was walking down that Paris street buck naked, the cheetah by her side. She had no leash for it, just her will. She was Josephine and Touissant and every other fronting, foolish brother she had ever known was the cheetah. She stopped and knelt and said something in French that made the cat stop, and she placed a diamond collar round its neck. All around her female-acting Frenchmen and their jealous wives watched her. She could hear each and every murmur. The Champs-Elysées was her campus and the people watching were an audience before which to perform. Everything in Erycha's dream was the opposite of the real world, where she sat in a far corner of the banquet hall next to a boy who had straight-up lied to her about himself and to whom she had been lying ever since just for the hell of it. Nobody was watching them. Nobody knew they were at the campus. Their only connection was the false one that they had created in their conversations that day. In the fantasy, she strolled slow and naked down the street, her walk a dance, her nakedness a basic beautiful truth. In the fantasy, she didn't have to worry about lies or class segregation or whether her grammar was completely proper. She spoke exquisite French in her dream.

The difference between dreams and lies dwindled as the night wore on. Touissant determined to go through the motions with the girl even though he knew she was doing the same thing, writing notes back and forth, talking to him when she had to, dancing with him when she got tired of sitting in her chair too long. But she was living in her thoughts, living in a silent conversation with her own desires, just as he was. He was even more centered on himself than she was. He was only thinking about himself now and about what would come next for him: in less than a week, he would be in New Orleans, at yet another college orientation. This one would be at Xavier University. He had family all over the South but mostly in New Orleans. He had ancestors buried there who had lived and died well before Emancipation. But he had yet to visit the town. He thought about the campus and all the black people that would be there. He thought about the cedar-skinned Creole girls and wondered if it would be easier or harder to talk to bayou sisters with heavy accents and different slang than with this person from his own hometown. He imagined that he would catch on to the New Orleans chat instantly, that some deep hidden part of him, combined of his Southern heritage and whatever else was working inside his soul, would vibe with the ways of the people down there. They would be familiar to him in a way that he wouldn't be able to understand or explain. He would just know them. That simple. It would be home out there, he thought, a return to an old home.

He wrote her one more note.

What if God told me to lie to you? What if He wanted me to meet you?

He didn't know where that line came from, if he had heard it somewhere before, in a church, on television, or the radio, or from the mouth of some kid trying to talk one of his sisters into a date. He didn't even know if Erycha went to church or even believed in God. He knew he didn't. But he passed her the note anyway.

you dont talk to god

Dance, Erycha had learned somewhere, was a story. That was why, though she had trouble admitting it aloud, she now intended to dance as little as possible and to think and to write about dance until she had filled volumes with a philosophy linking movement to culture and solitude. There were reasons for this decision that in sum was a story all by itself. It was a story she was living, though, and couldn't even talk about, let alone put down on paper. If it was a conversation, it would be one that nobody she was likely to spend time with could follow. If it was a movement, it would be something post-modern, probably some sort of desperate painful lunging on her back on the floor. She didn't see that going over well at the banquet. Instead, she tried something subtle.

She waited until the DJ exhausted a few dance and trance and hip-hop tracks. She thought how half the time the girls doing modern dance looked like old folks trying to do the gator on their backs. She thought about clubs in Los Angeles she had only heard tale of where the dancers could leave people motionless and in awe, their ideas on a dance floor were so good. When the first staccato beats of "If I Was Your Girlfriend" began and Prince began to speak and then sing, she got up from her chair and looked at Touissant. He stared back at her unmoved but interested enough not to take his eyes from her. It wasn't long before a slim girl in jeans and heels began dancing in her space. The girl danced close and wanted Erycha to come even closer. But Erycha was a solo act, despite the presence of a partner who flowed and shook and melted into her every time Prince came out of his pleading falsetto and dropped his voice into normal register.

Erycha was used to men dancing close and the girl was really no different. She was a shadow of movement, a likeness and a following all at once. She was willing to bend not only to the beat but to her partner, whereas Erycha, who led, told a story unshaped by the song and independent of her partner. Her body described the knife resting with its blade up right where she'd left it on the table in her small apartment. Her movement was not flow, but a strolling aggression that bent the girl in the jeans and heels this way then that and anticipated Prince's vocal changes so that she was ahead of time. She vogued her way into Prince's highest registers and sauntered her way out on the downbeat. She cut one dancer so quick and cold he didn't even know he'd been upstaged, his lame Chicago-step parodied and discarded, his partner distracted by a deep laceration that he had neither felt nor seen. Then the boy's partner stopped dancing with him and simply watched Erycha.

Erycha kept on dancing, first with the girl who had approached her, later with the girl who had left her partner. Erycha glanced at Touissant now and again. He was watching her.

In fact, he was captured by her glances. Her looks, even when they were brief, were demanding and fierce, but incredibly sad, too, like nothing he had seen before. In the parking lot after the proceedings had come to their close, she looked at him with eyes that said she wished not to be lied to, but knew that even her dreams were lies, that everything she had ever wanted was one way or another unreal. They both said goodbye and then she turned and walked away, strolling through the poorly lit lot. And he couldn't stop staring after her.

Vision Myth

————

The same instant his granny died in her Fresno hospital room, Touissant woke feverish and confused three hours to the South in his bedroom in his home in his suburb an hour east of Los Angeles.

He could hear his sisters downstairs. He listened until the sounds turned into words and made sense: they were leaving with Ms. Johnston and Ms. Johnston's daughter to go to day camp. The bedroom wall stopped swimming and solidified. He rose and suddenly the fever pain wrenched him deep down, and Touissant, who believed that he would live forever, felt starkly, completely alive.

His fever rose like the fires in the San Bernardino Mountains, a homicidal element flashing up against the living world. He felt two quick acid ropes scour his lungs. When he finally half-crawled his way down the stairs and his mother told him about the death in the family, he vomited on the living-room floor.

She looked at him with a blankness that Touissant had never seen in her eyes. "I got no minutes for this," she breathed. She put her hands on her hips and did something that made her throat sound like it was purging itself. Touissant knew that his getting sick was the last thing the family needed right now. He knew his mother was already counting out the cost of the trip to Fresno, gas money, the funeral fees, the inevitable breakfasts, lunches and dinners that she and her husband's degrees would somehow be expected to pay for. He understood why she was frustrated and didn't want to trouble her more. He wished he could chase the fever spiriting through him right out of his body. He watched her clean the mess, and saw how she glanced back at him furtively to judge whether he would vomit again.

"You need water," she said.

Touissant nodded.

"Water. Hot water. Vitamin C. An antibiotic."

In the kitchen, she rang out two vomit-soaked towels. Touissant turned and watched his dinner rice and clumps of congealed cinnamon and little undigested relics of vegetable and turkey fly wildly from the towels like water shaken from a dog. "Is that what's inside of me?" he asked, unbidden.

She stopped. The question caught her in full motion; a stopping question. Questions without answers were an inheritance down from his dad, but they annoyed his mother; the realities of a childhood spent picking fruit and cotton in the Central Valley were as simple and inarguable as the sun and had left her no minutes to ask why life was this way or that. "You sick, or just strange?" she asked. "You sit there." She pointed to a spot at the near edge of the living room couch. "Peace and be still there. Don't wiggle around. Don't move. Be still."

Touissant did as he was told. Not a sweet woman really, she was a healer, a leader, a mother. But look for your coddling and little self-esteem stuff elsewhere, his dad liked to say, look for it where you gonna find it. His dad's mother, the woman who had gone to her Lord before the sunrise, knew kindness and knew how to rear children with kindness. Touissant's mother was very different. He was starting to notice important differences between women. All his life, black women had seemed like so many sisters to each other, all of them as similar as his twin sisters were to each other, a universal feminine. He was starting to see past that now.

She heard him shifting around and ordered him to be still. "Your stomach idn't settled, idn't close to settled. You gotta let it settle. Sit back down."

Touissant obeyed and after a moment accepted his stillness. She was right, too: the longer he sat in place and the more fixed and motionless his body, from his toes to his intestines to his closed eyelids, the calmer was his stomach. He wasn't even aware that his eyes were closed until a drawer jarred open and the metal of knives and kitchen utensils sounded against each other. Then the door shut hard, wood blasted against wood. Then he knew his eyes were closed because he didn't know which kitchen drawer had been opened and closed, or who had opened and closed it. He tried to look around and saw only heat waves streaming without progress or recess, thick fluid fever lines where his sight should have been. Then there were shadows the color of faint ink blots that came and sat atop the waves. There were faint shadows where the kitchen table and the center island and the living room clock and the couch that he sat upon should have been. He wondered where his dad was.

"I'm tellin you the situation right now. My son, the fever, the unresponsiveness, the convulsions. I'm tryin my best to help my son. We're tryin our best. My husband's mother died this morning. He's not himself. He's not slept, hasn't had any water or food. We're tired. And now my son—." Touissant's eyes came open and he saw his mother's sculpture-hard face. He could hear her speaking fast and panicked. He saw her intent eyes, eyes harder than her face. Everything about her fixed on the problem that Touissant had become. "Goddamn. Is his chest rising and falling? *Yes!* He's convulsing. Why are you asking me that question? If his chest wasn't rising he'd be dead. He's obviously alive! Do I want an ambulance? What do you think? My son is writhing on the floor like an epileptic. My husband, a full grown man, cain't keep him still. Is anything coming from his mouth? Do you mean, is he expectorating? Foaming at the mouth? Lady, what kind of question is that? *No!*" She yelled at the woman on the other end of the line. "He is not foaming at the mouth! What kind of crazy question—my son does not have rabies. This is the situation: he's convulsing, his muscles are seizing, his eyes are open but he's not responding when we try to talk to him. He may or may not really be conscious and aware right now."

Touissant's heart turned into a kicking fetus. His chest was the heartchild's womb, demanding out with all the beating violence it could bring. His heart went faster and faster. "Shit," he heard himself say from some point distant from his uncontrollable body.

His dad's strong but soft-palmed hands gripped him and stilled his writhing. "You hear that, Lilly? You hear that?"

"What, Bobby?"

"He talked. He responded."

"He's talkin," she said into the phone. Then to her husband: "Rub his chest."

His dad pulled Touissant's shirt up and his soft palms went along his narrow chest, kneading his tensed torso and abdomen. Touissant's heart rate slowed, but sweat rafted down his skin in hot forceful currents.

"They say," his mother knelt next to father and son, "it's probably some sort of febrile seizure."

Touissant jerked out of their grasp and coughed up a chunk of phlegm and stomach waste that hit the carpet and did not move. Everyone gazed at the clear block of vomit.

"God-damn," his mother said. "Damn. Damn. Damn."

The voice on the other end of the phone blared incoherently.

"He coughed up somethin," his mother began. "He coughed up somethin clear as day and solid as a brick. We need an ambulance."

Touissant was still now. His seizure having subsided and the vomiting having emptied him, there was nothing left but to be still. His insides were hollow. He wanted the ambulance.

"You are telling me," his mother challenged in terse, measured words, "that there is no ambulance? Am I understanding you correctly? Then why did you ask me if we needed an ambulance just two minutes ago? What was the purpose of that question?" Her hands went into a brief seizure and she dropped the phone. The answer at the other end of the line resonated throughout the living room: the question about the ambulance had been procedural. Its purpose was to assess degree of urgency. That no ambulances, paramedics, or emergency responders of any kind were available did not preclude procedure. Procedure had to be followed to assess risk. When she picked the phone up again, Touissant's mother laced into the woman: "You tryina tell me ain't no ambulance, no paramedics, no emergency responders whatsoever? Because the state closed down the gotdamn fire station?" She dropped the phone again, this time purposely.

"Recession," the voice on the other end of the phone said.

Touissant didn't know what a recession was except that it seemed to shut down fire stations, lay off paramedics and ground ambulances. He wondered what recessions did to hospitals, doctors and nurses. In a city an hour east of a city that actually mattered, he figured the recession might kill a whole medical system.

For reasons having to do with their jobs and collective bargaining agreements and the economy, which he didn't understand, his parents could get medication and have their teeth fixed through Kaiser Hospital, but had to go to County Hospital in emergency situations. The family drove to the County Emergency Room, where a fat male nurse whose breathing Touissant could hear from up the hall placed him in a wheelchair, told his parents to bide their time in the waiting room and pushed Touissant a few feet before leaving him in the chaotic hospital hallway. He could hear his parents complaining just over his shoulder and knew that they hadn't followed the nurse's orders. Touissant watched the fat man wobble out of view. He remembered his granny all of a sudden. Not that she was dead, *that* he hadn't forgotten. What returned to him was the memory of a story she had told about his dad swallowing a coin. She was still a young woman then and his dad was just a child. He had been to a downtown fair and had brought home the bronze token he found in the dirt below a row of rickety bleachers. Somehow the token got into his throat.

She took him to the Cook County Hospital Emergency Room. (Had to hitch a ride with a neighborhood man because her husband was outside the city somewhere breaking in the new Thunderbird that would soon carry his restless ass and his whole family to California.) At the hospital, the assigned nurse left the boy and his mother in the first available hallway, much as Touissant had been left by the vividly unhealthy county hospital nurse. His granny told Touissant how that was the first and last time she had seen men chained to a wall and examined orally and rectally with flashlights. These were prisoners from Cook County Prison, trucked in after nightfall for their check-ups. It was the first and last time she saw a man stabbed through the neck yet still alive enough that he was explaining the basics of football and the Bears defense to a young, innocent-looking female nurse as she wheeled him down the hallway. She had seen many other things, of course, that were just as shocking, the Southern marigolds in bloom before springtime and black soldiers arriving back from the War with their backs straight and human rights on their lips, and union strikers in Chicago and Mexicans in Fresno beat near as low as any Mississippi Negro. And it was not the first time that she had seen newly dead corpses. But it was the first time her son had seen anything so frightening. Elderly folks expired in their wheelchairs, young men dead on their stretchers with body parts only half-hidden from view, their limbs still trembling slightly when a nurse or doctor would rush past. It was the first time he had seen dead men.

Touissant didn't like the idea of trembling corpses in Cook
County Hospital. He looked around the San Bernardino County
Emergency Room: Up and down the hallway where the nurse had
left him other white- and blue-coated nurses idled and walked and
sprinted back and forth between their respective responsibilities.
Now and then someone who he figured was a doctor by the stetho-
scope hanging from his pocket would maneuver through. Wheelchairs with flu-ridden kids and infirm adults crowded the hall,
making movement a difficult talent, part pushing, part cussing, and
many acts of agility. The wheelchairs, piloted by medical profession-
als, family and friends and by the patients themselves, spun this way
and that, dashed up and down, came and went. Two gurneys were
parked at the very end of the hall. Each was a mantelpiece outfitted
with a fallen flag: blankets covered what Touissant thought might
be dead people. He could see what looked like the outline of a long
nose, open lips and two bony knees underneath one of the white
hospital sheets. The second stretcher was a little more obvious: Touissant could see where the blanket sagged back into what looked like
a man's large round head. A faint patch of red was visible where the
blanket sagged. The dead man had a hole in his head.

He remembered how his granny's story had ended: the hospital hallway scared his dad so deeply, she said, he actually digested
the coin and cured his own self. By the time her husband and his
Thunderbird got to the hospital, the crisis had concluded. But when
Emmett Till was murdered not too long after and the body was
brought back North to Chicago and lain in state at the Southside
church for public viewings, he refused to go. Lines stretched for
blocks on end, black folks come to see the symbol of white man's
evil. But her boy thought the body had a ghost in it and might start
moving, like the bodies on the stretchers in the hospital when people
got too close.

Whether he had wanted to or not, his dad had seen something
important in Cook County Hospital, Touissant knew. What he

had seen was scary. It had made him hate death forever. But it was important as knowledge. And now the boy realized that he had seen and learned something, too: a few days from now, in Fresno, at the funeral, his granny's corpse, lain in her casket, would not be the first dead body his eyes would know. He had seen death already, a few days before he was supposed to, in a random way that had nothing to do with funerals or churches or family or love. He had seen two corpses and there was no going back from this. He imagined his granny's body, how the preparers would have the make-up imperfectly done on her face, one side smudged and darker than the other. A Sunday church hat with roses but no marigolds crowning her head, sprigs of her white hair falling like unmowed blades of grass from beneath the Sunday hat. And an old frayed familiar dress to lay her to rest in. It would be a different way of dying than this under-a-sheet, mouth-open, hole-in-the-head hospital stuff. Her skin would not be a discolored shade of green as he imagined was the fate of the corpses in the hallway. Her temple would not be caked with blood that seeped into the sheet set over it. Her death scene would be a world away from what he was seeing now, but not because it would be perfectly planned and brought off. It would be different because the proper hat and flowers and things placed upon her would be put there with love and memorial knowing. These corpses didn't have luxury like that. They were simple corpses. The boy's young mind wrapped itself around death and the different deaths of loved and unloved people.

Now Toussaint knew he would never die. Not only had he seen the hidden dead, he had had a virus steal into his body and try to kill him from the inside out. The virus had become a fever and the fever a seizure and the shape shifter had fought deep within him the way diseases and bullets got inside and killed people every day. But his body was not dying. His mind and imagination were not dying. They were fully alive. He felt more sensitive to every moment, every smallest piece of his life, every beat of his heart.

The fat black nurse, who had skin the color of new pennies, returned with two hospital-white blankets, which he laid carefully over the two gurneys at the back of the hallway. Now neither corpse could be seen. Their subtle outlines were perfectly hidden. Satisfied with that, the nurse wheeled the boy who knew that he would never die into the examination room.

Riding home in the backseat of his dad's new car, Touissant said nothing. His dad was driving and his mother was talking. He could tell that his dad was gearing the car up and down, testing its braking and acceleration and the basic precision of its design to trick his mind into thinking about something other than Granny's death. Meanwhile, his mother was talking in that way that meant she was absolutely sure that the things she was saying about the twins' day-camp schedule and about the doctor's orders for monitoring a child after a febrile seizure were of great importance.

Touissant didn't know what to think about. His granny was dead, he knew that. His memory of her rested peacefully amid his many thoughts. He remembered that in the examination room the doctor had told his parents that it was probably the extreme summer heat of the Inland Empire, as compared to the milder summers that Touissant had experienced closer to Los Angeles and the coast when they were still in college, that had caused the seizure. The doctor's advice was not complicated. Too much heat was bad for children, keep cool.

Touissant looked up at the sun above the San Bernardino Mountains. The sun controlled everything. It was God and the Devil. It brought seizures and killed children, as well as all the other weak things in the desert. Afternoon now: the sunscape was retreating a little at a time, dying over the mountains, allowing for evening and nightfall. Then the temperature would drop like a shot bird. And the desert would become unpredictable under that darkness, a mixing of summer and winter, everything roasted and dry but simultaneously stiffening up with the sudden wind and sunless air. Even in absence, the sun was everything; its absence as powerful as its presence, bringing cold and flu even as it scorched the earth and left the land dead and fallow.

Touissant saw a lizard perched atop a stop sign. It was a gray mannequin, the most still of all living things. Further up the way, he could see prairie dogs moving as fast as his dad's car between their dug holes and the tree-tall tornados of dust spontaneously born of the pressing heat and hard low winds. Touissant wondered what the prairie dogs were running from; he wanted to believe that they were running for the same reasons that people do, the way his great-granddad maybe had done all those many years ago with the government coming for him to take him to the War. Maybe the prairie dogs were full of pride and anger and imagination just like Major Freeman. Maybe they were trying to outrun the sun, just like the old man had tried to outrun whatever it was he was really running from, whether war, or white people, or marriage. Those absolutes stood alongside the sun and the world the sun had made: this desert. So big, the desert stretched with the sun, on and on and on. From greater San Diego, up to the Los Angeles Basin, up to Northern California and burning out to Arizona, Nevada, Utah. The desert went on forever, an infinity of dirt and rock and low scrub and small, hard defiant life. The desert was so vast, so vast. Vaster than the pages torn from every school book lain end to end, so vast. Maybe ants living in tract home walls and roadrunners chased from newly driven fence posts and coyotes exiled to the dry gulches and prairie dogs and lizards and woodpeckers and skunks and rattlesnakes and bullfrogs were as prideful and bold as all the black folks with their money right, who had come to this hot, raw place. Maybe everything alive in this forever endless desert lived in defiance of it. Survival. Maybe that was the secret of what his life would be, something about survival.

They passed the Buddhist temple, with its always-lit lanterns rowing either side of the long walkway leading toward mysterious elaborately engraved doors, and turned toward their just-bought home. The car rolled into its new driveway. The house was their little temple; its simple three-quarters square, one-quarter pyramid design rose from the earth into dangerous light. Touissant felt absolutely blessed. His sisters were waiting in the driveway. He wasn't sure how they had gotten back from day camp so early or why they were waiting in the driveway. He didn't care how or why, he was happier than ever just to see them, his family. The car pulled forward and the twins stepped aside in unison. The garage door rose electronically. Dea and Kia were smiling sad smiles, the sunshine living on their perfect teeth and penny-colored skin.

In her dream, turning eight was wonderful past wonderful. The dream was a large dream and it came to her in such detail in the September night that she felt like it had belonged to her all along. She saw her parents taking her to the circus right down the street from their apartment. But when they parked the car and got out and held hands following the crowds into a high dark tent it was like entering a new world. The walk-up to the bleachers was paved with dirt that people kicked into child-sized clouds as they hurried forward. The dirt hung in the air as dust particles creating a thin, continuous veil across her vision. The tent dome ran upward in arches of dark red, dark gold, dark green, dark sunshine.

They sat in the front row only a few feet from the center ring where the action was to take place. Ushers and vendors wound through the busy aisleways. Then a bugle cried out of the darkness and a deep slow drumroll began. More instruments began to play: trumpets, tubas, a sad clarinet. A funeral march anthem played through the tent. Erycha stared over the ring, across the tent toward where the sound seemed to emanate, but she couldn't see the players at first. They were still shrouded, invisible. The funeral march played on, its deep, gutter-low groove rumbling the bleachers.

A woman appeared at the north end of the tent. Spot-lit outside the ropes of the ring, she wore a sequined dark yellow gown that flowed all the way to her ankles. Her fat fingers sparkled with little diamonds, her headdress plumed in pale green feathers. "Soul!" she sang in full sudden ecstasy. "Soul!" The music rose like something headed into the sky. "Soul universoul . . .

> "One of these mornings bright and fair
> Goin'a take my wings and cleave the air
> Pharoah's army got drownded
> O Mary don't you weep . . ."

And as her singing reverberated through the still, thick air a buzz of anticipatory talk started to flow through the grapevine of bleachers. In time the word passed through enough lips that it found its way to Erycha and her parents, and they passed it between each other like a burning coal: "Here comes the band, here comes the band. South Care-lina State. The truth!"

"Drum major," the singer said, her voice descending even further out of female range, into a low, sweet slow tone. "Drum major, now, what's goin on?"

Stillness: the spotlight alone moved. Wandered away from her and panned in ever-diminishing illumination across the north and northwest end of the tent until it fell away completely and full gloom accompanied stillness for a long moment.

"Drum major, c'mon now. I been asked you, what's really goin on?"

The spotlight triggered back, this time at the southern end of the tent, just over Erycha's shoulder and aimed down along a passageway of suspended dust that flowed out to the very end of the tent itself. She turned with all the rest and looked to the swirling dust beam.

"Drum major, girl, you comin out or not? Now, these people *been* waited."

The trumpets blared forth again, the clarinet called out in its light and lonely voice; then the rest of the brass section and the cymbals and the drumroll barreled on, all gut-bucketing forward in slow lurches. Subtly, new melodies and an unfamiliar rhythm arose.

"I likes what I'm hearin now. I likes what I'm hearin. Ain't this your cue, boy?"

A small black shadow appeared at the very furthest edge of the spotlight, its slender semi-rounded shape like a shy small cat come out at daybreak. It slipped forward a step. Its white and gold tassels gleamed in the illumination. But it paused there, in a recess between slip and step and stride.

"Drum major," the singer said, "Please! Get to steppin."

Suddenly the music reeled out of blues, past jazz and into chaotic Southern bounce. Roiling across the space and bringing the crowd to their feet as if they were all one mind in motion, one body in dance.

The drum major sprang into view, a small but awesome frightening figure dressed in white, gold-tasseled shoes; immaculately blue-jeweled and yellow-fringed pants; a sky-colored shirt with bold-embossed letters over the heart: University of South Carolina State.

"The South Carolina State marching band, y'all!" The woman's voice rang out. "Make noise!"

The drum major's face was invisible between a high tight collar and the furred feathered top hat that started somewhere around the eyes and seemed to reach ten feet up in the air. Metal wings extended from its sides and back, like silver flames, seemingly weighting down the hat and the drum major held beneath it that much more. The drum major's head tilted down and the wand he carried at his side swung like a militant third arm, every last thread of his momentum concentrated into propulsive step, like dancing on an earthquake fault line. Erycha didn't know whether to dance or cheer or do what she really wanted to do, which was coil up in fear at the newness of it all, when the major danced past her and led the band into the center ring.

They arrayed themselves behind their leader, so many peacock plumes. The music pulled back and settled itself in a bed of down-tempo trumpets. The drums and cymbals silenced. The melody returned to its first funeral lilt. The drum major came still and stood corpse rigid, his thin shoulders forward, arms at sides, legs close together, all military precision and rigor. Erycha looked on. Her fear began to wane.

Sometimes Erycha fantasized herself in the role of a princess and sometimes even a queen, but now she wished she could be the drum major at the center of the circus orchestrating its wild careening movements. People took their lead from the drum major. They did as the major did, moved as he moved. They even went silent and came to attention when he went silent and still and brought his wand down motionless at his side.

Now, the drum major raised the wand slowly and the spotlight rose. He held the wand high like a standard in the sky. Seconds extended themselves like days. Everyone waited on that wand to drop. The drum major tilted his top hat forward and the plumes shook like so many dancers. He sliced the wand downward through the air, bringing it back to his side. In the distance, an elephant roar drowned out the band altogether. At that call, the drum major leapt over the ring ropes and quick into the dark, invisible. The other band members followed and the spot-lit stage fell empty for a moment. The elephant sounded his one booming note again. And then he and a fleet of his brothers came rushing up from the east end of the tent, up a steep incline and into the light of the circus.

Fine cedar-colored sisters rode the elephants, straddling their gray backs with lean exposed legs. Suddenly one girl in a shiny gold dress hopped to her feet atop the elephant and the crowd let out a collective gasp. Then the girl bent forward at the waist like her muscles and bones were elastic tape; she angled her forehead down onto the elephant's neck and brought her hands down on its back and executed a perfect handstand. Her tiny dress fell inverted over her upper half and she held the pose for a good minute, perfect as any ballerina, atop the romping elephant. The elephants arranged themselves in a tight circle at the center of the ring, the girl reassumed her straddle-spot and while the elephants roared exultantly a red, black and green flag was produced from somewhere and Carthage was conquered and Hannibal's spirit was anointed emperor of all known worlds.

When the elephants and their riders exited, recorded music began to blast from the subwoofers perched in the high corners of the tent: hip-hop bass blending with atmospheric chords. "Ladies and gentlemen," a male voice rang out. "Next up we got a real treat for you. All the way from BK, Double-Dutch Dynamite!"

The strange beat quickly segued into an EPMD instrumental. "BK to LA."

Two girls and four boys cartwheeled into the ring, waving jump ropes like nunchucks. The six split into sets of three and the girl threw two of her ropes to her opposite number. Then they slipped the jump ropes to the boys at either side of them and began to dance like over lines of fire as they quickly complicated their steps into a whirlwind of runs and walks and an incredible backflip where one boy shape-shifted in the air and reformed a beautiful blackbird only to land on his feet a boy once more. The song finally broke down, instrumental, then isolated drums, and then the sound of a record shattering rang throughout the tent and the double-dutching girls feigned exhaustion and fell to the ground. All movement stopped. The next song wailed up and the performers, save one, somersaulted from the ring, jumping into darkness, their bodies dissembling way up there in the black heights, before finding themselves feet first on the ground almost outside the light, cakewalking away.

The World's Greatest Double-Dutcher sat down in the middle of the ring wiping pearls of sweat from his brow. The other double-dutchers ran from the stage. The spotlight trained on its only visible subject: the boy.

"Chil'." The familiar singer's voice issued out of a space Erycha could only call nowhere. "Chil'!" The boy's eyes widened and he stopped wiping his brow and sat up ruler-straight. *"Baby,* what are you doin in those *street rags?* Didn't I teach you away from all of that gutter music? I wanted you to be a bonafide drum-major, a bonafide black leader. But look at you, wildin in the streets, showin-out. I won't stand for it!"

The boy shot to his feet, rigid as the drum major.

The spotlight beamed in with a different golden color that held the boy within it like an intimate and revealing embrace. Now the audience could see the thinness of the body and fine delicate soft lines of the face. A syrup of sweet late laughter overtook the crowd as they realized the trick. The boy who was a girl leapt to her feet and executed a couple quick step moves tilting her hatless head forward as if finding new freedom or feeling the intangible weight of sudden fame.

Then: a tiger's piercing scream sheering through the tent like a record scratched with a machete. Bongo drums began to beat far off. The spotlight hovered idly over the ring. Then four tiger cages were wheeled mechanically into the ring. A tall, high yellow queen traipsed in after the cages. She dangled a long cat-o'-nine-tails in her long fingers. She let the whip trail along the ring floor. As she went past each tiger's cage, the animals acknowledged her with a waving paw, a wagging tail. She cracked the whip against the bars of their cages and the tigers flinched. Having greeted each animal, she came to the middle of the ring.

"Riana Guyana Moore, people, Riana Guyana Moore: the *only* African-American tiger tamer!"

The tamer produced a foot-long gold key from her suit pocket and began to unlock the cages one by one. The tigers sauntered out and at the gentle suggestion of the cat-o'-nine-tails they formed a diagonal line stretching from the east end of the ring to its northwestern edge. She let them stand there for a moment, easy as the day they were born. Then she whirled the whip in the air and shouted imperatives in German: the tigers obeyed, rising to their hind legs with their mouths agape and front paws surrendered useless in the air.

She kept them in that pose for what seemed like forever before cracking the whip, dropping them to all fours. She strutted a path between them, a fifth feline, her head high, her back a half-moon arc, her heels stabbing the ground with proud cat contempt.

She glided like that all the way out of the ring, completely out of sight and by some invisible order commanded the tigers to reenter their cages and allow themselves to be borne mechanically off.

The spotlight wandered away from the ring and settled on the band, tucked in a deep corner: they eased into a funeral dirge for the departing animals. A solitary drum beat in the background. Then the band shifted into a liquid interlude, the drums washing under in the saxophone's rush, waves in passage. A clarinet cried up out of the inchoate depths and the band began to play the accompaniment to its own funeral, its own death, field songs and swing, and rhythm and blues, in an effortlessly epic movement.

The drum major staggered back to center-stage. Hatless still, in a tattered shirt and shorts and pathetically barefooted, she collapsed in the middle of the ring. The circus stopped. Everyone stared at the spot where her band had danced and played and the animals had performed and the children, she among them, had shape-shifted; they stared where their girl lay.

Finally, the singer's voice returned. "Girl? Daughter?"

"Yes."

"Daughter, remember God. Remember His word. His word is love. His word is the truth and the fire."

"Yes," she said again.

"We dance, we sing, we speak, we breathe, we walk and live in His light and in His service alone."

On Erycha's birthday morning, her mother gave her a lemon cake, an entire cake all for herself. This was a unique gift. She tasted the tangy frosting first and later the candied crust and sweet bread. She was very thankful for the cake, for being one day and one year older, for the prophetic vision God had granted her.

She prayed the candle flames down and sat waiting for her father, who had left some time before the bitch from welfare visited, to come home.

The smog blew in from Los Angeles and when time turned to deep summer and then from summer to September, the pollution would collect along with the heat and be like a wicked dome closing over the valley. And it was always hot. August was supposed to be the hottest month but it always turned out that September was the killer: day laborers were liable to collapse and die out in the fruit fields. Old grandmas would get it easier, pass out in their gardens. Young single mothers were a natural temperature gauge, pushing their baby-strollers either fast or very slow or not at all depending on how high the heat waves shimmered off the ground. Actual heat indexes cost too much money so people became their own indexes; they knew hot from hot and that sufficed.

There would be fires in the mountains and fires in the valleys as the dead brush succumbed to the sun. Then the air wafted in a perpetual state of recovery, after the burn.

In those early days when Erycha was still a child, time passed but change was an imperceptible movement. Like the earth's rotation, it went unnoticed. From day to day and year to year the same strange mother and stranger-father lived on, abiding each other, fighting each other, vexing on each other. The same small, close-quartered community of blacks went on seemingly changeless. Folks went hungry, scrounged jobs, worked, enlisted, left for the other side of the world, and came home. The schools and the courts alternately pampered and screwed them. The economy cycled up and down, pivoting upon their prone bodies fixed at the base of the system. They cussed the greedy white man, the godless homos and the job-takin Messicans. They struggled, made do, developed skills outside the legitimate economy that controlled Monday through Friday and immersed themselves within the imperiling worlds of weekend work. They took three buses to take one job, played maid, braided hair, bootlegged anything popular enough to be bought twice. They provided the freaks from across town with their girl and boy and cheap pussy. They were raided by the police, got locked up, went away, came home, shot and cut each other in their front yards over drug money and other bullshit, defiled their community, messed-over their kin, passed along diseases like they did their last names.

As with every community, they were collectively close-minded, treating anything new as a trespassing cancer. This was an attitude that had less to do with people themselves, because their neighborhoods routinely housed the poor, the foreign, prostitutes, transvestites, drifters, than with the new spirit and ideas of troublemaking individuals: to say that there was no God, to submit that men who fucked men were still men, to decide out loud that the thugs in their midst were all damn Uncle Toms so worshipful of money that they thought nothing of selling their sisters and poisoning their people, was deemed not diagnosis but sickness itself, even as the community shut itself away and coughed up its lungs. Yet somehow within that closed-in space the natural goodness of folk always survived and walked on past the Devil: they bore each other's children and raised youth that were not their own, prayed for one another, did for one another, did for the least among them, and actually practiced what politicians and professors fat-mouthed about from far away. They built the Central City Mission, their own small haven for the least fortunate among them. It was they who tore down the crack houses and ministered to the lost brothers and sisters that could still be saved from their ceaseless beasts. They laid hands upon and governed as best they could a world outsiders had long since condemned.

But their beliefs were set and immovable, as rigid as Italian ballet. The seasons spiraled around and around and nothing changed.

This inviolate world was such that Erycha hardly noticed as her body began to curve, forming a new outline, hips, breasts and female fullness. She had no idea that she was growing out of more than old clothes, that one day all she would have to do would be to walk down the street or open her mouth and raise a question to find herself spiritually exiled. Then she would have new names given to her. White girl. Educated bitch. But for now that was a long way off. For now she was still just eight and nine and ten turning eleven and eleven turning twelve and summer nights she laid her rounding body down and slept naked on her naked mattress, satisfied enough that she never had nightmares, never needed dreams.

By the time Touissant turned twelve, East Highland had evolved into a beautiful bedroom community. There were rows of palm trees columned like the slats in a shut gate across the length of its high hill. That hill, itself simple nature, had been made into a statement, dictating a separation between the East and West sides of the town, with the homes and the health food stores and the Buddhist temple along the hill's long incline representing the city's East, and the apartments and pawn shops and supermercados and community centers and small store-front churches in the flat lands the West. Not only the hill but a freeway separated the town's two sides. Grandiose two- and three-story homes threw their block shadows down the length of Highland hill and onto the ghetto beyond the freeway, and when the smog would lift after afternoon, the biggest houses and prettiest palm trees stood in shadow, dark traces of a class statement.

The home a state university music professor (Touissant's dad) and county hospital administrator (Touissant's mom) could maintain stood toward the bottom of the hill. But the important thing was to be on the hill. Staring beyond the hill at the snowy mountain range that shone in the early sunlight like blue-white pyramids reaching for the sky, Touissant figured there must be some reason, some logic to it all. Not just the hill and how it divided his little town into the wealthy and the kinda-wealthy and the not wealthy at all, but everything else, too. Like the mountains. Why did they exist? And the snow? And the palm trees so close to the snow? And the desert so close to the snow? Why were there places so strange that they could bring winter and summer and mountain and desert, and life and death, all together along one plain of sight? Why were people born where they were born and why did they die where they died? Why and why and why?

Touissant gripped the event flyer tight in his sports-shirt pocket. His sisters had made a pastime out of leaving invitations to concerts and shows in random niches in the house. They were no longer content to drop the laminated flyers on the living room floor or on the bathroom sink, but had progressed to wedging the things in windowsills and dropping them into flower pots and placing them inside old books that would spark their interest for five or ten brittle pages before they moved on to the next unlikely excitement. Most of the flyers advertised events by foregrounding a half-naked girl posed seductively. Touissant knew that the guys who wanted the twins half-naked at their parties gave them the flyers and he knew how uninterested the twins usually were. He made mental note not to hand out raunchy flyers to pretty girls when he got old enough to do that sort of thing.

But one flyer caught his attention. It had been left in one of the violently large old war novels that Touissant's gramps had passed down to his dad before he died. *The Young Lions*, the book was called. The flyer was sticking out from between pages 190 and 191, which was impressive in and of itself. Even if the advertisement had been as nondescript as all the booty-shaking flyers that found their way into the family library, he would still have remembered it for the amount of reading it implied. Either that or one of the girls had placed the flyer there just for the sake of it. The invitation itself was unique: a forum open to the public to address chronic violence in the neighborhoods of San Bernardino and West Highland. Touissant had never thought much about San Bernardino or West Highland. That area was off-limits for reasons he had never much considered. He understood vaguely that the area was blighted, recalled vaguely Dea and Kia's offhand remarks about avoiding shows staged there, noticed still vaguely how much they seemed to know about places where they said no one should ever go. Now he wanted to know more. He hid the flyer in a place where no one would find it, and he committed the date, time and location of the event to memory.

On the bus to Seccombe Park, Touissant watched as a little girl and two little boys play-fought with each other. The kids were maybe nine, maybe ten years old. Both boys wore blue bandanas, which they flaunted like pretty scarves around their throats. Touissant knew from investigative news reports on television that these kids were Crips or playing at being Crips. He imagined a bunch of tiny children trying to do a cartoon drive-by: they would have on their blue bandanas but would be unable to see over the steering wheel or lift the gun out the window.

The bus was a block away from Seccombe when he heard a soft popping sound come from where the little kids were play-fighting.

The girl lay on the bus floor, playing dead. One of the boys stood over her, shooting her lustily with a cap gun, filling her body with imaginary bullets. After a minute, an adult on the bus yelled, "Hey! Stop!"

The kids looked up and stopped their play. The boy put the cap gun in his pocket and retook his seat on the bus. The girl stood up. The boy untied his blue flag and dusted her off with it, smoothed her hair where her artfully winged and braided cornrows had become tousled and loose.

When he reached his stop, Touissant looked around Seccombe Park for blue rags like the ones worn by the boys on the bus. The gang symbols were not hard to find and came in red as well. Tied around throats, wrapped around waists, knotted on wrists and worn round heads, it was obvious the gang members were as interested in advertisement as the event organizers. Touissant knew nothing about gangs except what journalists had told him. Those journalists had gone heavy on menace but light on real information: he had come to understand that gangs sold drugs and killed each other and killed innocent men, women and children on a regular basis. But there had been no news stories about gang members mingling at the lake, participating in anti-violence events. He wondered if the journalists had gotten it wrong, or if the organizers at Seccombe had made the mistake. He wondered whether it was a good or bad thing that formal security was nowhere visible.

There also weren't any Mexicans there. Black people of many descriptions, from gangbangers to kids in school uniforms and folks in their work clothes, crowded the park, but there were no Mexican gangbangers, no Mexican freelance thugs, no groups of young Latinas with their figures falling out of their outfits, no older Latinas dressed like they were headed for church, no self-important middle-aged men in business suits or rugged work uniforms. Touissant had only seen this many black people in one place when the family went to visit relatives in Alabama, which made him feel good and bad at the same time. But he also knew that however he felt about black people, San Bernardino was a Mexican town. Most of the gangs were probably Mexican gangs, not black gangs. How effective, then, could a forum organized to stop violence be without a single Mexican?

A man the color of parchment paper and dressed in dashiki and sombrero began talking loudly about just that problem: "This party is supposed to be a chance for reconciliation, redemption." The man was strutting through the massing crowd talking to no one in particular, everyone in general. "The black gangs need to make peace with regular folk. Regular folk need to make peace with the gangs. The po-lice need to make peace with the folk and the gangs. Brown

folk need to unify with black folk. The po-lice need to unify with all
the peace loving people here. But they ain't here! The Mexicans ain't
here! The po-lice may be here, but they ain't showin they faces! We
can't have true reconciliation without all parties present."

Touissant watched the insular cliques of gang members and young
women and middle-aged women and elderly women. They began
talking louder, doing their best to ignore the man. Obviously he was
not held in high regard in the neighborhood. Touissant looked back
to the flyer: former USC All-American, NFL defensive back and
San Bernardino native Vincent Deveraux had organized the event.
Below the title of the forum, its date, time and location, the athlete's
figure loomed imposingly upon the laminated card. He was dressed
in a business suit, not a mess of contradictory ethnic clothing. His
face was drawn and stern. Touissant overheard a few girls whispering about the NFL player, wondering when he would appear, what
he would look like in person, if his girlfriend would be present. The
athlete was the kind of man people responded to. He had respect,
unlike the man in the sombrero. Touissant hoped Deveraux would
take the stage soon and get things started.

The night was desert cool, desert dry and windy, and most of the
girls were wearing jeans or conservative dresses. The jeans, hugged
tight to their legs and asses, were more revealing than the dresses.
Some girls were plain-looking, others very pretty. One by one, he
watched as the prettiest of the girls brushed past him and into the
vicinity of the older guys, the gang members and the unaffiliated
brothers. Being attractive, he quickly realized, was no prerequisite
for a girl to ignore him. There were no prerequisites. Everybody
ignored him. Even one very tall, very gawky girl about the same age
as him, with a jutting emaciated collarbone and eyes that looked too
big for her skull, walked past and gave Touissant a disdainful once-
over with her insect eyes. He watched her go stand with a group of
other loud and unattractive girls: at least all the ugly ones stay in one
place, he thought to himself.

Touissant had come to the neighborhood forum to learn about the violence so close yet so far away from where he lived. But he had also come to meet people, especially girls. The grasshopper-faced girl looking at him like he was the ugly one was not a good sign when it came to meeting girls. He spent a minute telling himself that it was the absence of any but black girls that was holding him back. He told himself that he didn't know how to relate to black girls, at least not these ghetto black girls.

Then he noticed a pretty honey-colored girl: she was standing alone just like Touissant was. She had big eyes too, but they were different somehow. Big soft doe's eyes. Those eyes mooned off into the distance, probably wishing after something she couldn't have or had yet to find. Touissant wanted to go and talk to her. But then he thought about all the things that could go wrong; a leave-me-alone look, a put-down, a jealous gang member boyfriend dismembering Touissant in public. He didn't get up and go over to her. His fear and pride were invisible hands holding him in place.

After a while a butter-faced Black-Filipino kid came and sat next to him on the bench. The kid was two or three years older than Touissant, but he seemed just as ignored. "Sucks we can't smoke out here," the kid offered. "I got a dime 'a weed but cain't share it with nobody. Cain't smoke it in Seccombe my own self."

Touissant was confused. He didn't know what marijuana and dimes had to do with each other. "Huh?"

"Undercovers. You know what I'm sayin. The NFL nigga who put this on has undercover po-lice all around this bitch."

"Really?!" Touissant suddenly felt safer.

"Yeah, black. This is on some inner-sanctum illuminati shit, know what I'm sayin?"

Touissant had no idea what the boy was saying now.

"The forces that are behind *every thing:* they about to imprison and disappear Tupac, Michael Jackson, even Quentin Tarantino! The NFL is part 'a this leviathan, too. It's a billion dollar industry. This nigga was at USC, too, which is like a farm for the rich, where the rich grow richer. When you start dealin in that big money, you gotta sell your soul to the illuminati devils." The kid's eyes were Kool-Aid red. "It's crazy, black man. Crazy. Crazy."

"Um," Touissant began.

"I can tell you don't smoke."

Touissant shook his head.

"Prohibitin this weed is the worst trick, black. The worst. You can commit murder in broad-ass daylight on G Street an' pose for a picture with the nigga you just killt an' get away with it. But if it's an unprescribed substance, oh hell nah. Fuck this shit, man. Fuck this shit." He hawked up a huge loogie and spat forcefully. Then his small, thin body convulsed in spasms, coughs, gasps.

Touissant was pretty sure no undercover security personnel were in attendance. And he didn't want to catch whatever physical or mental illness was consuming the kid, so he quickly jumped from the bench and melded back into the thronging crowd.

"In San Diego, there were sixty-two homicides this past calendar year. In Toronto, there were seventy-five murders." A man with a face like forty miles of bad road all rained-on had taken the makeshift stage in the middle of the park and begun to speak into a handheld mic. He had not introduced himself. He seemed to assume that people knew who he was; that, or he didn't care whether they did or not. It took Touissant a moment to realize that this was the man on the flyer. the athletic star of the city, the organizer of the event. But after that first instant of non-recognition, he noticed the depth in the man's shoulders and chest and the piled biceps and the absolute leanness of his face. That severity in his face was parts toughness and concern and Spartan conditioning. "While in San Bernardino, our hometown, there were sixty-eight homicides. This means our town's murder rate is almost seven times as high as San Diego's and more than twelve times as high as the big city in Canada. It is much higher than Los Angeles's murder rate and nearly as bad as Watts and Compton." Several whoops and turf-calls went up from the gang contingents. "Are you finished yet?" Deveraux asked. The crowd went completely silent. "My question," he asked, "is simple. Why?"

Touissant waited for the man to answer his own question the way his teachers did when none of the students cared to talk. But he did not do this. He stood on stage, arms crossed, comfortable in the breach that he had opened and placed his question inside. Touissant looked at Deveraux and thought about his gramps, who had passed away so recently: Deveraux had that kind of presence, the kind of presence that walked forward, the kind of presence that would linger even when he was two months dead.

A hand finally rose from within the quieted crowd. "Gangs," the hand answered.

Remembering the blue and red bandanas, Touissant had no trouble believing that.

"Jealousy," another hand said.

"Yeah," yet another hand called out. "Jealousy."

"Jealousy?" Deveraux asked.

Heads nodded, one after the next.

"Yeah," the woman who'd raised her hand first said. "It ain't just about red an' blue. Some 'a these boys will kill their own color over some jealousy shit. They'd kill *you,* Mr. Deveraux, just the same like they do each other, if they thought they could get away with it."

"Hmmm," Deveraux said.

"It's random," the woman continued. "It's black on black, blue on blue, red on red. It didn't used to be like this. Now, you don't even know what they might be shootin over. Could be a Crip kill a Blood but not even nothin to do with gangbangin, could just be somebody flirted with somebody else's bitch."

"Let's try not to curse," Deveraux said.

"Amen," several women in the crowd murmured. The man in the dashiki and sombrero called out, "Amen, brother."

"Race!" someone else said. "Speak on race, Mr. Deveraux."

"This isn't a sermon," Deveraux admonished. "Why don't you speak on race, young lady."

"Black an' brown," the girl said. "The Messicans hate the blacks. The blacks is mad cuz these Messicans pushed us outta L.A. An' now here they come wantin to push us outta fuckin California!"

"Keep it clean. Keep it clean."

"The Messicans think they better. They learn how to talk English an' don't wanna speak to a nigga for nothin. Don't even wanna live in the same apartment buildings as us. We move in, they move out, start callin G Street, Mount Vernon, this whole area Lil Africa. They be all up in them trailer parks, them lil barrio spots; an' we all up in the cheap-ass apartments. So you start to thinkin, let's keep them Messicans on that street an' that street an' that street. Turf. You know what I'm sayin?" Touissant understood what she was saying. "Cuz we ain't got any Messican friends, we don't know them from Adam. You stop carin what happens to people you don't know except when you see one of 'em holdin down a job you applied for an' they cain't hardly talk English. Then you thinkin unclean words."

"Right." The athlete nodded. "Right."

"An' there's hella skinheads out here, too," the girl kept on. "We duckin nigga haters an' the cops. You been seein the same convict folk yo whole life, same issues, same problems, an' ain't nothin to do but *be hot.*" A line of warmed-over laughter ran through the crowd. The desert air hung still above them. "So you starts to thinkin, maybe I need to get me that gun. Maybe I need to carry with me that gun that I already own."

"And from there," Deveraux concluded, "drama results. Children die. We can't have our children dying."

"And it's not just the kids," a tall kid with glasses added. "A lot of the worst perpetrators be forty, fifty, sixty years old. Look at the streets, man. You can't blame the kids for everything. You have these old people who were part of the crack wars, you have the mental house evacuees, all these geezers mumblin to theyselves, showin-out in the street, doin drugs out front of the elementary schools. How would you like it if one of these old crackheads was your grand-daddy?"

Never, Touissant said to himself. Whatever his gramps's flaws, his womanizing, his egotism, he had never disgraced the family. No one ever had to worry that a Freeman man would be strung out in a crack house. Touissant pictured a family tree, its branches severed and lying pathetically on the ground. He was so fascinated with his family history, he couldn't imagine wanting *not* to know his heritage. But now he knew that there were people whose families had disgraced them so bad there was no redemption possible.

"Berdoo, man, always been this way."

"Not always," Deveraux countered.

"Like when was it different?" the tall kid challenged.

"Yeah," the crowd called. "When?"

The boy was probably just angling to get at more girls, Touissant figured, probably wanted to present himself as some kind of hot young rebel. Not a bad strategy. He wished he had come up with it first.

"What year were you born, brother?" Deveraux asked the boy.

"1977."

"Well I've been here a little longer than that. I remember '76: that was the year San Bernardino was named as an All-American city. We had Norton Air Force Base. We had Kaiser Steel and Route 66."

"Route 66 is white people shit!" someone screamed. The crowd cheered.

"Then," Deveraux continued, "the Base closed. Kaiser closed. Money flowed east, to Highland, to Redlands."

Touissant noted the target subtly placed upon his suburban community. He thought about the palm trees lined up in perfect symmetry along the top of Highland hill. He thought about the three-story houses behind the trees and the mountains like blue-white diamonds overlooking the houses and shadowing the impoverished valley. He was starting to receive some answers to all his questions about how his privileged world had come to be.

"Always happens to the black people!" the same screaming voice screamed again, "We always gettin shorted!"

Touissant knew he didn't belong here: he was like a rich white person in this community. He had nothing in common with these folks. He had never been shorted. Nothing had ever been taken from him; everything had been given to him.

"Just shows," the thin kid said, "that it wadn't our generation did all this." The kid waved his hand at the decrepit landscape of Seccombe Park. It was nighttime but the panzer-green lake water and the ducks that the stray dogs caught, gutted and left to decompose in the grass remained visible.

"OK," Deveraux conceded. "But I don't think you can do much with a sixty-year-old crack fiend. He's too far gone. She's too far gone. But the children can always make a better way. Let's get back to this issue of jealousy."

"Let's speak on the Crips," a Blood offered.

"Let's speak on the Bloods," a Crip shot back.

"Let's speak on jealousy," Deveraux said again.

"There's jealousy within the sets," one gang member said. "A lot of the violence got less to do with the sets goin against each other than status inside the gang sets. Dudes tryina move up, get points, you know. Men always gon' fight over bitches, gangs or no gangs. They doin that in Beverly Hills. But this is on some contract shit, na'mean?"

By the look on his face, it was clear to Touissant that the athlete didn't know what the kid meant. If a grown man who also happened to be an athletic hero and a native of the ghetto in question could not understand its cratering culture, there was no way a teenage boy from the suburbs who had had to lie to his parents about visiting the public library just to get across town would be able to understand the poverty and violence that haunted black life. Touissant wondered if he would ever understand black people and their endless problems.

Deveraux tried to retake control of the dialogue. "The main thing that I want us to take away from this talk and this get-together is that we'll hold a forum like this weekly, every Sunday night. I've got a conflict-resolution counselor who's worked in Selma, Alabama, and Northern Ireland. He'll be here next Sunday. You can get dressed up, go to church in the morning, come to Seccombe at night. We're gonna bring Sunday back, y'all! But, seriously, people, we need resolution to our issues that's in words, not guns. It's good that we're identifying problems, now we need to solve them." Deveraux paused, taking in a long deep breath. "Now," he said, "these gangs that the young man in the crowd was referring to. These gangs." He sighed. "Gangs," he said again. "Gangs." He seemed lost in his mind all of a sudden. "Gangs," he began again. "These gangs."

Touissant thought about his granddad's stroked-out mind losing its center and order, flying free through memories and stories, reality and fiction, all the way back to a painful Alabama childhood that his consciousness had long ago forgot. The father who had fathered him in Jackson, then gone off to Tuscaloosa and sent for child and mother there, making them nomads just like him, the whole family and family upon family forever on the run. Raised by two loved but abandoned women, he never forgot the first pain of a switch against his back, the cordwood flaring against his baby fat, the pain his mother's hands made against his ass, back when they still went by the theory that spanking a child hard enough made him sleep good. And the way the fields stretched out every morning, every night, past the rising sun, past the setting sun; endless and overwhelming. And the way the white side of town bordered and bounded his life, the white tight finite space hemming in the even tighter smaller black world. But his childhood was good, too, in the gaps between the big hard facts. Like the way the wind whipped the cotton in the afternoons, scattering white tufts through the air, where they finally fell apart. His first tentative adventures beyond that tall cotton and into the city: church Sundays, where a wagon became a carriage, a mule a mighty steed and his brown suit-and-tie the most princely airs. The women's paper fans seemed more like majestic palm fronds transported from Rome, or Paris, or California. And the preacher: the preacher, the preacher, the preacher laying his game about the neighborhood and right morality and the Lord. Good Jesus. These recollections from boyhood would mix indiscriminately with his adolescent memories: by the time war was declared, he had already made friends with violence and even though he didn't give a shit if the Japs won the Pacific or which group of white people got to claim Europe, he enlisted. He wanted to do to armed men in the light of day what Alabama did to him helpless in the dark. But instead he spent the war crossing water from killer island to killer island delivering supplies under heavy fire, still just running and ducking, trying to stay alive. And when he came home from islands where black and Jap corpses stopped stinking he got so used to their smell, he started reading war novels that depicted nakedly the hatred and violence that formed and ruled the world. *From Here to Eternity. The Naked and the Dead. The Young Lions.* Blood on those pages. Those books and all the swimming and running he'd had to do made him wonder even more about his father: America was a scrapping angry nation, yet there was nothing America loved more than a running nigger. Running niggers were non-violent by necessity and didn't need to be court martialed, or imprisoned, or anything in particular. Soldiers with guns and black militants were problems to be dealt with, but niggers on the run were nobody's problem but the Lord's. Yet if the story about the man was true, his government actually went after him because he was a confirmed pacifist. It didn't make sense. So he kept reading, kept running all the way to Chicago, all the way to California, and kept telling that story most all his life, trying to tell the truth in the lie.

But he wore out. One day, maybe, the spirit of all that searching exited his body. Perhaps it was that sudden; one day, the spirit was gone. After all, it was a fact that at the end of his life he no longer owned any books. He no longer read, no longer ran. The first stroke: silence. The second stroke: stasis. Paralysis. His joints were on strike now, refusing to work for him. They were so many colluding unions of limbs working to bring the owner to his knees. He became physically half a man, with half a voice, half a brain, and far less than half his memory. Then the third stroke, and whatever happens to a man when he dies.

By the time Touissant stopped thinking about his gramps, the community forum had ended.

People were emptying into cars and onto walking paths. Mr. Deveraux was picking up trash around Seccombe. Another big, well-built young man and a couple of the nicer girls who had stayed behind were helping as well. A little light-skinned, red-haired woman who seemed to be Deveraux's girlfriend stood aside and watched them pick up the trash. It was sad to see the peaceful people pick up trash when he knew they would always be picking up after everyone else. Touissant noticed the three kids from the bus; they were running around playing tag now, smacking each other with their little kid-sized blue bandanas.

It was a sad end to a well-meaning event. And Touissant wished that people had taken the football player and his program more seriously. But of course there was no way to force people to do what they weren't committed to doing. They just did whatever they felt like. People were difficult that way. Touissant walked back to the bus stop and boarded the first thing headed east. He never went back to Seccombe, and it was a long time before he knew whether Deveraux's dream had come true or not. It would be a solid year before he thought about the football player and the forum in the park again, and then it was only because of an article in the local paper. A series of gang injunctions in San Bernardino that prohibited known gang members from congregating had led to the destabilization of the black gang sets throughout the region. Apparently, the forums in Seccombe had been surveilled by undercover policemen who had taken pictures and even learned the street and government names of the gang members in attendance.

The law enforcement sources cited in the article hailed the forums as one of the master strokes leading to the injunction policy, but the truth was that the injunctions exclusively targeted blacks and left the dominant Mexican gang sets to run wild. The new policy worked to decrease the influence of the gangs but actually increased vice crime and violence among unaffiliated freelance dealers and pimps and jackers. The injunctions created a far more unstable criminal class and led to a disturbing crime wave that spread west into Rialto and east into West Highland.

All in all, Touissant decided that he wasn't a fan of the football player or his event or the ultimate consequences that flowed from the movement to stop the violence. He had never been a sports fan, but after reading that article and thinking about its implications he stopped watching NFL games altogether. But in the back of his mind, the idea of a consummate athlete who was also incredibly smart and strategic and charismatic remained enticing. A person like that could change the world, or at least his community. That dream never really left him. Deveraux had used his powers strangely, to disastrous ends; but that didn't mean that some other scholar-athlete who happened to be as much a thinker as a physical specimen couldn't use his super-powers for the betterment of his community. In fact, such a hero could learn from the failures of the past and do things differently and actually create the community that he wished for.

He exited the bus and walked down his home block. He was imagining the twins impatiently calling him to dinner: "Toui-ssant!

Toui-ssant!" They were the sirens in myth calling home the hero. Their voices were harping and beautiful all at once. They spoke his name with the urgent devotion that they would later reserve for babies and diamonds. Touissant imagined himself returning home a rising sun in the universe of his small suburban community. He had been to distant lands and seen so much. He was a man of experience and accomplishment now. Shining armor, garlands at his feet, ladies he was not related to crying his name, the men of the town acknowledging his regal right.

The future was beautiful, he concluded, as he navigated the treacherous suburban streets, past the Buddhist temple, around one corner, then the next, and finally home. As he unlocked the front door and strode inside, he noticed how subdued the house sounded. The voices and movements of his family were muffled, indistinct. Strange welcome for this triumphant return. In the bright morning of his mind this wasn't how it was supposed to be: his return should be the most exalted in all the land. His white steed should rear majestically.

"Touissant?" he finally heard one of the twins say, in a tentative voice. It was the kind of unsure sound that revealed nothing but the distance between speaker and spoken to: he couldn't tell what she might be thinking or feeling or the expression on her face, or even which one she was. All he could tell was that she was speaking from the kitchen. Then she added, "Hey, Mom, he's home."

"Is that Touissant?" his mom wondered, also from the kitchen. "Tell him to turn off the porch light."

"Turn off the porch light," the other twin ordered.

Touissant turned it off and closed the front door behind himself.

"C'mon," he heard his mom saying, and he knew she was speaking to him directly now. "C'mon, sweetie, and sit down for dinner. We've been waiting for you."

He obeyed. Went into the kitchen where the nondescript dinner sat cooling, chicken cold, pie cold, corn cold and pale yellow. He looked from his mom to his dad, who had already begun to eat, and the twins, who were looking at him with deep black reproachful eyes. There they all were: the whole family. His mom looked thoughtful but it was hard to tell what she was thinking. She was tapping her fork against her plate of food, chicken and cornbread and thin cobs of pale corn. "C'mon," she said again, "We can't eat until everyone sits down. That means you, Touissant. You know the rules."

The rules, he noticed, didn't seem to apply to his dad.

"Now we gonna pray." She sighed. But she didn't close her eyes and she didn't fold her hands. Touissant looked around the table again: the twins were staring back at him, his dad's eyes moved between his plate and the people at the table. There was no reverence in their open eyes and unclasped hands. It was a bad way to receive a man of experience.

"Who's gonna pray?" Dea asked.

Everyone shrugged, no one answered. None of them actually believed in God. After a while he noticed his dad smirking around the corners of his mouth.

"Well," his mom offered, "who wants to pray over this food?"

His dad sighed.

The twins pouted their lips and stared into their food like the prayer was hiding in the chicken.

The silence lengthened, continued. Now the only sound was the rhythmic knocking of his mom's fork against her plate.

"Touissant should say the prayer!" Dea suddenly blurted.

"Yeah," Kia seconded. "He was the one who *came home late* and made us all *wait to eat!* Anyway, he always prays the prettiest prayers."

Touissant tilted his head back and thought about his recently deceased granddad and his deceased great-grand, probably still running in the afterlife if an afterlife actually existed, and about all the people apparently enfolded in violence not more than ten minutes from the Buddhist temple that watched over his neighborhood. The ghetto wasn't more than ten minutes from his neighborhood's sound walls, but going there was the longest trip he had ever taken. The ghetto across town was somehow further away than his relatives on the opposite coast. His dad said something to the twins, told them to stop vexing their little brother. But Touissant wasn't listening enough to be bothered. He was trying to think of something significant to say about the worldwide misfortune that was not the exception but the rule of life. He wanted to say something for all the people now living directly in peril in this place, in this dark time. But the words were gone. His gift for language was dead. He knew that even if he did pray, there was no God and there was nothing that talking to the air would do to change the nature of things. There was nothing he could say that would change the unforgiving divisions between places and people. All his fortunes were so little, everything he had been given seemed vacant rendered against the world just a few miles outside his suburb. He found himself unwilling to pray.

Erycha's mother taught her that the things of earth were the things of earth and that the things of the Lord were some-way different as they weren't things precisely, but instead beyond explanation, let alone possession. She taught her about the eternal truth of God and the temporary truth of everything underneath Him. And Sundays she took her daughter down the road to the Central City Catholic Mission, and there amongst homeless and orphans and HIV/AIDS sufferers she learned to cross herself, to swallow down Christ's body and blood and not to trouble too much over the differences between Baptists and Catholics.

One day a woman blacker than the tents of Kedar and the curtains of Solomon told her she could be an artist. People see me, the black ballerina said, and a flute begin playing in their head, they see me and see the Taj Mahal, a rattler in a bucket and a cheap dancing girl. When they see you, maybe they see that same cheap dancing girl, but that's where you will teach them, that us poor make the world at its fringes and invent beauty where nobody ever think to look.

Erycha needed money for ballet slippers. There were no great ballerinas without ballet slippers. In point of fact, there were no ballerinas, period, without slippers. Not only did ballerinas have money for proper footwear, they also had money to pay for classes and money to pay for pointe shoes and probably more funds besides. As a starting point, Erycha chose only to ask for the ballet slippers. She figured if she kept her requests small at first, maybe her parents would say yes. All the other inevitable costs could be put off for the time being.

It didn't seem like too much to ask to deliver the slippers with the $70 price tag from the display case to her feet. But as usual, her parents had their reasons to say no. Those reasons started at the top: President Clinton, they said, that man claimed the American economy was improving, that there were jobs to be had. But that only meant that if Erycha's parents wanted to turn Jamaican and work two or three low-paid hustles each and still make less salary than one real career would give them, they were free to do so.

Then there was the class: they had just finished paying for ballet instruction way off in Redlands. The class itself was expensive and had required ballet slippers and pointe shoes in addition to the initial fee, and when Erycha performed the basic floor and barre exercises in sneakers she ended up with a beginner's version of shin splints, a nagging pain running along each tibia. But even though she was healthy enough to continue, without the proper footwear the ailment was only bound to worsen. Either she had to quit or the full payment would have to be made, another unnecessary expense, with the inevitable result two shins that would feel like fire.

Then there was the robbery: her mother had recently been robbed in the apartment parking lot, in broad daylight, with the sunshine and her daughter as witnesses. This was another expense, another loss. That her mother had only been robbed of $50 and could count herself lucky she was even alive to complain about it wasn't the point. The point was that the more unnecessary subtractions, payments and thefts incurred, the fewer necessary things could be bought. So when Erycha asked about her slippers, the answer was emphatic: *"No, girl, what you think this is? I know we doin better than back in the day,* but c'mon now. That's rich folks' games. You wanna dance, you need to make the money to dance."

Rich folks' games. That was how they thought of ballet. And they didn't plan to finance any dreams. Erycha was barely a teenager yet suddenly financially independent. From her mother's complaints about her father, she understood that if financially independent persons didn't find work and had to depend on others to support them they would be considered unemployed, derelict and unfit for marriage. She already hated the idea of marriage, and the rest of it sounded bad, too, so she set about trying to find work.

Work. She had *been workin*.

All things are full of labor, she knew from her personal experience cleaning and cooking. All things are full of labor.

It was not work itself that was at issue, she realized, but what and how much was exchanged for it. She saw how hard the Mexican day-laborers worked, how early they rose and how late they went home, and she noted how poor they remained. She had seen her mother spend years working for poverty-level wages, barely enough to keep the family off food stamps. And she had seen the opposite math, too, how fast a thief with a weapon or a boy luxuriating on a busy corner could make sufficient ends to buy clothes and jewelry and pay rent. So what can I do that'll make me some real ends, get me paid? she asked herself.

Her first answer was that she knew how to braid hair and people paid good money to get their hair braided. Of course she braided her mother's hair and her mother braided hers and neither had ever paid the other because there was no use in passing family money when it would only be passed back in a day, or two, or ten seconds.

The one exception to all the free braiding done in the Evans home came when the rent wasn't paid and the refrigerator was empty and her father hadn't worked in Lord knew how long. Then her mother would braid other women's heads for money. Then braiding became an off-the-books profession without licenses or worker permits or taxation, just set up shop and get to braiding.

Now Erycha followed her mother's exception: she drew up tiny flyers on half sheets of paper and posted them on the apartment railings. "BRAIDWORK. EVANS APT. E-33. $10/HR. WEEKDAYS 3:00- 9:00PM. WEEKENDS 8:00AM-5:00PM. AND BY APPOINTMENT." The flyers were simple and straightforward. The location was close by, the fee reasonable, the hours convenient. She was trying.

Business came fast, but it also came with unpredicted drawbacks.

Her first customer was one of the corner boys, Ricky Carter. The day of the braiding, he walked her home from school and then up into the apartment. Then he started in, freestyling loudly, to Erycha, about Erycha:

> That shape, nigga
> That shake, nigga
> Makin me ache, nigga
> For real straight, nigga.

She set him down in a chair in front of the kitchen sink then went to work taming his natural, using her clippers here, her finger-nails there. As she worked she began to notice splotches of darkness building beneath her blue fingernails like a fungus or crust. His dan-druff was getting under her nails. "Your scalp's dry," she told him.

"Make it wet, girl."

"It's full of dandruff. Dandruff is dead skin flaked off from your scalp."

"A'ight, ma. No need to dog a nigga . . . Wait a sec', listen here:

Young
Innocent
That's how I gets 'em
trips 'em
then I rips 'em
OG mack, wit these, Crip-isms
Pimp, to death, or prison.

She kept working, mending his neglected head. Occasionally, he'd start in again with his low talk. She wondered where her father had gone to, if he had turned true Jamaican and found that third job to go along with his sometimes stints at the Mission and at the auto body shop. She wondered what he would think of Ricky when he saw him, and listened to him. Her father was an easygoing, forever lenient man, but, then, he wasn't aware that boys at school and on the corners had started to talk loose at her. He talked to women a little too loose himself, but Erycha knew that would have no bearing on how he would want people speaking at his girl.

Ricky didn't know any way to talk but loose and that made for a real problem. She knew braiding his hair would take three or four hours and that both her parents would be home before the job ended. Between the two of them, her mother was the fiercer, her temper quicker, striking harder. If she heard some of the things Ricky was saying about *her* girl, Ricky would have to jump quick.

She braided his hair as fast as she could. He probably wouldn't notice if his rows were a little crooked, or if this or that braid coiled a little too casually. She kept braiding. And far from complaining, Ricky didn't even seem to care when she drew the knots tighter than she herself could have endured without screaming. After a while she wondered whether he was even paying attention to what she was doing to his hair. Probably, he just wanted to be close to her and the braiding was the way to accomplish that. But she couldn't find anything special in their closeness, or in him, for that matter. He was just another boy, as flamboyant and silly as every other boy and man she had ever known. Even if he was different, better some sort of way, it wouldn't matter. She wasn't going to get to know him now. Her dad would be home any minute now. She narrowed her eyes, clenched her fingers over each braid and leaned in to finish the job.

She tilted her body over his braided head just so, and the added leverage the position gained her strengthened every pull, tug and twist. She was up close to him now, maneuvering his head left and right, up and down so that she could twist the braids tight and move on to the next without delay, like a puppet master dancing her machine this way and that. The minutes seemed to tick faster now. She stole glances at the microwave clock: at five p.m., it was still just she and the boy in the apartment. Then it was half past, then solid six, and still it was just she and the boy all alone together. Her work was reaping its reward: his hair was fast becoming the neat black picket fence of thug-beautiful braids that he had asked her for. Where before his ragged natural had simply flooded over itself in harmless old tufts, people could look at him now and think danger.

Funny, she thought, because she couldn't. To her, he was as harmless as a weevil in her cereal. It was only with the work of her quick little fingers that he could transform. Fearing him seemed silly, like a mother fearing the children she bore. She thought of *her* mother: *she* wouldn't be afraid of Ricky, no matter how his hair was done. Erycha leaned in closer, finishing the final braids, four, then three and two and one.

As she twisted the last braid, tightening it to the point of strangulation, she felt something stir at her edges. A vague then intensifying pressure on her breasts. She closed her eyes and paused over the final braid. She felt a coming warmth take her out of herself, and when she came back to her natural mind and her eyes were open again and she had her senses regained, all she wanted to do was lift her shirt a little and let him in. She eased over where he wouldn't have to tilt his head up to have her; she let him lift the shirt with his teeth and pass his tongue under the bra. And her fingers paused, hesitant between the braid and her bra, like two opportunities, knowing neither, feeling only him. Then she undid her bra.

She wasn't sure how long his tongue lingered on her nipples. It could have been a second; it could have been enough minutes to age her. All she knew was it felt good and new and warm. Then her father's brogans sounded on the hollow stair-steps. Slam, slam, slam, he came. It was another moment before she could react at all. Then she sort of swooned into Ricky chest first, then leapt back in the next instant. She found herself at the opposite end of the kitchen from Ricky when the apartment door opened.

"Hey, E-girl," her father called. His voice sounded loose and happy through the thin wall that separated the kitchen from the main room. Probably he'd been drinking. She hesitated. Maybe the alcohol would have him in a forgiving mood. But maybe not. Drunk men could get unpredictable so she really had no idea how he'd react when he came around the corner and saw her like this, with this boy.

Fortunately, he couldn't see either of them yet. She took her last free seconds to pull down her shirt, put her bra back where it was supposed to be. Then she stood stalk still against the thin wall, as if squeezed between it and some other immovable barrier. She arched her body between the real and the imagined wall, her swayback coming to a verticality beyond the perfections of ballet.

She stared at Ricky. He stared at her. His eyes were moving. He looked like he might bolt away any second. But she stood in her spot and he sat in his.

It wasn't until her dad passed into the kitchen that Ricky said something. "Yo' daughter had been braidin my hair, sir," he managed. His voice had an intense formality to it now.

"Good," her father said, "sir." He laughed the way he usually did when his day had been long and he didn't give a damn anymore. He looked from the boy to his daughter, back to the boy. "How she doin the job from across the room, though?" Now he was smirking at the both of them.

"I don' know, sir. My name's Rick Parker."

"A'right, Rick Parker." Her dad was still laughing.

"I'ma finish him in a second, daddy," Erycha promised. "I'm almost done."

"Well, get to it, girl. Don' make the man wait now."

"OK," she said.

"A'right," he said.

"A'ight," Ricky said.

Erycha came back to him one sliding little step at a time. Then she started braiding him again. She was sure Judgment Day would present itself before she redid that final braid.

She heard her father still laughing a few feet away. "Ya know, I had a ace boon coon back in the day named Rick. We played ball at Oakland Tech, football, basketball. Ricky Everett was the most absent-mindedest nigga I ever met! I'd ask this boy to loan me some ends, wait on it a few days, pay him back half. Ricky wadn't rich, he jus couldn't remember a damn thing."

Ricky laughed.

"Ricky Everett, Ricky Everett. I ended up havin to come live down here behind some stuff that boy done did, but that's another story."

Ricky maybe didn't pick up on the change in tone, or thought what he had to say was better than lingering over it. "I got a pa'tna like that. Man, I be prankin on my nigga Snow, takin his left-out things—"

"Why they call him Snow?" Her dad cut him off. "He alvino?" His voice was alive again. "I knew a couple cats who had that condition, scare you half to death the first time you see 'em in the dark."

"Nah. Not close. That nigga blacker 'n the back 'a my neck!"

They both burst out laughing hard—at the idiocy of names and friends—almost like they forgot where they were and how to act and the purpose of this whole production.

Erycha knocked her closed-fist on Ricky's head: the braids were done.

Outside the apartment doorway, she had no idea how to handle herself, what she should say, what she should do. What she wanted to do was tell Ricky to go away and not come back. But she knew her father was being drunk and inappropriate; he was listening to them and there was no telling how he would act if she did anything even slightly suspicious toward his new mentee.

"Thanks, Erycha," Ricky offered in a quiet voice.

They shared another meaningful glare.

"$10, right?"

"Uh-huh." She nodded in a cramped inflexible way. "Thanks. Bye."

For a long time after that she made sure when she saw Ricky to pay rent in warm smiles and long intimate hugs. Her reputation was still important to her then. Against her better judgment, she even let him kiss her. She even let him call her his girl. Anything to make sure he wouldn't spread word about what had happened between them.

That was her first and only attempt at braiding hair for money. Now she had ten George Washingtons to show for it, as well as a lesson in desire and a new boyfriend, who called at her from two streets down and showed up at her place unannounced and uninvited. A friend of the family all of a sudden, sometimes Ricky would just wander around the house, just because. All by his lonely he would wander, another loose and aimless brother on the premises.

He had a lot to say to her now. "Erycha, Erycha, Erycha," he said. "If you wanna make cash-money, don' try to get it how you livin, get ya'self from this Westside. Break East."

She didn't need the boy to tell her that. All she had to do was look up Highland Hill at the tilting palm trees and rich homes and the beautiful Buddhist temple to know that that was where the money lived. When she decided to look for housecleaning work there, she told herself the decision had nothing to do with Ricky's influence. The decision was related to the closure of the beauty parlor that she and her mother occasionally got prettied-up at. The place was shut down due to poor sanitation and the possibility of hepatitis transfer. She had made the complicated connection between the beauty parlor and her own braid work, she told herself, that was why she was trying something different. That was the only reason for her decision. Only that. Pure and simple. Nothing to do with what Ricky told her to do.

It took a week of bus rides and long walks and fast rejections and learning to lie about her age before a Mrs. Clarkson said, "What the heck? You know, my husband isn't home yet, but you know what, what the heck? I can tell you're a real strong girl and you'll probably love the work, so what the heck?" and hired her one day a week for a five hour shift and six dollars per hour.

She did not love the work. Nobody loves getting down on her knees and cleaning toilets and shower stalls with Ajax that makes her dizzy with each inhale; or dredging mysterious moist things from between floor tiles; or vacuuming perilous twisting staircases along thin stair-steps; or sweeping out crystal-clear cobwebs from the arches of vaulted ceilings; or constantly having to retrace her steps to pick up after the family's no-account lazy son who slept his days away on their couch. The son, in particular, annoyed her: all he did was lie on his back, watch television and drink beer. He told Erycha that he was twenty-three years old, had even graduated from UCLA, but was in no way interested in working for a living. He needed to rest, he said. Life should consist of more than working to eat at night and rising in the morning to work again, he said. Every-body, he told Erycha, should take at least one year completely off.

She looked at him like an alien after that talk. Even her father, who'd been born tired, had never gone an entire year without work; and his belly had never swelled to twice its natural size; his face had never bloated up like a blowfish from drinking beer day in and day out. This made living off welfare look like working three jobs, and Erycha couldn't understand it as a way of life.

But she told herself that he was part of the family, the Clarkson family that had provided her with a job. She told herself that many people who needed jobs to pay rent, not just buy ballet slippers, didn't have them, so she shouldn't complain. She found her way to the family bedrooms: first, the son's, which she found in a mess and left in military tidiness; then the parents', whose bed was already sufficiently made, a pretty king-sized arrangement set on high wooden legs with white cotton sheets woven into snowflake patterns. Frilled gold and purple pillows were piled out almost to the mid-point of the bed. Erycha pulled herself onto its outer edge and sat there, thinking about all the beds and floors she'd slept on and the one time she even slept in a sandbox, not because she had to, because not even crackheads had to sleep in sandboxes, but just because she had been to the beach by then and learned how soft sand was and wondered ever after what kind of bed it would make. She slept and dreamt, but when she woke the sand had climbed like ants into her clothes and between her teeth. Life was no dream.

She cleaned that house, beds and all, every week for a month and a half. As always with her, she was working hard, the only difference now being her weekly pay. Over those first six weeks, she earned $180, which was more than enough money for ballet slippers. But she found herself with far less than that every time she'd check her money jar: some of it, she knew, went to daily expenses like the meals her parents sometimes were too busy or unaccountable to provide, or the bus fare that was required to get across town. But she couldn't understand how such large sums disappeared so fast. It couldn't all be going to food and fares; it was a strange kind of math that kept her poor. Either her money jar had a hole that was letting the money down an invisible tunnel, or somebody was stealing from her.

It's always somethin, she figured, Always somethin.

The seventh time she cleaned the Clarkson house, the son fell asleep on the couch while she was vacuuming the living room. She counted the scattered beer cans on the floor beneath him in the path of the vacuum cleaner. As she delicately pushed the cans out of the way and ran the vacuum underneath his legs, that gluttonous pro-tuberant temple of a body simply rolled off the couch and fell onto the vacuum, impaling itself there. For a moment he just sort of lay suspended upon the vacuum like a fish snared by a hook. Then he let out a deep groan, "Oooooh! Oooooh!" that bubbled out through the house, and then he tumbled down to the floor face-first. Then, silence.

He lay there all afternoon. When Erycha got ready to leave for home at five o'clock, he was still lying on his belly, with only its subtle rhythmic motion to assure her he was still alive and breath-ing. She had put the beer cans in the kitchen trash can but now she retrieved them and tried to scatter them in the exact pattern that he had. That way Mrs. Clarkson would know why her son was passed out on the floor, and why her vacuum now had a bad dent in it. Then she locked the doors and left.

That night the apartment phone rang once, and a minute later Erycha damn near got yanked out of bed by her braids. Her mother was pulling at her and shaking her more awake than she already was. "Why, why this white woman got me on the phone? Gotdamn. *Sayin you stole from her?*"

"*Stole?* Who sayin that?"

"This woman. Mrs. Carson. That where you been goin?"

"I been makin money, I ain't steal it. I don't know what she about."

Her mother backed up a step. She took a moment. "Three-hund'ed dollars, this woman claimin." Her eyes grew softer brown in the unlit room. The baby fat had mostly gone from around her cheeks. She could no longer look tender or soft without trying.

What Mrs. Clarkson was saying was only what her son had said to her, that Erycha had thieved the emergency stash of money that his parents kept beneath their nightstand. According to him, Erycha didn't clean a damn thing, she just spent her work hours searching for places where the family hid their money. That was why there were beer cans scattered all about the downstairs living room and money missing from underneath the nightstand. It was also why he could spend his days in serene meditation, undisturbed by the loud noises that an honest cleaning girl would have made.

Erycha remembered the man who'd robbed her mother: his looming presence, the black bandana covering everything but his eyes, the gun in his hand. She could tell these folks about real robbery. As for her, she didn't take by unjust means, hadn't hardly even shoplifted but once or twice. The allegation was a sinning-ass lie. "Her son's a liar," Erycha said to anyone who would listen over the course of the next week, but that only included her parents and not Mrs. Clarkson, who summarily fired her from her position and reported the theft to the authorities.

Law enforcement came down and were about to start a serious investigation when the son preemptively confessed to the crime. He had no income, he explained, so how else was he to afford the necessities of food and water? The police weren't in the business of arresting the wealthy for minor theft or for child labor law violations, so the investigation ended before it began.

The charges were dropped, and Mrs. Clarkson apologized to Erycha and Erycha's entire family dating back to slave-times and forward to at least her great-grandchildren's children. She even offered to rehire her at $12 an hour. But by then Erycha had moved on to new employment. She mowed a lawn. Then she tried to sell her father's girl magazines. And when what money she made still disappeared faster than she could grasp it, she began scouting garage sales and pawnshops for a cheaper pair of slippers. But wherever she went, the answer was the same: ballet sounded like a fine lil bag, they'd tell her, but wadn't nobody practicin it round the way. Course she *could* trade in her ballet things for somethin more marketable like a curling iron or a few razorblades, how did that sound?

The sellers and shop owners were always more than glad to help her out in some partial way, but that way never seemed to include selling her cheap ballet slippers. The red pair in the mall's display case haunted her more and more persistently now. They weren't cheap and in fact they were starting to seem more like glass slippers than regular old dance shoes, but there was something firm within her that would not let go ambition, that stiffened and solidified the more she was denied.

Then she hit on the idea of walking people's dogs.

So many people were scared to walk their own dogs. On the sunrise side of the freeway, people groomed their pit bulls and rottweilers for a harsh world; some even fought their dogs the same as they'd play dominoes. In the East, the people stayed scared of the West, bought the same pit bulls and rottweilers and stuck Beware of Dog plaques on their picket fences. To live in the same suburb as one of these dogs was to risk death just walking down the block. Erycha had learned this somehow, and she knew, too, probably from the miscellaneous black truths passed down at funeral services, overheard at homecoming celebrations for boys back from military duty or prison, that there would always be good money in doing dangerous things, that a black man and even a black woman could always stay alive and stay paid if they were willing to risk their lives.

Erycha walked dogs all over town, from the darkened Eastside orange groves, up and down that steep hillside and across the freeway through desolate Westside streets. But she didn't so much walk those dogs as they walked her. The mastiffs and rottweilers regularly doubled and even tripled her in weight, so there wasn't much she could do if one wanted to shit in the middle of a busy intersection or decided to explore a flower bed. Once, the Great Dane she was walking took a deep interest in the shuttered beauty parlor's outdoor display of fake flowers. Nobody had wanted the flowers so after the closure they just sat outside waiting for fate to take them away. The dog turned her toward the flowers, toppled the display, messed around in it and emerged with a garland of plastic roses round its neck. It might as well have been their wedding day, the little girl and the giant dog with the necklace of fake flowers, because everybody watched them walking that day. Everybody had a look to give or something to say. When the corner boys saw them pass, they forgot their usual catcalls and laughed like the dirty dogs they were. Ricky, too. Erycha ignored them and kept moving. The sun set in bright red and dark orange, its last light mixing with thick unyielding smog and the first shades of black night.

And that night, she went first to the Central City Mission, then to her room and in both places she got down on her knees and prayed out the bitterness that was in her soul: God wouldn't give her good luck, let alone dignity. The prize she quested hid in plain sight, just out of reach. As soon as she earned money it disappeared like her pockets were holes or a burglar lived in her money jar. He subjected her to humiliations. He subjected her to the closed thinking of her parents and her community and suspicious white folks. He brought punishments to her that were out of line with any sin she could possibly have committed.

When He has tested me, Job affirmed, I shall come forth as gold. She recited that line to herself after she slipped into bed, hoping it would help her fall asleep.

———

In the morning, she woke unsaved and broke open the pillow casing where she hid her money now. There were nine ten-dollar bills in all, more than enough to pay for her slippers. That afternoon she found her way to the mall and gave her money to a tall, threadlike ma'am who peered down at her with all the bewilderment of a classically trained ballet teacher. ("You, my dear," the instructors liked to tell her, "are what we call shapely." All sighs and surrenders. "Well, goodbye to alignment!") But the woman eventually subdued her surprise and handed Erycha the slippers.

She cradled those slippers like she would her child, all the way home.

Suddenly, she owned what it had taken her so much time, so much coveting and questing to attain—but now a new problem arose: the slippers were all she'd sought, but they were far from all she wanted and needed for ballet. She knew that buying the slippers was only a first step, a first step necessitating so many future steps that she could only imagine how many dogs she would have to walk before she came to the end of the road. There were pointe shoes to purchase, then classes, then full-time enrollment in the Performing Arts School in Redlands, and somehow she would need to do something someway about her shapely swayback. All of it would cost money, and she had no idea how she could continually make more of it, only that she would have to. And her days spun out endlessly in front of her paved with the gold that her journey would exact.

Then she remembered she had an appointment to keep: this time a bizarre old bird who wanted her twin Dobermans walked at 6:45 p.m. on the dot, around her block six times, no more, no less. Erycha wondered what kind of dogs needed disciplining like that, at 6:45 p.m. precisely, six times around exactly. She wondered how scared an old lady would have to be to own twin Dobermans. But money was money. Best not to ask too many questions.

She took the bus across town, picked up the dogs and left it at that.

At first, it was easy going. The dogs obeyed her pulls and jerks and didn't even strain against their leashes when the first poodle sauntered past. Maybe that rigid routine, six times, no more, no less, had made the dogs more disciplined. They were the best behaved she had ever walked.

But then she lost count. When she came past the old lady's house again, she wasn't sure if it was for the fourth or for the fifth time. She yanked on the dogs' leashes again and felt them acquiesce, slowing their pace. They were so well behaved! It was really too bad that their mistress was afraid to walk them: their chests looked sunken, their coats discolored and disheveled; one was short of breath. So she decided that the best thing she could do for the poor old things would be to chance going around one time too many instead of one time too few. After all, who knew how long it would be before they got their next walk, their next glimpse of sunlight? So she went around what she judged to be one time too many.

And as she was nearing the mistress's front lawn, a tall, good-looking boy flanked by his drooling rottweilers came gliding down the sidewalk. He held their leashes too loosely, as if his good looks alone would make them obey. Seeing him so cool, so full of glide, she stopped and stared. Then she realized that it was the wrong time to stop. She tried desperately to rein the Dobermans back. But they refused. Then their resistance turned into a headlong dash up past the mistress's front yard and straight toward the rottweilers. One of the rottweilers gave an exclamatory bark—not warning but anticipation. The beautiful kid looked up and tried to pull his dogs back. But Erycha could see right away that it wouldn't be enough. The dogs' heads were the size of hubcaps, their chests rippled with power. The rottweilers shot forward and the Dobermans shot forward and both their handlers were carried along now, their bodies bent like sprinters just out of the starting blocks, their speed increasing exponentially. The boy managed to turn his body sideways and hold onto both his leashes, steering his dogs off the sidewalk and into the street, and the girl tried to dig in her heels and wrap the leashes more securely round her wrists. They might've even avoided one another except that when Erycha wrapped the leashes round her wrists her dogs sensed the change and pulled forward with even greater force. They angled against her weight into the street where the rottweilers were now being dragged backward by their master's hands on the scruffs of their huge necks. The dogs leapt skyward. The heavier body of the boy was flung underneath them and the lighter girl flew above. What happened next she never figured out. All she knew was when she finally came to rest in an unincorporated patch of soft dirt and fleeing ants she was lying flat on her back, lying there no different than if she was still in bed shading her eyes against the first light of morning. She squinted and looked out at the silent empty street. The dogs had disappeared. The boy had disappeared, too.

She knew something was lost. She was certain some possession, she wasn't sure what, had gone missing in the ruckus. She tried to stand up and look for the lost thing, but something wasn't quite right. She felt unsteady on her feet, her vision was clouded. Whatever it was, it was small and she was having a hard time making fine distinctions between all the little things on the ground: specks of sand, gravel, ants, little black bits of paper crumpled into small twisted-up balls. She dropped back to the ground, angry that she couldn't find what she had lost, angrier that she couldn't even remember what it was she was looking for. She sat on her butt and searched her hands through the soft dirt, blinking and looking and searching and lying flat and closing her eyes when things became clouded again, and then raising up and starting over remanded to the original frustration and confusion. She didn't know how long she stayed there in the dirt, only that she eventually gave up on finding whatever she'd lost. Then she heard a voice distant above her calling down, "Are you OK?"

"Huh." She answered vaguely. She opened her eyes again.

"Um, what's your name?" it asked. It was her derelict prince, she realized. He had returned from wherever he'd disappeared to. Maybe he was what she had lost. She was angry at him for disappearing and happy he was back. She found it temporarily impossible to say what she meant. "My name?" she asked.

"Yeah, what's that name?"

"Me?"

"What state are you in?"

"Who? Whose state? Shit, whatever."

"Hey, I'm only asking the questions they ask football players before they give them the smelling salts." He laughed. She didn't see the humor. "When's your birthday?" he continued. "Day and month and year."

Challenged by his laughter, she sat up again: "September 13th, 1983." She stared up at him defiantly. "And I'm fine, thank you very much." She thrust her chin forward in a tough pose and tried to focus, but everything still flowed liquid and impermanent.

"Really?" The boy shook his head. "Happy belated birthday."

She vaguely remembered a birthday, possibly her own. She vaguely remembered her parents making a fuss, maybe to do with her, but maybe not. But she couldn't remember an actual birthday celebration either with them or with Ricky, who was supposedly her boyfriend now. Either it was her memory or her family, one or the other or both were broken. There were dark open-cut spaces in her mind where happiness should have been. What she could remember was the day before the birthday. The argument in the apartment: the half-said things and the ignorance and hiddenness that were all she had ever learned of her family history. Her dad talking loud from the other bedroom, Get a grip, girl. It's just fi'ty bucks. Stop actin like I killed Jesus. Her mother countering, E'rything's *just* somethin.

Fifty bucks this time, a hundred the next. Your daughter's born-day is tomorrow an' you bout to help that no-account, for what? From the kitchen now, her dad's voice banging through Erycha's bedroom wall, I'ma take care of it. Pursuing him into the kitchen, her mother's voice sliced ice cold through every apartment wall: you always say that, but we wouldn't have shit but chicken an' Newports here if it wadn't for me keepin track 'a the money. Shit. I don't know where half this money be disappearin to. You ain't spendin *my* money nowhere but the swap meet. His back against the wall, you really gon' make me double back on my nigga like that? Then her mother yelling, Yes! What he ever done for you, for us, but get you caught up an' sent down South? We wouldn't even be here if it wadn't for his ass. Back in their bedroom now, her dad fully on the defensive: don' you understand, it was a war goin on. If it wadn't for that man, them West Oakland niggas woulda had me strung up. Her voice faint but cutting, from the bedroom, the door closing behind her: so, what you tellin me? That played-out jail episode more important 'n Erycha's day?

Erycha remembered how she only learned who got the last word in the argument two days later when her dad presented her with a pair of pretty high-heeled black and gold shoes embroidered with sequins. They would fall apart if she ever took them onto a dance floor but might be nice to wear on a date if she ever got to go on one.

The boy smiled his disarming smile and helped her up out of the dirt. She clutched her ballet shoes as he walked her to the bus. When she wobbled on the top step and dropped her fare on the floor, he steadied her, picked up the coins and offered to see her home. All of a sudden, he was too nice to say no to.

The bus ride back into West Highland was slow and full of stops. Afternoon passed into early evening. She let the time go listening to the boy explain that it was always trouble to walk the Dobermans past his pack of aggressive pets. He told how the dogs had shaken him off like water. How it was only when their brawl found its way into a neighboring flower bed that its owner came outside with a water hose and got control of the situation. And how the old lady had tottered out next and retrieved her Dobermans and shooed the neighbor back into her house. How it had taken him some time to walk his animals home, to turn around and come back and see to Erycha. He looked at her, resting his soft brown eyes on hers. "You looked familiar," he said.

Night's shadows swam down his face. The occasional streetlight lit him up then dwindled across the bus's metal railing and floor. She wondered if she actually knew him from somewhere. She wanted to believe they were connected some way, but she doubted it. He didn't attend her school. He dressed too proper and spoke way too proper to be one of Ricky's friends. So how could she know him?

He asked her what her name was again.

She gave it to him.

He told her it was a pretty name.

She thanked him.

She decided she liked him but felt distant from him, as if a destroyed space were between them, blacking out real talk. She wanted to tell him more about herself but something in her held back, told her it wouldn't do any good to try to relate across whatever it was that was between them. Maybe the space was the city itself: she was headed home going West, he would go East. She waited for him to say something.

The bus passed under a bright red sign reading Highland Mall. His regal black face went red, each detail electrically emphasized. She could see the ignorance in his eyes. She knew he was younger than Ricky and more of a kid than even she was, much more ignorant and innocent than she had ever been. She stayed silent.

Finally he said: "So, walking dogs, that's your thing? Why that?"

She still felt the oppressive wall between them. Then the echoing sound of the bus gearing down and coming to its next stop. Her eyes fell from him and his from hers, and they looked ahead toward the bus stop where they were to get off, the vacant lot that was one half of Del Rosa Avenue. She knew she could get off right here, that she could say she was OK, walk off the bus by herself and he wouldn't stop her. But she didn't. She didn't leave.

The bus was moving again. She found herself sitting, riding, staring blankly past his eyes at the Westside's shuttered stores, vacated lots, unlit streets, the whole damn thing running on and on, spilling out poverty. He stared back at her and they locked there, neither of them exiting the bus at the appointed stop but holding to the ends of that unknown ground that divided them.

"Walking dogs is your thing?" he asked her again.

"Uh-huh."

"Why?" he asked again.

"Cuz." She opened her mouth to say more and then stopped. She didn't say anything until the bus came to the next stop. Then, "I been tryin to make money for my ballet. First, it was braidin hair, but that wadn't workin out. So I tried cleanin houses, but the homeowner accused me, lied on me that I was stealin from her. Then I tried some more other things, which, some worked, others was trife. I got them slippers I needed, though. But that was only the beginning."

"How much money have you made?" he asked her.

They got off the bus together and went and stood under a street lamp. She could see his face now. He was dark but not beautiful, she decided, revising her opinion. A boy would have to do something beautiful to be beautiful.

"That's the thing about it, the confusin thing about it. I make the money, then it ain't there when I wake up or come home. It's like my money jar got a big ol' hole in it, or somethin."

"Wow."

"But I love ballet. I cain't just give it up."

"You could do something less expensive. Like stepping. My sisters step."

"I do ballet." She stared across the street down the way a little at the Del Rosa Apartments. The piled petals of a dead rose. "I'm tryina be a ballerina, not just another chick dancin hip-hop. But it costs, na'mean? You wouldn't understand."

He was quiet. Then he wondered aloud: "If you're so poor, why not find out who's stealing all your money? It's not disappearing on its own, right?"

No, it wasn't disappearing on its own, Ercyha said without speaking to him. But she told herself it wasn't as simple as something stolen from her: a million hands were on her money. She had been robbed from, from the day she was born. "Nigga!" She snapped at him. "Nigga, don't try an' tell me."

He fell back like she'd cut him. The expression on his face was confused and innocent. It was his innocence that had brought him here; it was his innocence that led him to ask that last question. He was young. But she had been exposed. She had seen and experienced things. Worldly business she wasn't supposed to know, she knew. She knew that her parents had not met the way they told her they met. She knew they hadn't come South for the reasons they gave. She knew she had been born to this earth in circumstances different than she'd been led to believe. She didn't know why she was here, or any of the other stuff, but that would come with time too, she knew, one painful detail after another until there would be no space left free and blank.

There were a lot of things about her parents she wished to know and didn't know and probably would never know, but one thing she did know about them was that her mother controlled the money. Her mother wasn't about wasting money and wasn't about letting anybody under her roof waste ten cents, let alone hundreds of well-earned dollars. So, if her parents, for all their close-minded, simple ways, weren't the culprits, and if God made no miracles and no mistakes, if money didn't simply disappear down magic passageways, then where had it all gone? Only stupid old Ricky, shit-talking, bullshitting-ass Ricky, the boy whom she was bound to by desire and fear, remained as a suspect. In fact, he stood alone as the culprit. But if she exposed him, she exposed herself. If she called him a thief, he would shrug it off, take his place in line with all the other little criminals. But if he slutted her out, nobody would want her coming around anymore.

Her dilemma was something fierce. She felt things closing in on her. Short on time, on space, on air. She needed to get away from the well-meaning boy, escape his searching questions. She shook her head at him and jumped out into the street, spun around a speeding car, and danced onto the opposite sidewalk. Then she started running. Kept running. Ran until the boy was long gone. She kept running, even though she'd escaped him. Kept running. Ran until she was well down Del Rosa Avenue. Now she was at the far end of the apartment gates. She slipped between the slender rails and the whole time all she could think of was robbery. Robbery, robbery, robbery.

Across the lawn and cement walkway that led to the back end of the buildings, she was still moving like something was chasing her. Climbing the stairs to her apartment door, she suddenly, finally stopped running and found herself in a pause, deadfooted, looking down at the street: the boy from the bus was gone and now she could see the corner boys posted up, sentinel strong, some huddled together, some strolling back and forth outside the apartment gates, others idling in the streets on the lane lines between moving cars. Robbery. The word flashed in her mind. She stopped at a window. She saw some kids in loose jeans and white T-shirts run a Mexican guy's pockets for his wallet, loose change and whatever else they could seize. Then they disappeared down an alleyway into the neighborhood cuts. Robbery. She saw the Mexican walk out of the alleyway and onto Del Rosa. He spoke to two other Mexican men, gesturing at his emptied pockets. The two men just nodded and kept their hands in their pockets. They ain't his friends, Erycha thought. He thinks it's like that, but it ain't like that. Robbery, she thought to herself. Then she saw Ricky. Then he saw her. After a second, he smiled, baring his teeth, and blew her a kiss. She could see his thieving nature working its way inside his affection, inside the kiss, snaking into her. Robbery, she thought. He motioned to her to come back down to the street. *Robbery!* He motioned at her again and she nodded against what she assumed was her will.

And back on the street, he held her tightly around her waist. She felt what it was to have male hands inside her intimate space, that hard soft confused comforting wanting touch. She felt protected and bare naked all at once. He kissed her and she responded a little.

Inside the apartment she could hear dinner unfreezing in the microwave, whirring like a rutting vacuum cleaner. Her dad was fast asleep despite it, splayed out snoring on the family couch.

Then above all the other noise, she heard the voices of women. From the kitchen, her mother and her beautician girlfriend from the below-code salon were chattering away like birds vexing in a cage. *Idn't it terr'ble what the city's come to? Criminality wherever you turn.* Speak on it, girl. *You see these young men, just hangin around like there ain't nothin else to do when they could be earnin money honestly at a job.* I see 'em, too. I see 'em, too. *Been robbed my-own-self, right outside that door and in broad daylight too.* How to control these young boys is a mystery. Doubt if God knows. *God may have abandoned black people. Wouldn't blame Him neither, with all the mess that goes on.* And your daughter right here, gotta witness it all. *And my daughter right here, gotta witness it all.*

Erycha started listening, but then the truth lit up in her mind how black people could speak against criminality and wrong and wickedness all day, but never did much to take it decisively out of their world. Everyone, herself included, allowed worldly sin into their most intimate spaces. She had seen—in this very neighborhood where she was born and loved and neglected and half-raised—black folks accommodate everything from stillborn children, to illness, to outright murder, and poverty that simply didn't have to be, and Lord knows they didn't hardly do a thing about it. No, she thought to herself, black people just ain't studyin protection too hard. We sittin down with danger, down at the table, and we lettin him stay in the house, no different than we accommodate troublesome family. That's why I'm out here gettin caught up like this. That's why I'm gettin stole, *stolen* from like this. Because my people won't protect me. Because I don't know from sin how to protect myself.

She decided not to pray that night.

And in the morning she woke early and instead of getting dressed for school left home in her night clothes and went down to the pawnshop that opened at seven a.m. all days and she sold her ballet slippers for as many razorblades and rubbers as those shoes could bring.

II

Children's Stories

B ut there were good times too. Before Ricky stole from her and before she sold her slippers, there was the time that the small-minded ballet teacher at the dance studio in Redlands went out of town for three weeks and two twin sisters stepped in as her substitute. The sisters didn't complain about Erycha's curves because they had more curves than Erycha could imagine having. Their bodies were free spirals whirling out and in and out again. The sisters didn't fit within ballet's thin little lines and the sisters couldn't care less. Their self-confidence was obvious.

The sisters didn't tell Erycha that she couldn't dance ballet or that she was best suited for lower forms of movement. Their encouragement implied the opposite, that ballet was only one among many styles, that there was no hierarchy of forms and no last word on beauty. Her body was already right. Over the course of those three sessions, the girl's desire turned not just from technique but away from ballet and for a while all she wanted was to be as graceful and gorgeous and confident as the sisters. During the three Saturday mornings that she spent as their student, Erycha became more engaged with dance as an excitement, an art, a craft, a moment of wonder, than she had ever been before or would ever be again. She was thirteen years old. She felt beautiful when either of the two instructors took time with her, stretching her, pressing upon her hamstrings, kneading her restricted calf muscles, turning her hips out for her in a way that was careful and sensitive and demanding all at the same time.

The twins knew a lot about flexibility and contemporary dance in its many forms, but next to nothing about ballet. Erycha didn't know that the girls had gotten the job through their father: Professor Freeman was a tenured professor at the university where her small-minded ballet instructor worked as an adjunct lecturer in the dance department. The Professor had wandered over to the Dance Building and dropped a number of hints about how his daughters needed instructional experience if they were to bolster their résumés within the academic art world. While he favored the idea of the twins team-teaching a modern dance class under supervision from a professional dance instructor, he also wasn't too particular. When the adjunct requested, for undisclosed personal reasons, to take an extended leave from teaching mid-semester and Professor Freeman offered to provide a substitute for the instructor without monetary compensation and without telling administration about her absence, the trade-off was natural. Where with professional supervision the girls would have been expected to teach the class systematically, with the sole focus being on ballet, this way they opened an experience altogether unexpected and more beautiful.

At the third and last lesson that they conducted, the twins began class by introducing their family to the students and the many parents who brought their daughters to the studio each Saturday morning. Erycha's main impression of her substitute instructors' parents was that they smiled much more than the adults she was used to engaging with. They were also better-dressed than most people over thirty, especially as this was the weekend and most adults considered the weekend the only chance at freedom that life still offered. She liked the twins' parents as much as she liked the twins themselves. She wondered why her parents couldn't be more like this, why the kids she knew whose parents were much worse than hers, abusive, drug-addicted, imprisoned, all the etceteras, never got to see adults who were comfortable with themselves, comfortable with one another, in love with one another, just doing their marriage thing without being all dysfunctional about it.

The twins introduced their parents by full name and professional title. Then they sort of gestured at the boy that the parents had brought with them. He would be known as "little brother," they said. For his part, little brother never raised his eyes to look at the dance students who had congregated in a standing circle around him and his parents. Erycha thought it was a little strange that a boy about her age wouldn't want to look at a bunch of teenage girls in skin-tight leotards. Probably gay. But if he were gay, wouldn't he be interested in the dance studio? Little brother didn't even glance up and say hi. Erycha wondered if he was as attractive as his sisters and figured he probably was. But she couldn't tell with his head turned down. She figured by the way the boy held that stance, his feet so firmly planted, his eyes so intently fixed on his feet, that it was less shyness than indifference that kept him from showing his face.

The class itself was good and then it was over, and she sensed the end of something. She knew the twins could quickly forget her and that she could, even would forget them, too, first their names, then their faces and familiar bodies, all forgotten. Then she would forget that they had ever even existed within the world that she knew.

And then there was the Spring Break of their junior year in high school: the visit to Oakland.

Erycha went on the trip North because she was under mandate. Her mother was trying to retie bonds that had broken between her and her daughter and her and her family up North. When she was a little girl Erycha went with her mother to the Central City Mission almost every Sunday. Receiving the Word of God was a good thing but it was hardly the only benefit: there was the time spent together walking up to G Street and the time at the Mission amidst so many prayerful strangers and the time it took to walk home. What they had had together was time. But she couldn't remember the last time she'd been to the Mission on a Sunday, nor the last time she'd taken a walk with her mother. Now a five-hundred mile car ride was required to do what a simple walk up the block had given them before: time together and alone. Even worse, Erycha knew that she didn't really want to be there and only went because she felt obligated.

Touissant went on his trip without mandate but simply out of an anthropological interest in the history of his people in California. He loved history in all the shapes it took, and his many elderly Bay Area relatives represented a remarkable living history. They had come from the Deep South states to Oakland and the other port towns of the Bay Area to work in the World War II shipyards and factories. They had survived and outlasted legal segregation, the War, white flight, the Black Panthers, Black Power, police terrorism, the crack wars and urban gentrification. Black California was an isle in an archipelago of histories.

The trip meant different things for the girl and for the boy. For Erycha, it was a tedious shit-smelling drive up the 5 Freeway, the seven-color sky constantly threatening a rain that California-style never came, just darkened the hot stinking earth. All this for the irrational end purpose of going to a ghetto even more squalid and violent than the place she called home. Deep East Oakland. The flat lands. Sobrante Park. One road in, one road out. She had visited Sobrante once before, the last time her mother had tried to reconcile with her family, and was familiar with how the same group of dudes posted themselves in front of the liquor store that marked the entrance to and exit from the neighborhood. 24/7/365, apparently. It was like they were private security or something, holding the line between the outside world and the world of their insular little neighborhood. Erycha wasn't sure why Sobrante was designed the way it was or what motives might really cause a community to be so closed off that it formed a ghetto within a ghetto and a deep recess of neglect. It was a reality she didn't understand and didn't want to learn. She chose to read all the fiction.

For Touissant, the trip was a one-hour flight and a five-minute drive into a nice little suburban East Oakland neighborhood where the streets were lined with evergreen trees, the modest one-story homes were well-kept, and most of the residents drew Social Security. The home where his parents had arranged to stay was itself an historical artifact: it stood as one of the first black-owned homes in all of East Oakland. The elderly couple that had bought the home in the 1940s were still very much alive and busy with the present day, but they were also proud of their past and liked to tell about how they had paid for their first stove with their last five dollars only to have it damaged by the rocks that the white people threw through their front window. How the kindly Portuguese family next door had loaned them money to buy bars for their windows and a dog to guard their lawn. How the red-lining of arriving blacks and the departure of whites had initiated a period of decline for most of the surrounding neighborhoods, but never on their streets, never in their home. How they had come through it all, together, with their backs straight, with a foundational investment in the golden state. Their stories were only the beginning: their friends and children stopped by randomly, all hours day and night, a true community that shared kin and history and fresh-caught fish, wagered goods and time as much as money on cards and horses and dominoes, and told story after story.

Touissant only left the old house to run errands, he was so interested in all this.

One afternoon, both children were sent to the corner store. For Erycha, it was the store past the dangerous-looking liquor store that marked off Sobrante Park from the rest of East Oakland. For Touissant, it was the convenient little spot that the elders had made a habit of sending him to several times a day. He didn't mind: the store was interesting in its own culturally specific way. For Erycha, her trips to the store were an annoyance because they required her to skirt past the men on the Sobrante corner who tried to talk to her and get her number and called her bitch and white girl each time she kept her head in her book and ignored them. For Touissant, the trips were funny little vignettes in his visit, where he could overhear arguments about Black Jesus and Tongan Mormonism and underground rap music, where he could watch the Moroccan storeowners compulsively dust their prayer rug and fiddle with the old transistor radio on top of the cigar shelf, which brought in only static. At first, he expected that they had the radio tuned to a frequency just out of range of the call to prayer. But one time one of the men rattled the radio just right and a local college basketball game came on.

Inside the store, Erycha waited in line, her thoughts deep within Jane Austen's delicate, if still difficult, world. The store was filled with men and she knew that most of them, Muslims included, were probably judging her by her ass. That was all the more reason to imagine her body transported to stately old aristocratic Britain, where the worst of things was light work compared to Oakland. Someone wondered aloud if the new girl with the white headwrap and the strange high school name imprinted on her sweatpants was just a visitor or here to stay for good. She didn't help them solve the mystery, just kept on reading. Well behind her in line, Touissant couldn't see the name of the high school on the girl's sweatpants, but he did notice that she was reading. He couldn't see the title or the author of the book she held in her hand, but he knew by its size and the portrait of prim gentlemen and gowned women on the cover that it was one of those very old British books about people too rich to work and their arranged marriages and all that. Strange, he thought. He had read one book by Jane Austen, *Sense and Sensibility,* for school and it had been so boring it made him wish he was illiterate.

He wanted to talk to the girl with the modest white headwrap and the book in her hand, but since he didn't know anything about the book he knew he would just come off the same as any other guy

looking for an in. Better not to. He knew by the way she held herself so still, like a dancer with her back poised taut curving up from
an invisible floor, that she was in no mood to talk. He had seen his
sisters hold themselves just that way in the presence of men they
didn't care for. There were other ways to start a conversation, to draw
her attention, to light up a bright place in her mind where she could
see him as special in some way. But Touissant was only beginning
to learn how to do more than study people for their histories and
cultural signs; he didn't yet know how to relate in ways that would
make people feel alive and vulnerable and open all at once.

He said nothing. He watched Erycha pay for her bundle of groceries and leave. The light that flowed through the store's open front
door was so incredibly bright that she disappeared into it as she left
and he never saw what book she was reading or her face. Out in
the open air, the girl saw the same incredibly brilliant sunshine and
wondered at the difference between the Bay, with all its cold bright
sunlight, and the hot gray colored place that she was from. Somethin good in the hood, she thought, smirking. Somethin, fi-na-lly.

And then there was the time they met in a dream: they and everybody else in the lost world were wandering about a lush garden
bounded by a four-walled bright blue sky. They were asking each
other for answers to the mysteries that their brothers and fathers
and grandfathers and men even older than that had left them with.
Missing soldiers and runaway parents and people shot dead in the
street and quiet men, who allowed their families everything but their
innermost thoughts, found life and revelation in the questions that
Touissant and Erycha and all the other searchers asked and answered.
The people hugged each other, thanked each other, found comfort
in knowledge. Touissant learned things that no family tree could tell
him about Alabama and Mississippi and New Orleans and about his
family there and the story of his great-granddad on the run.

Erycha saw her father, her young father, watching her mother sleep and wondering at the secret in her belly. She wasn't showing yet, but he knew. A man feels it when his woman is pregnant, feels that baby in his own guts. He'd heard that from his Mississippi kinfolk. Erycha saw him looking at her through her mother's shirt and skin. She saw him incarcerated and in fear of his life in the pen. She saw him sent down state like an auctioned slave down river, and how he emerged from that drowning water at the halfway house and then at the Mission and then in the home that her mother, who had followed in his wake, made as if bound to him, chained by her dreams and by a newborn daughter. It was a dream of bondage but at least in the dream she knew how her world had come to be.

III

They brought bolt cutters to break the bolts and a hammer in case the bolt cutters didn't work. They brought Windex to wipe away fingerprint stains and gloves to conceal their fingerprints, and black clothes so no one would see them messing around up there with the door that led onto the high school's Clock Tower roof. The one girl said, yeah, definitely, most definitely they was gonna get to the roof and couldn't no security guards stop 'em. Another was talking about hanging their socks and bras from the awning once they got up there. That sounded like something that would be funny the next day. But then there was this other girl—Erycha didn't know her name—she said it was the stupidest shit ever. Freshman type shit, she sniffed. And freshmen bitches were the dumbest bitches livin.

The front door leading into Tower Auditorium was already unlocked so they got inside real easy. Then all they had to do was climb four empty flights of stairs. On the third floor, the Mexican janitor was singing from down the hallway.

"Messican music." Quincia laughed.

Lindsay laughed too.

Erycha laughed as well, but she laughed because she actually understood the song the janitor was singing: it was a corrido about a drug runner and his demanding mistresses. The runner kept having to make trips North because he had a different woman in each barrio and each one was determined to be the star in her dusty little version of heaven. She thought how Ricky was sort of like that, an up-and-coming hustler with cash flow, a girl-getter. She hoped the corrido ended with the drug runner selecting his smartest girl, moving her from her mother's house into her very own paid-for mansion. He would also need to tell all his other ladies to get ghost.

She was feeling good. Maybe the feeling came from hanging out with sophomores and juniors. Maybe it was to do with getting to know her new step squad teammates Quincia and Lindsay. It was Quincia who had found out that Erycha could dance and broke it down to her that ballet was some cold Caucasian bullshit, the only style of dance where the dancer had to get up on her tiptoes with the melody instead of down low where the rhythm was. It was all about tiptoes and straight lines and flatness. It was just too proper, Quincia counseled. The only fun dance styles were the ones where girls didn't have to be all proper: like stepping, where you could get low and curvaceous and cold beautiful with it. Erycha, all of a sudden, agreed. She learned to like stepping. Even if it wasn't as high artistic as ballet, at least it was fun. That, in the end, was why she had started stepping and why she was sneaking onto the Clock Tower roof right now. It was fun and not proper.

Erycha did improper things all the time, but they weren't much fun; praying in anger wasn't fun, arguing about money wasn't fun, and having sex with Ricky on the regular wasn't near as fun as it would have been if her mind wasn't always preoccupied with life-concerns and birth control complications while he was giving it to her.

She let the sophomore and the junior and the other girl go ahead of her. All the girls were wearing black on black sweatpants and shirts and do-rags. Those, along with the Windex and bolt cutters and black gloves were pieces in the master plan. They'd be harder to spot in the dark that way, so the logic of the scheme went. But Erycha had wandered around campus enough times after step squad practice to know the school got empty long before dark. No one, white, black or blue was going to get caught because there was no one except the singing janitor around to do the catching and his mind was down in Mexico with his gold-digging broads and the drug dealers who loved them. They might as well start clapping and stepping and making the ground talk back to them, they were so free.

I n his dream, Touissant could see his black shadow running ahead of him. He looked over his shoulder at his pursuer, a black shadow without a face chasing after him in long, fast strides. "Touissant," the shadow at his back shouted. "Touissant. Why you runnin?"

No, Touissant thought, No. He was fast but not as fast as the shadows that bracketed him. The shadow behind caught him and pulled him to the ground. They wrestled there, striking each other with concussive fists and elbows. But the man was full-grown and stronger than Touissant. He gained leverage, rolled the boy onto his stomach, straddled him and wrenched his arm out of its range of motion. Touissant gasped in total pain. "Who am I?" the man shouted. "Boy, who am I?" Touissant's body tensed hot with anger. He saw white, the color of death. The voice was his granddad's voice. He didn't know why he wanted to kill the man, but he knew he wanted to kill him, make him disappear. He tried to think what to do with his free arm that would disappear the man. He convulsed his body and wrenched around and punched at the shadow and hit something that was hard and ungiving knuckle-first so that a shooting pain radiated down the bones of his hand one at a time and brought him awake, cold with sweat and trembling. He remembered to open his eyes: his bedroom, quiet and dark and alone. Outside his open window the Buddhist temple rose up, many-roofed, many-spired, like a hand and fingers reaching after the stars and moon.

Now the sun was battling through Highland's afternoon smog, declaring its fierce existence. Touissant shaded his eyes, and now he could see the mean smile working in little spasms, interrupting the smooth line of his sister's jaw and cheekbone. He had given Dea's phone number to a boy on the high school football team. The football boy didn't seem to understand that Dea had graduated, was about to start school at USC and only dealt with men now. Touissant didn't seem to understand this either. But she was about to teach him.

Touissant didn't say he was sorry, just ducked the right cross he knew he had coming.

Missing with the right, she managed to connect with a left upper-cut to his chin. Touissant reeled back in his seat and tried to make himself into a ball and unbuckle his seat belt all at the same time. She threw another combination, but he blocked it and now with his body free he lunged at her, punching her in the shoulder. She pushed his light body away from her and squared him up for another blow. Touissant tried to get the car door open so he could at least get out and fight her in open space, but Dea's hands were quick and in a moment she'd slashed him across the nose. Touissant tasted blood on his teeth and spit it out. His nose was bleeding. He opened the car door, fell out into the street and then he lay there wondering if he should get up and run or if he should fight back. She had a skill and aggressiveness he couldn't match, her body was thick and strong and four important years older than his. He was aware of his sunken chest and narrow shoulders. He rolled onto his side figuring he could slide-tackle her and get her on the ground. He swung his leg out, catching her high-heeled shoe and bringing her down. She screeched and fell. He pounced at her instantly, but she rolled out of the way just as quick and started kicking him in the stomach. He threw a punch that tangled in her hair and made her scream and kick even harder. He was winning now, but the kicks were becoming so violent that he spit out the pebbles that had gotten up into his mouth, and for a moment as they flew away in balls of shining saliva he was afraid the little rocks might be his teeth.

Touissant's sisters were twin vipers now, long slen˙ʟr gorgeous and mean, twins in their pretty faces, twin twosomes of long legs, developed breasts, rounded backsides and entitled attitudes.

The summer marked for them a final moment before college. Other than warding off high school boys and boxing their brother, there was nothing to do. They slept the days away, often in each other's arms and each other's beds, as if no space existed between them whatsoever. Like you couldn't work a wisp of air between them they were so close, even when they were asleep. But nights, they managed to wake and to sneak away to places unknown and far enough away that they rarely returned before dawn. For a while, Touissant had no idea where they were sneaking away. He was a well-behaved fourteen years old so he barely knew that the hours after midnight and prior to daylight even existed, let alone why Dea and Kia would want to use them to sneak out first-floor windows into waiting sports cars. Unlike his parents, who were too busy with their jobs and his care to wake at the drop of a high-heeled shoe on tiled floor or the slow, near imperceptible opening of the library room window, he heard every movement in their escapes and returns. He would go to his second-floor bedroom window, which faced directly onto the street below, and watch them dash through the unreproving shine of streetlights into an idling vehicle; he would watch them return under fainter dawn light, a window's skillful breach, a stiletto's smallest sound. Every night, he wondered where they went. He wondered what they did that made them so tired in the days.

"They sleep so much, they might start growing again," their father laughed. "Get tall enough, they might be supermodels. Make some real money."

"They're getting the sleep in now because they know USC won't let 'em," their mother said. "They can spend their summer however they want to, long as they handle their business come fall."

Like Touissant, the twins were vessels of potential: all they had to do was be brilliant when they arrived at college. That was all anyone asked of talented children in their world.

"Where do you guys *go?*" Touissant wanted to know.

"Out," Kia answered guardedly.

"Yeah. Out," Dea said.

He noticed that where before they had only acted as one, now they seemed telepathic.

"Why do you care?" Dea sighed. She went and closed the door so that the conversation would stay in the bedroom. She looked at Touissant the same way she had right before she had swung on him in the car earlier that summer.

"Yeah, don't you have, like, better things to do than watch what we're doing at three in the morning? Like sleep?" Kia questioned.

No, he shook his head. He didn't have anything better to do at that hour. He wanted to do whatever they were doing, or at least know something about it. He wasn't trying to upset their routine, he was just curious. But there had always been this unbridgeable gap lying between the twins and him, as if their two-ness versus his solitary inviolable individuality prohibited any real connection.

"When I was your age, all I did was sleep at night," Dea said. She made her eyebrows arch in regal condescension. Touissant knew not to take her looks too seriously.

Kia mimicked Dea's glare.

"It's not like I'm snitching on you," he maintained. "I just asked a question."

"Snitch." The twins hissed in unison. "You sure as hell won't snitch."

"I promise, I won't."

"You better not."

"I said I wouldn't."

"We'll make you learn a new dance if you do, boy."

"Like I said . . ."

"See, that's why we can't tell you anything, because you'll snitch."

"Look," he said, holding up his fingers one after the next. "Think about it: I already would've told if I had wanted to. I don't need to know where you guys are going to know that you're sneaking out without permission. I could already have told Mom and Dad. Whether you tell me where you all go has no bearing on that; if anything, telling me will make me less likely to tell." He paused and ran his tongue along his lips with predatory satisfaction. "If I was going to tell, I would've when I found that piece of blue cloth stuck in the windowsill."

"Huh?" the twins asked.

"Look at your blue dress." Touissant nodded. He knew they wore one another's clothes interchangeably, and that his little piece of evidence would implicate both girls if their parents ever saw it. It was really just a little rag of blue thread from the hem of the dress, hardly worth the mentioning, but he enjoyed the intrigue that its revelation lent the episode, like a plot twist in a nineteenth-century novel.

He yawned and watched them hurry to their shared closet, rifle through their shared wardrobe, through their many mini-skirts and mini-tops and blouses and dresses and strapless gowns and velour leotards until they found the blue dress. Indeed, it was rent at its edge. Kia looked to Dea, who looked back to Kia. Then they looked back to their cold-eyed little brother and they seemed to understand that there was no chance of recovering the evidence from him, that matching wits and words with the boy was an effort bound for failure. They were gifted girls but that gift was in music and dance, not deduction or rhetoric. They couldn't argue their way back into control of the situation. Their conniving little brother had out-thought them and managed to get what he wanted.

They realized, in unison, that he would come with them the next time they went clubbing.

The boyfriends were right there waiting for them when the girls and Touissant sneaked out the house, over the fence and across the driveway. The two boyfriends nodded respectfully at Touissant as he hustled into the little sports car. "What's up, young G?" Dea's said. "How you doin, homie?" Kia's greeted.

All Touissant could see of the two men were their shaggy dreadlocks and dark, creased faces. This equated to experience in his mind. He imagined the little car tipping from side to side as they headed down the freeway, its progress altered by the imbalance between innocence and experience, and the twins somewhere in between.

"Hey, bruh," Dea's boyfriend said, "I know a dude knows some security at the club. Said he could get us in no problem." He looked over his shoulder at Dea as he drove.

"My sister and I can get into any club in the world," Dea responded. "Yes, we're *that* fine."

"Amen to that," the boyfriend said.

Kia's boyfriend added, "Lots 'a bouncers wouldn't let us in wit three under-aged people. Not 'less the hoes were suckin his dick."

"Well, maybe the dudes will need to get on *y'all* knees to get us in," Dea shot back.

"Hey, young G, you boogie? C-walk? Stroll? What's your dance of choice?" Dea's boyfriend tried to change the subject.

"No," Dea snapped. "No, he doesn't like to. And you're not going to teach him any gangster dances either. That's foul. Touissant doesn't dance."

"Yeah," Kia seconded, protectively. "Leave him be."

Without warning, a huge neon sign loomed overhead, capturing Touissant's attention. Club Cash, it read. A Jamaican dancehall beat droned through the building's open doors.

The club was the kind of abject scum-dumpster that had long characterized the Inland Empire, so low-end that neither identification nor blowjobs were required for under-age people to gain entrance. The security just let everyone through. Inside, the boyfriends still wouldn't leave Touissant be. The point of clubbing, they said, was having fun, dancing and drinking. If Touissant wouldn't dance, he would have to drink. While Dea and Kia moved around on the dance floor, the two men passed the time by testing the kid's tolerance. A sip of this, a shot of that. Touissant had no idea what he was downing. All he knew was that some of it tasted smooth and good while other drinks were so harsh that he would almost gag as the liquid fell through his throat. As he drank, he listened to the men describe in analytical detail the advantages and disadvantages of various drinks, their effects and potentialities in all kinds of circumstances, from the bedroom to the bathroom. He stood back against the bar, observing: Club Cash was a moving mural of flashing bright colors, short skirts and baggy jeans, and dances that looked like sex. The twins moved from partner to partner and always back to one another. This is how they express themselves, he thought, not sure whether the dances that looked like sex were a good or bad thing. Maybe some things, like music and dance and sex, weren't actually good or bad but something else beyond judgment. He tried to sort through his thoughts and impressions, but it was all too fast and new to understand.

He let the music wash over him, everything felt now, each sensation fresh. But just when he had started to move to the music, letting the drums and bass line mold his spine, he felt something surge up from his stomach, up to his throat. He remembered the flu, the way his vomit felt like a rope of acid in his throat: the liquor rose from his stomach, returned to his throat, burned his lungs, demanded to rise up and revolt out onto the dance floor. He hurried toward what he thought might be a bathroom, and the next thing that came clear to him was a mass of waving dreadlocks like dancing Africans grooving before him and a voice saying, "C'mon, blood, heave it up, heave it up. Won't do no good if you don't eject that shit."

It was Dea's boyfriend.

Touissant felt the pressure in his throat again and spun back around to the toilet. Then he felt better.

He could hear Kia's boyfriend's panicked voice saying, "He done? He done yet?"

"I don't know, ask him," Dea's said. "You got anything left, homie?" he asked Touissant.

"We cain't just sit up in a women's restroom like won't nobody notice," Kia's hissed in return.

Touissant looked around: everything was so clean except the toilet stall.

He stayed awake too long that night and the hangover hit him while he was still awake, etching pain into not only his movements but his thoughts as well. When it was finally time to go home, he fell asleep in the car and dreamt that he was running again. The shadow that had been his granddad was gone, but the shadow ahead of him was still ahead of him and it was still running faster than he could ever imagine running. It was Major Freeman. He was young again and slender and even in his overalls, it was apparent he was long and country-strong in ways Touissant could only hope to become. He fled down an industrial back alley, through the basement of a factory, ducking strangely angled metal pipes and beams, then into a cramped kitchenette over and past children and a woman sleeping on a thick-carpeted floor. Then they were running through a forest of mossy low-hanging trees. The air was moist and thick all of a sudden, the humidity settling down all over the body like a heavy girl with child-bearing fat and curves riding a man. Touissant saw his great-granny, ran past her like a signpost; then there was a pretty girl the color of sunlit beach sand, and then she was gone, left behind, too. Then they were in a small shack and hurtled headlong toward a cavernous big black woman who stretched out her arms toward them. They surged into her embrace and ran through her and came out her backside. Then they were beyond the shack. They kept running and hit swampland and then the mouth of the Gulf rose out of the near horizon and the shadow careened toward it. There was nowhere to go but into the water. Touissant told himself he had no choice but to jump in, but at the water's edge he stopped.

The dream was out of his mind before sunrise; but when he told his sisters everything that he hadn't dreamt but that had actually happened that night at the club it was enough to make them suddenly protective and principled. They weren't above trading punches with him, and they liked it when their boyfriends took liberties with them, but no man who violated their little brother was worth their minutes.

The sports car never came back after that either in daylight or after dark. And Dea and Kia actually spent the final weeks of July in the house nights.

Then they found a new friend to replace the boyfriends. He was a skinny unattractive white kid named Tim. He sported uncombed, mop-like hair, ugly spectacles and awkwardly spaced freckles. It was one thing to have freckles, another for them to tatter the face like scarification.

But he majored in electronic and experimental music at an institute just outside L.A. during the school year and spent his summers facilitating projects with vocalists and bands. Though a prolific composer on his computer, he didn't play an instrument or sing, facts upon which he would discourse at charming and self-deprecating length. He won the sisters over and in no time they were recording tracks and hanging out on beaches and boardwalks and nightclubs together. They were quite a combination, Touissant thought, with latent malice, this strange triangle of beauty and white nerdiness, talent and white musical appropriation.

With Tim's unexpected appearance, the Freeman house became inundated with new-wave-experimental, industrial-experimental, house and dub and trance-experimental, hip-hop, trip-hop and dancehall, African, Bangra and West Indian-experimental musicology. The sounds were disorganized and inconsistently rhythmic and sometimes startling beautiful; they were also so loud they cracked the glassware, rumbled the floor and walls and made reading impossible.

The parents decided they loved the music and that Tim was a very nice young man, while Touissant decided the opposite and withdrew to locations within the house that were further and further from the noise. He remembered his dreams, the black men, the running away. He didn't know why he had run from the black men, but he knew if it had been a white man doing the chasing he would have turned and fought. He was sure he would have. He recalled the urge to dance at the night club, and how the deeper urge to wretch up his insides had attended and finally superseded it. More and more, he was coming to dislike music, in particular the way it brought people together and created strange alliances like the one that developed between Tim and his family the summer before his sisters moved away.

It was not Tim but Mrs. Freeman who decided the twins should have a going-away party. Tim, as well as Mr. Freeman, just made themselves useful: Tim arranged a score for the party out of his volumes of unpublished work, and Touissant's dad wrote out half the necessary checks. Touissant's mom, though, not only wrote out her share of the checks, she also sent out e-mails and did up flyers and put up banners and balloons, ordered a caterer and talked the neighbors into blocking off the cul-de-sac for the special night. She organized a neat schedule of events and oversaw Tim's selection of music, and essentially planned everything down to the finest detail.

She even planned around her unengaged son, making sure not to involve him any more than he wanted to be involved.

Touissant was her pride, her last and most distinctly gifted child. She had long ago given up on trying to understand or relate to him. Instead of worrying about that fact or reading books on child rearing, she simply decided that his talent couldn't be divorced from his difference, that in fact the essence of some gifts was not in the unity but the separation that they wrought. She couldn't love him the same way she loved her girls. He was different. With him loving was letting him be.

So he managed to keep to himself, to stay an outsider to the event. When the guests began to roll up in their cars and park all about the cul-de-sac and filter into the street, the driveway, the house, he was stationed in his familiar perch at his bedroom window that overlooked it all. From there, he could see beyond the neighborhood and its sound walls all the way out to the dry river basin. And beyond the basin, the freeway and the western half of Highland stretched away and away toward the horizon and the setting sun.

It wasn't until long after the sun had set that the party really started. Half the suburb was in attendance by then, either thronging the street or crowding the front yard or eating and drinking inside the house.

As the night wore on and the food and drink wore out, the guests left the house in a steadier and steadier stream until only Touissant was left there. Then he could see everyone out in the street, all his sisters' admirers, from the adults come to congratulate them to the boys trying to date them. He could hear Tim's score resounding throughout the neighborhood, the soundtrack to a whiteboy's discovery of multiple musical diasporas, the music of the slums transplanted to the suburbs. It sounded much better than Touissant figured it should. The music was rolling like an ancient thunder, with long, deep bass lines and hybrid tonal riffing and melodies to cry over. Down below, he could see shadows on the street. The shadows were dancing and talking and doing whatever with seemingly unconscious joy.

He lay in bed for what seemed like hours listening to the twins' long musical goodbye. He got sleepy and felt himself falling away. There was that pre-dream detachment of brain from body that came right before the end of consciousness and the beginning of mystery, so that now, for a wonderful moment, he could choose between thoughts and feelings and not have to confuse the one with the other. He was courting sleep, running after it without quite catching it, letting it run ahead a little further, a little further, not wanting to be completely conscious nor drop away into black oblivion. It's perfect like this, he thought, as long as you can choose between thinking and feeling, one then the other, but not both.

The music lowered in pitch and a new sound rose up: the twins were singing. It had been so long since last he'd heard them sing, he'd almost forgotten what their voices sounded like. Now they sounded brand new.

> My Je-sus, Je-sus!
> Christ, Christ,
> My mornings and my nights!

He got out of bed, went to the window again. In the early Highland years, he'd still been small enough to climb into the windowsill, sit there and look out at the known and unknown world. But now he was older and all he could do was rest his forearms on the sill and stick his head out through the open frame and wonder about the mess in his mind.

He could see the girls in the lit driveway, which functioned as a sort of illuminated stage for them. Their faces were prettier than ever. Their flowing black dresses contrasted that light and set them off in a combination of color and darkness. They seemed to waver on a slender edge between one thing and another, between this moment and whatever would come next.

Out the corner of his vision, Touissant saw a black slash flee along the road. He looked after it and then he knew that even though he was awake, his dream was coming back to get him. The shadow wasn't running away, it was returning; lit by the walkway lanterns of the Buddhist temple, it sprinted up the outer road, up the cul-de-sac, a blur weaving between the people below, leaping through the night up to his window. Now he saw him in full clear view: a young black man with long red shreds of someone's hair coiled tight as chains around his hands. Touissant did not move, but shut his eyes and ran away.

Erycha was a dancer without a dance floor. That's how she thought of herself, a chemical outside its element. It would've been one thing to pop-and-lock or step or breakdance. Breakdancers, especially, had it good: their dance floor was a piece of cardboard and a street corner or an abandoned warehouse or somebody's garage. Maybe she would have to figure out how cardboard and a ballerina could dance together.

In the winters, the Mission held a talent show to raise funds for stopping violence or AIDS or something, but she never competed because she knew it would turn into more of a popularity contest than a real talent show. Besides, there was no way for her to compete; other than the steppers, the only talent at the shows was the little half-decent rappers. Ricky was in that group and that was the only reason she even paid the talent show the slightest mind year after year.

Rick had a troubled relationship with the talent show. Every year it treated him wrong. The last year he competed, he had an entire entourage of young girls there to support him. So did almost all the other little local rappers. But one out-of-town kid, who came to the show alone and didn't even bother to tell the crowd his name, dug Ricky's rapping grave and threw him inside. He locked eyes with

Erycha and told her that the only time her dude saw a hood was when he put on his jacket, his whole hardness was fabricated and tainted, fuck Ricky's freelance hustlin, might as well go sell bean pies with the Muslims. Watching Ricky have to stand there, hearing the well-honed shit he had to take without any chance to defend himself, and noting how the whole crowd, including all his girls, turned on him, actually hurt her. She found herself alone with him behind the stage curtains. She wondered how the nameless unknown knew that she was Rick's only real girlfriend. Probably something about the way she watched him. The whole thing was wrong, but appropriate. She cuddled her man and nipped at his chin with her lips. Despite herself, she'd grown painfully close to him. He wasn't exactly the person she dreamt about. But his reality was close to hers, and he cared about her, and it surprised her just how much she could return that feeling and care for him, to the point of pain.

She gazed through the thin, revealing curtain that separated stage and backstage and rendered everyone visible to everyone else: she looked out at the crowd and noted the blue and red and purple bandanas and how each cheer had its own color, blue or red or purple, always matching, never broken. The unknown rapper would be dismissed, too, because he was unaffiliated, as was Ricky. The show, as usual, had degenerated into a turf squabble between gang sets.

"Ain't that but a bitch," Ricky muttered. By the same time a year later, he would be hustling so hard his only talent show would be in the streets. He was tough and creative and independent, which was enough to make street money, and a boy with even a little cash, a car, a place to stay, no convictions on his record, wasn't going to find himself unpopular. That street money would be his walk in the world: a kid with cash and immediate options. Erycha could see ahead to how things would probably be and she figured she wouldn't be his only girl for long. She could see Rick moving on from her, on to somebody who would cater to him all hours and keep his place clean and be there for him at the end of the day and not trouble too much about the silent competition with every female halfway attractive and lonely.

She looked up at him, pecked his chin again. His jaw and in fact his whole face was filling out, growing even and strong. She was fifteen, which by numbers meant he was eighteen now. He was becoming something like a man now. She wondered if it would be a total mistake to try to have him to herself.

"The second round contestants are," a wavering, slightly scared speaker announced, "Ladainian and Rocky J.J. and . . . Marquise!"

Turf calls resounded above the music. Neither Ricky, nor his opponent, had been selected.

Erycha held her man. "Unfair," she whispered to him.

But later, after the talent show was over and she had taken herself home for the night, she decided that the real unfairness wasn't what had happened to the unaffiliated rappers but rather the talent show's basic exclusivity. Ricky would be more than fine as long as he could stay alive and free. She wasn't too worried about him. But now that she was away from him and her head was clear of stupid romantic thoughts, she thought about what was acceptable in her world and what was denied outright. That the talent show denied much more than it accepted was obvious. Rapping and stepping was everything there. The boys rapped, the girls stepped, and that was it. She straight-up hated rap music, but stepping she actually enjoyed. Every time she danced with some random step squad and felt the energy earthquaking across the stage and into the crowd, she realized that this was actually what people wanted to watch. And she felt the threads of ballet fraying a little more in her hands.

It was what it was. She understood. Ballet had never done anything for black girls, so black girls weren't trying to have time for it. Stepping was home truth while ballet was another world entirely. But as easy as Erycha knew it would be to let go of ballet, she also didn't want to be bound up by invisible, communal ties and bindings. Leaving ballet behind would guarantee that bondage. She wanted to leave it behind, yet she still wanted to be part of the otherworld that it called her to. She wanted to work out the contradictions that dancing led her to. She needed to talk to somebody about these things, to speak on what she wanted and how that agreed and disagreed with what her community wanted, and about the smallness of youth culture and the wild troublesome loveliness of black culture, and how she was reaching after the strands of all these many things, the strands getting thinner and thinner at her fingertips. She almost picked up the phone to call Ricky, but then didn't. She knew how that would go: either he would lead the conversation into things sexual, or she would try and explain how she felt and he wouldn't understand.

She wasn't exactly waiting on the next talent show so she let her feelings go silent, and then what at first was a conscious decision turned into a complacent silence. Months passed without that conversation.

Then late one night her parents woke her with a fight so righteous and dangerous she was afraid to get between them. From her bedroom, under her covers, she could hear them yelling through the closed bedroom door.

"That was the line! That was the line!"

"What line you talkin bout? Makin up non-sense!"

"Oh, it's nonsense for me to wanna know where my money done went?"

"I a'ready tol you where it went? What else we gon' speak on?"

"I need to know *why*, Morris! *I need to know why!*"

They careened as one injured body from bedroom to kitchen.

Somebody kicked a wall or a table and cussed so hard the word didn't have a gender.

"Fuck."

"This ain't bout no lil money, Evy. You know it ain't."

"Hell it ain't. You gambled that shit away like it never existed. Like it never existed. Fuck you it ain't about no lil money!"

"Don't curse at me!"

"Don't raise your voice at me."

Back to the bedroom. The door slammed shut so hard it fell back open and banged like a gunshot against the out-facing wall.

"You still holdin on to that original sin, ain't you? Jus' a'mit it, jus straight a'mit it."

Either she didn't admit it, or her admission was too quiet for Erycha to hear.

"You still mad I defended blood when he was bout to get killt. Jus' a'mit it. You mad I saved the man."

"Man?"

"My boy."

"Your boy wadn't no man an' he wadn't worth takin no assault charge for, gettin you sent down here on some 'for your own safety' shit procedure. Be damned. I was pregnant, Morris. You was locked up. I gave birth. You was locked up. Your daughter was born. You was locked up."

"Yeah, yeah, I know I's locked. I know you's pregnant, too. I know you gave birth. Shit, e'rybody an' they momma know you was pregnant an' gave birth an' fuck an' whatnot 'cept—you done said that shit so many times to so many people don' need to know it, don' give a damn that they know it, it'a be a miracle if the President don' know it. You even keep tellin _me_ you was pregnant like I don' know the story my damn self."

"Do you? Do you know what it was like carryin that child alone? Deliverin that child in County without no man, no family, no one but that doctor an' them bitch nurses lookin down at me like I'm some no-account lil black hooker? Do you know what it was like to leave e'rything I known to u-nite my daughter with her father, even though now I know you wadn't worth the paper my bus ticket was printed on?"

Another door slammed. Her dad's voice rang out in the tinny quality with which everything said from the bathroom reverberated. "Nah. Nah, I don' know what it's like to be with some man ain't worth shit. You don' neither."

"Do you know how *it was?* Do you know what that did to me? Do you know what that did to our daughter?"

"To Erycha?" Erycha could all but see him shaking his head at her mother and smiling uneasily. "Well, hell. Maybe I don'. Maybe I don', Evy. Maybe that's why you fierce as a mufucka." He laughed, awkwardly, high and thin and off his balance.

"I just care." She brought out the words like each deserved its own sentence. "I cared because I had to. I had Erycha. But right now I'm almost past caring. I almost just wanna walk, leave you here to mess this situation up more 'n you a'ready done did."

Something clattered against tiled floor. They had moved rooms again.

"You act like all I do, e'rything I am be negative. You act like I'm scum on the earth. When was the last time you remembered to be glad I love you, glad I love Erycha, glad I work, glad I pay some these bills?"

"Them all things you s'posed to do."

"It's somethin. But you talkin down to me, Evelyn. Talkin down. You got any idea how shiftless niggas out here be? I'm a good man. Yeah, I got flaws. Shit, world's flawed as a crooked circle. But I does mines."

"Which is what? Besides the casino?"

Her voice was lower now and Erycha could tell they were not speaking from across a room any longer, but close up, the way people do before a real fight. When he spoke, her dad's voice had that knotted up sound, like he could barely pull the words out his throat for anger. "You act so, so innocent. But I remember you from the jump. I remember you tellin me, 'Momma keep me all shut up in church, not knowin nothin but a prayer.' You used to thank me. Now you wanna act like I kidnapped you."

"Morris." His name came out her mouth so low and tense it almost bit. Then what sounded like glass shattered against the far wall.

"Goddamnit!" she heard one of them say, but wasn't sure which. "Why you did that?" It was her dad. "Why? Cuz you cain't take me speakin back? You cain't take me sayin what I gots to say? You cain't take me bein a man?" His hand hit the kitchen table, thick strike.

"I never said you wadn't no man."

"Might's well have. Do you know what it's like to be up in one 'a these Cali jails, girl? All these Messicans runnin shit. Aryans, too. Guards evil. I had to fight for that boy or be dead my damn self. His peoples woulda done me for not steppin up. Only mistake I made was bein in jail, steadily goin to jail. You don' know what it is to be no nigga in jail, I don' know what it is to carry no child: we even."

"You actually gon sit up here, before me an' God, an' say somethin that stupid? I got nothin more to say."

"Me neither."

Another object broke against a wall or counter's edge and fell to the ground and broke again.

Erycha knew it was when things got quiet that things got worse. She came out her room with a quickness: she was in the kitchen, wedging herself between them before she knew what she was doing. "I'ma call po-lice on both y'all!" she screamed. "Y'all too damn loud!" she added, though she was the loudest by far now.

She felt their bodies give and fall back. Her mother swiveled on her bare heel, turned away and walked to the opposite side of the dark kitchen. She was muttering something, grating out sounds too low to be heard. Her dad was even quieter as he stepped back and went over to lean against the stove. He was looking up at Erycha, shaking his head, looking down, saying nothing, looking back up. Then he dipped his shoulders, spun around and punched the wall. The blow was short, fast and explosive enough to take a woman's head off her shoulders. The stucco and most of the kitchen wall above the stove and below the cupboard became a crater.

That was the end.

Everyone went to bed then, like he had solved something.

It was rare that she had actual dreams, those full-born things that arise in the unconscious dark night. But she had made a habit of waking early and sort of letting her mind wander into what she could only think of as waking dreams. These waking dreams usually involved dance, and, when not about dance, they furnished dark magically enhanced versions of all the men she'd ever known, better teachers and principals, better security guards and social workers, better liquor store owners even, and better Muslims and Christians and Catholics and better fathers and a better Ricky than she had ever known. But the morning after the fight, she woke late and her mind did not wander. She came to already knowing she needed to talk to Ricky. She needed to tell him how she truly felt; not with screaming and not with sex, but in the close, quiet, eye-meeting way that grown folks were supposed to handle their serious business. When she met with him later in the day and began to talk, Ricky actually played his part to perfection, listening to her with all the quietness and seriousness he had in him, biding patiently, waiting for whatever she wanted to tell him. But the more she talked, the more she surprised herself with what she didn't say and didn't tell him about. She didn't tell him about her parents' fight, or about the story behind their fight. She didn't tell him how nervous and agitated she felt most days. What she did tell him was something she'd never dreamt she would say, which was that she wanted to be with him, straight-up, no back-lookin: she meant it, too; Ricky was her boy because she wanted him more than anything else she could touch and hold. She wanted to be in his world even more and deeper than she already was.

That was the morning he asked her to come stay with him.

Man, Erycha thought, maaan, you know my situation. You know what I want. You know what I have. You know Ricky got me set up all nice in this lil two-room apartment house. You know how much I always wanted to be out my parents' place. How they vexed me. But you know that this idn't heaven neither. It starts to feel small, cramped in here. After a while I feel like I'm maintainin in what seems like four feet of space with this wild-ass lil kid and not a thing to distract my attention except the occasional police raid or shooting. So maybe you can understand when I tell you I cain't just deal with lil one's foolishness the way Ricky be tellin me a strong black woman gotta. What's he know about strong black women? Is he one? Ricky actually knows more than he lets on, but he don't know any more about females than the next nigga. Deal with things like a princess be more like it, if I had my way.

If this place were her palace, Erycha figured she'd have her hair braided free of charge every weekend and she would control who came and went. She could show Ricky's little brother the door when he acted a fool, and decide the standards he would have to meet before he would be allowed back in. If you need to bounce off walls all day long, lil one, she thought but didn't say, you best find somewhere else to do it. What she actually did tell the little boy, who Ricky left her with weekend days when she was home and he was out hustling, was: "Go outside. Play. Exercise. It'a make you stronger."

But he just turned his black marshmallow face up at her, stuck out his soft bottom lip and stared. The boy got lovely big brown eyes, she told the man who lived in that space Ricky could never occupy, that wanting, needing part of her mind where nothing but imagined men and imagined destinies resided. But he don't try to use 'em to get over on me like a regular ten-year-old would. Nah, he just be starin, makin his lip big, lookin at me like he hates me.

"You heard me, get outta my bedroom."

"You ain't my daddy."

"Ain't your moms neither, but you still gonna listen."

"You'd be a bad mom."

Man, she thought, just listen to him. She remembered her unmade hair and wondered where her do-rag had run off to. She pulled her knees up to her chest. Then she reached for the heavier blanket and put that over herself too and completed the process by pushing lil one so that he slid his butt off the edge of the bed.

"You ain't my mom!" the boy screeched. Then his voice grew quieter, softer. "I listens to my bruva 'cause we related, plus he take care 'a me. You don't do none 'a that."

"Your brother out makin them ends. I'm his voice while he in the world."

lil one was standing in the bedroom doorway now. Short as a shadow. Almost gone. "Nah," he said.

"Nah what? You think we livin here for free? You don't have a job. I don't have no job. Ricky be workin *all day* so you can stay outta foster care. Somebody gotta keep things straight while he out grindin, right? That's me. Erycha."

"I listens to my fambly," he insisted.

"Then go find 'em. Shit. Go see what they got waitin for you." Erycha threw up her hands. "Please. Leave me be."

She put the pillow over her face and prayed for a miracle. A small one came to her when lil one stepped out and closed the bedroom door behind him.

It was ten long minutes before she even took the pillow from her face. So tired, she said to the man in her thoughts, so tired, I guess. I always thought that after I moved out my momma's place and found support things would be so much better. That I'd at least have my ballet paid for, my hair taken care of, some small desires met. But, then, life. At least lil one's gone though. Now I cain't hear him outside the door. Maybe he's playin with that dog Ricky found. Maybe *you* came through, scooped him up, delivered me from this premature motherhood.

She got out of the bed slowly. It was almost eleven o'clock but she wasn't dressed or showered or anything. It was Sunday. The weekend. But she knew these were only excuses, excuses that the men in her life, her dad, Ricky, would accept and even live by themselves, but that the more perfect man who lived in her mind would reject. He'd see excuses for what they were: lies letting her not face herself, not be anything more than this couple miles of lazy, low-ambition Negroes. It's pathetic, right? she thought, dependin on men the way I do now. Me, who's moved away from home at sixteen. Me, who's emancipated myself from a bad situation. Me, the good girl with the good grades. The one doin e'rything right, never expected nothin from my parents, let alone a boyfriend. I *been* strong. But it's one of those things, man, it gets lonely. Today's our special day: Sunday. Rick don't make it all Fridays, but he never puts nothin before Sunday service, not even his other female, that O Street bitch whatever her name is, Mexican bitch. We go to noon church, we eat late lunch there an' we come home with the Lord all in us. Be at peace, no matter how loud lil one plays. It's the best thing in my week, better than anything.

Sundays, I cherish. The rest 'a the week, even Saturday, no tellin. But other times are good, too. Not always. But sometimes. Like the time he convinced me to tag the sign outside Victoria Arms. That was stupid fun. While we was doin it, this skinny nigga rolled up on his bike, didn't pay the taggin no mind. I'm thinkin, ah shit, is this one 'a them lil territorial hyper niggas Ricky says be set trippin, tryina make him give up his money? Hate those gang-affiliated kids. But the boy was cool. Wadn't representin no one but hisself. Just tryina sell us some incense sticks. Romantic, he said. Nahright. Boy had blazin gold fronts. Then I was thinkin: he must be practicin to move down the way an' pass the collection plate at that frontin-ass Pentecostal Church. But then he lit the incense, let it burn in the air an' it was the strongest most unapologetic most sexual sweet cinnamon-sugar smell.

The frontdoor opened and lil one walked back inside. He dragged behind him the dog he had found out on Victoria Street a couple weeks prior. Whenever Erycha saw the boy and the dog, the boy dragging the dog by its chain, the dog looking like it was going through convulsions from the rough treatment, she thought about how much better a pet a reptile would be than a dog. A little lizard would do, an iguana would be even better. Iguanas especially and reptiles in general let their owners live in peace and didn't tear through a house like they were still feral. She imagined an iguana peacefully perched on the side of someone's wall, eating the rose petals that dangled there. It was sort of picturesque to her, in the same way that ballet was picturesque, part of its beauty always coming from its difference, its stillness, its poised strength, its harsh sharp scales and lines.

"Be careful with that thing," she cautioned. "I think it's angry at you."

"He took a crap in the street, all up close by the Mission," lil one reported. "But he know not to do no mess inside."

"You was at the Mission? You get anything?"

"Nah. Couldn't, cuz, like I said, he took a shit out front. "

"Don't cuss. You know you ain't sposed to bring the dog inside the gates. You could get Ricky an' me in trouble."

"You cuss." He slapped the dog upside its head till it sat down on all fours. Then he looked up at Erycha with that not-cute, not-young stare of his: "See, he'a listen. It's just, we ain't got no real dog chain. My bruva won't buy one. He tol me just go snatch up a good bike chain, use it like it's a dog chain. But it ain't the same."

I don't like that, you know what I'm sayin? You understand why it's plain wrong for Rick to be tellin this young boy to thieve things?

Through the open window she saw the dirt of the driveway rise like hot vapors: Ricky was pulling his duster-looking vehicle to a fast screeching stop. lil one dropped to the floor. She watched as the dirt cloud dissipated and then she could see Ricky on the march. His tightly braided cornrows had dust and sunlight all in them, dirty and lovely. He had something behind him, she noticed, something he was holding over his shoulder and out of view. She watched as he used his free hand to tip back the flower pot and get the key.

She went over to lil one where he knelt with the dog and flicked his ear. "Why you wanna act all paranoid? Act happy, your brother is home."

"It's a bike chain, though," the child hissed.

"You want a bike chain, I want diamonds. Ain't nothin perfect."

Ricky's key caught in the lock.

He smiled and came to her, kneeling before her like her future husband, putting his left hand on her knee. He kissed the separate fingers like jewels in a chain. "Still wearin them boxers, girl? The tank, too."

"Slow day." She shrugged. "Slow day." She messed at her hair a little, with no results. "Them your boxers, remember?"

"Most e'rything you got mine one way or another."

Ricky raised up and pushed her down on the bed beneath him. She opened her legs and clung to his shoulders and held tight, and right then—with her fingers starting to dig into him, because she'd learned that that was always the test, if her man would let her mark him, or if he was saving his body for someone else—that was when she felt the silk frills: my new dress, she thought. It feels like a blue dress.

He started sliding the tank top down her shoulders.

He kept sliding the tank top down her shoulders.

"A dress," she said.

He stopped moving over her.

He stopped sliding the tank top from her.

He pulled its straps back up.

"You like your new dress?" He took his hands off her and flashed the thing in front of her as if it were more than it was. "Saks, girl. Not no San Bernardino Outlet Mall. Bought it just now. You gonna try it on?"

Her mind went two ways, yes and no, but his eyes persuaded her. She pulled the dress from his hand and held it up in front of her like she was modeling it in Saks. It was the sky before the smog, *that* blue.

"That still your favorite color, that shade?"

She could see him through the dress, the material was so thin. She wondered, What'll happen when the wind blows, Marilyn Monroe? She could imagine it whirling with the motion of her body, a halo borne about her hips. The dress was way too delicate for stepping, but perfect for something more refined. She was sure she could find good times for a good dress. The problem was, she wasn't even sure she could accept it.

"Is it the right color?" She could sense his tension rising ever so slightly.

She knew what she should ask: why? But she didn't know whether she could. It was a bad time for that question. But she thought about the prostitute knifed dead and burned blacker than an African down in an H Street alleyway. She thought about his friend, Snow, recently caught-up and sent to Chino Prison. She thought about how much she worried over Ricky every time he left in the morning. She thought of his family, his little brother living with them, his sister ducking Child Protective Services out in Moreno Valley, his mother derelict as ever in Watts, probably still smoking crack and selling her pussy. She thought of her boy, Ricky, that boy constantly scared of law enforcement, constantly stashing money and drugs, stashing his gun, stashing whatever bootleg shit he happened to be selling in air vents and pipes, under bushes and balanced on tree branches, and in the makeshift safe he had created beneath the apartment sink. He even asked her to hold something once. She was sixteen years old and already she had held drugs, walked whatever it was, she didn't even know what it was, down the street to a grown man in a small, dim apartment house with an air conditioner that hummed like thunder, and she had to pretend not to be scared. What was she doing living on this edge, supported solely by this boy who was clinging to the same edge without the slightest support? What place did she have in this life? How could she be part of his world and be anything more than the scrambling hoodrat that he was? Stop thinkin, she told herself. He just gave you a gift, lil heifer. Lotta females would kill for that dress an' a man good enough to give it to 'em. That's a gift, girl. Be good. Say somethin appreciative.

"I ain't ask for no dresses, Ricky."

"Well," he leaned back, sizing her up, "that's basically the idea behind a surprise present, ain't it? Surprise. Nahright? You know, you shouldn't have to beg for e'rything you get."

"Sorry, but I gotta bring out the b word, Rick: I ain't ask for no dress, I only asked for you to be on time for church. And don't talk yet, I a'ready know what you bout to say an' what you bout to do, you fittin to leave on me 'cause e'ry time you gimme somethin nice, you bout to bounce an' that's fucked-up, scuse my language. It is, though, you know what I'm sayin? But, you know, the thing of it is, until now, it was never Sunday."

His face did not change. "You wanted jewelry?"

Maaaaan, I shoulda shot him. That's what a man would do, right? Went an' got you a gun an' shot his ass. Is that what you woulda done? Killed him? Would you kill a man? Truth is, I didn't even slap him, I listened to him instead. He reasoned it out real smoove, that Sunday service must not be that important to me either since it wadn't like I was all dressed up an' racin to the door. I wadn't dressed at all, just waitin on him. Either I was layin for a fight, he told me, or I wadn't tryin to get to church too hard no-way. "It's not fair you bein passive-aggressive an' shit," he says. "How'm I gonna react when you actin like a big ol' contradiction? C'mon now, Erycha."

I don't know what he means by all that so idn't easy to argue with him without just cussin him out, an' that really ain't me anyway. You know me: that's not me. I don't wanna turn my place into some ghetto-type situation where all people do is start screamin, then progress to shootin each other. Just because we live in the hood doesn't mean we need to act hood. That's why even though I shoulda shot him, I didn't even scream on him. I tried to think things out instead an' after a minute, it started to seem like he was right. But a part of me felt like that would mean I was a hoodrat my own self, immersed in this mess. I couldn't take the dress, but I couldn't give it back without wonderin why I wadn't givin back the key to the frontdoor while I's at it.

Ricky shifted his focus. He shouted through the closed bedroom door at lil one. "I'm this close to evictin that dog my damn self. Did you know it's been crappin in the dirt outside?"

"It's my protection," lil one yelled back.

"I protect you." Ricky got up and opened the door and walked into the main room. "What you need protection from anyway?"

"You don't know till you need it."

"Protection. Who you is? The President?" Ricky laughed. Then Erycha heard something serious enter his voice. "I been lettin the dog hang around because you like it, you care for it. But you gotta care for it better. These 'partments is only rented, but we gotta treat 'em right. They ours even if we don't own 'em. They might's well be our property 'cause it's us who lives here. And, who knows, one day I might be buyin, renovatin places like this."

lil one didn't know what to say to that. It had probably never occurred to him that anyone who wasn't white or born rich owned shit or had claim to anything. Food stamps. Section 8. Handouts over handouts over handouts. That was the world he had been raised up in. Erycha wasn't even good at accepting gifts from her man, but she worried lil one had the opposite mindset. lil one prob'ly thinks Ricky's crazy, she thought. Which he is. But he's not crazy for tryina own things. Not because he knows there's more to life than this ghetto mess. That's the good part about Ricky: he wants to have things. He cares. She walked out into the main room.

"I hate this place," lil one mouthed off, "I liked Watts better."

"Well, if Watts is heaven," Ricky began, then changed course again: "Like I said a'ready, it's a issue of pride in property. Folk prob'ly tol you this before, but maybe it'a help if you hear it from me."

No, Erycha thought, no, Daddy, it will not help.

"Some white man own this whole bitch. He own e'rything you can lay yo' eyes on from here to forever. But that ain't forever. There used to be Indians out here. White man took they land. Why ain't you listenin? Raise yo' head up, lil nigga. Like I said, this was Indian man land. White man done took it from him. White man can get took jus the same. That's why niggas is goin to college now, or we becomin entrepreneurs like myself. We gonna own things, na'mean?"

Ricky looked hard at the small uncomprehending boy. There was real frustration in his eyes. He couldn't say what he wanted to say exactly the way he wanted to say it. The boy would never learn because he couldn't teach him.

"Listen here," Erycha tried. "What Ricky's sayin is, whatever white guy owns this place, it doesn't matter so much. This place is ours in that we live here. Livin is ownership. It's ours because we here. So we might's well take good care of it . . ."

Maaan, I'm this close to fallin back to sleep again. Ain't that but a bitch? I don't know if I should fight it, or just let the tiredness get inside me an' take me down. I'm thinkin to myself, who really truly actually wants to be a strong black woman, what them words even mean, doin all the work an' takin all the mess? I can do without that. Lay on my back an' get presents brought to me like a princess instead. Get my hair braided free of charge while I'm at it, while I'm dreamin. I think that whole strong thing is prob'ly just some ex-cuse for when you cain't live any better an' all that's left for you is to do the best with the mess you got. See me layin still here. Look at me. I even make my fingers lay still. My eyes been layin still and closed shut ever since Ricky told me I had passive aggressions and I didn't slap him. That was before I decided he was right. Now I'm back to lyin here, in his bed, in his apartment. The dress is chillin beside me like Ricky would if he was with me now, except that he would wanna touch me, wanna fuck, an' the dress don't even care if I touch it. Bought an' paid for, it ain't nothin no more. I want it to touch me the way I would want Ricky to touch me, maybe even more, it is so beautiful. A dancer's dress. But it just lays there like nothin, or like a question, or like a demand, or a come-due debt; I'm not sure, I'm not sure. Maybe it's me who needs to make the first move and touch it. Take the initiative. Tell Ricky the fuck off. Tell my parents the truth: they need to stop fightin that fight they been fightin since the day I was born, or go they separate ways. Tell e'rybody in this town to get grown, or get gone. Get a lotta folks gone out my life that way. Shoot, could even tell lil one's mom she needs to start actin like it, give the boy bus fare back to Watts.

That would solve e'rything, right? Then my life would be perfect, with no friends, no family whatsoever. It's kinda one 'a these no-win situations, go one way, get messed up, go the other way, get the same. It's lose-lose: either I accept this life, or I'm without. Makes me see your genius, Dream Man, 'cause you never ever ever make the first move, do you? You never ask me out, never take me nowhere, never buy me nothin, nor tell me how I'm prettier or smarter or dance better than all them other girls in the world. Nah, you just let me go my lonely way. You just let me wander in this world. Let me be neglected. Let me get with this dope boy. And now where are you? Hidin? Holdin back? Waitin, like the Savior to come rescue me? Nah. You somewhere else, tellin another girl she smart, she pretty, she gets to have this an' do that an' be here an' go there. You'll never be with me. This is why I hate you even though I love you. Because the smallest thought of you fills me with sadness. If you ever came to me, I'd care more about my braids than Jesus. So it's prob'ly a good thing you just in my mind, a figment of my imagination. If you were real, I'd be writin lil love letters to you, throwin 'em in the trash can just so I could write you again. I'd be callin you all day, leavin you messages on your phone, talkin silly shit about how I couldn't stand life without you. I'd be runnin to you whenever I was in a situation an' didn't know the way out. And I'd be dyin somewhere below the love, somewhere below the desire, thinkin I'm lost, I'm lost, I'm lost. Because nobody can make me happy except me.

All my stories end the same, they all end the same damn way. I keep gettin taught, keep learnin the same ol' lesson: I only got myself. Cain't rely on a dream, cain't rely on a dream man. I cain't even rely on my parents they so chil'ish an' selfish. Always squabblin. I sure as hell cain't rely on Ricky. How that boy plans to get outta this hood in somethin besides a po-lice van or a pine box is beyond me. I love him, but it's somethin I cain't deal with. I gotta leave him. Gotta leave so many things. Even gotta leave you, love: because you born from the same poison, you just taste sweeter. That's why I'm sayin goodbye.

"If you got so much money why you drivin a hooptie?" lil one asked Ricky. "You should buy a Escalade," he added.

"Nah," Ricky said, grasping for a critical explanation that he did not possess. "These 'partments here, they long money. Escalade, nah, that ain't even makin money, na'mean?"

lil one shook his head. He didn't get it.

"Depreciation. You know that word?"

lil one shook his head some more.

Ricky was getting very frustrated: explaining financial and proprietary concepts to this child wasn't as easy as strong-arming a scared suburban kid in a drug deal.

Erycha listened to their endless discussion and decided to get out of bed and resolve the matter once and for all. She knew Ricky understood the twin concepts of appreciation and depreciation. He had scheming smarts that kept him alive and successful. He was just totally uneducated and so used to dealing with problems by force that he was unable to define or explain anything. And lil one was as deeply difficult a student as she had ever known. But she figured kids, especially this particular kid, needed to be taught about money and ownership or else they would turn out like her parents, who were still renters, still children within the economy. She worked her way out of the mental space of her dreams and desires and back into the space of common knowledge and communication. She began in, telling lil one, "Appreciation, you can understand as the ownership of a thing that rises in value. A thing that rises in value after you've taken ownership of it. Depreciation is the direct opposite—"

She started to say more, but her words were immediately drowned out by the sudden, sheering deceleration of a fast-moving car. The smell of burning rubber entered the apartment. The car came to a violent halt. lil one was already on the floor and scrambling for cover. The dog was scrambling for cover. Erycha looked to Ricky, who dived to the ground in the next flash of a moment. Erycha hesitated. Then, as automatic gunfire broke out the window of the neighboring apartment house and shredded its surrounding wall, she just stayed where she was, standing, perfectly motionless.

Erycha knew pure luck alone had kept her alive that day. lil one was from Watts so he knew that a car screeching to a halt like that was the reliable sign of a drive-by come to fruition. But she should have been just as alert. Erycha knew the way the smell of gunpowder hung in the air right after a shootout. She knew how the heavy odor of kindled brush mimicked that scent every summer during the annual fires, and she knew how to tell the difference one from the other. San Bernardino and its Western corridor into Highland was now the most violent area in Southern California and one of the most violent places in America. Drive-bys were common. Killings were common. Not to dive on the floor when within range of gunfire was suicide. Stray bullets left people just as dead as shots that found their intended targets. But out of shock or fearlessness or cluelessness, she had done nothing to protect herself and had survived unharmed.

Later, she could think of no real explanation for why she hadn't hit the floor except that she was just so divinely pissed-off at Ricky, at the fear she suddenly saw in his eyes right before he dove for safety, that she forgot to protect herself. That fear she saw told her he thought the gunfire might be for him. Now she knew even more than before that this kid with fear for eyes was not the man she dreamt of. She didn't want to be with someone who was scared that he and those around him might be shot and killed at any moment. She didn't want to live with a drug dealer. And she definitely didn't want to live with a drug dealer who would hit the floor to save himself without protecting his girl first.

Show, don't tell. Best not to explain through words but actions that she simply wouldn't tolerate living under siege. She wasn't trying to subtly hint that Ricky find a safer career or a safer place to live or anything like that. All that type of change took more time and effort and retraining than she had minutes for. Ricky might not have time for all that either, which was fair enough. She didn't want him to change a thing about himself. She didn't hate him the way he was. She cared for him. She just wanted out. He had left her unprotected and that was unacceptable. He was smart enough to do that math. So the next morning without discussion she packed up all her things except the new dress and went back to her mother's apartment. Simple as that. Her parents didn't question why she was moving back in, just helped her with her things. Simple as that. She didn't bring up the original sin argument that drove her away in the first place, just let it all be. Simple as that.

But after a week gone from Ricky, things got complicated: she wasn't only moving out but also cutting off everything that connected her to him, from sex to conversation. Erycha was severe the way a black woman needs to be: when she was done, she was finished and there was no negotiating with a dead end. That he actually tried was only evidence of just how different the two of them were and that he didn't understand where she was coming from or where she was trying to go in life.

He showed up one day in a three-piece Claiborne suit and a beret that right away she could tell wasn't off the Outlet Mall rack but bought from somewhere like Nordstrom's, Neiman Marcus, somewhere expensive like that. "Hey, girl," he said.

She was surprised to see him, surprised that he had come by, surprised at just how different he looked in the expensive clothes. He looked like a man on his way to work at a downtown office, a lawyer, maybe. She had no words.

"I been readin."

"You been readin?" She worked at the knot that held her hair in her new headwrap.

"Yeah. Not for you, though. Not to impress you or nothin. For me. To step up my entrepreneurishness. Mackaveli. *The Prince.* You know, Tupac's favorite book. It's where he got his tactics, his strategy."

"Huh." She stared at him, confused and unsure what to say.

"Men must be either pampered or anni'lated," he said. "All armed prophets has succeeded, all unarmed ones has failed."

He went on like this, memorized quotation after memorized quotation. It took a long minute before she got that he was speaking close to verbatim from *The Prince* itself. It was a book she knew of but hadn't read and didn't intend to. Nothing from what she'd heard tale of it, including Tupac's love, interested her in the least. Still, Rick stayed there on the doorstep, all grown-up and professional-looking in his Claiborne, with a serious look on his face and a bunch of anti-social quotations committed to memory.

"Gotta love it," he said, about what she wasn't sure. Love was out of the question, that she wasn't confused about.

She remembered how easily he could remember rap lyrics and saw the roots of this performance. "What else?" she asked. She stopped messing with her headwrap.

"Men are so simple," he went on, "a deceiver never short of victims for his deception."

Erycha sighed. As much as she still cared for him, she wanted to deceive him into leaving right about now. His new hero, Mackaveli, came off like the kind of hard troublesome brother who would do well hustling and bootlegging and thugging, but who wouldn't make life any easier for his people. He sounded a lot like Ricky, in fact;

independent-minded but selfish and rough as hell when he wanted to be. She knew how this kind of thinking worked: it got people shot and killed every day. Mackaveli might as well have written a book about black-on-black crime because his philosophy explained it near to perfection, except that he had left out the part about how it was especially easy for black folk to deceive, coerce and kill other black folk because they ate alike, drank and smoked the same stuff in the same places, talked the same shit, walked the same streets and stayed in the same damn neighborhoods with each other. Mackaveli wasn't helping anything; he could go to hell as far as she was concerned.

As for Rick, he still believed they were meant for each other, or something like that. But she remembered how he had stolen her money, how he had kept other females, and all the ways he'd messed her over. He wasn't all that smart, she decided, just very creative. But she was done.

When he finally did leave the doorstep and went out Del Rosa back to his broken-down duster, Erycha closed the apartment door and went into the bathroom, where she had been refashioning her braids before the interruption. She took the new headwrap off and played it through her fingers, feeling along the indentations that her cornrows made in the cloth. She was trying to remember where exactly she had been in the process of her braidwork before Ricky came through. Braiding hair was as much an art as anything else careful and beautiful in this world. Erycha had too much respect for the precision that the work required and the way it would leave her looking for weeks on end to approach it with half her mind. But she was having trouble focusing on her hair. She was thinking about the headwrap in her hands, its long thin transparent white length: it bridged the space between the boy and her braids. It was a connecting tissue, or it was just a pretty little thing; or something more than just that, the flag of her dispossession, or the sign of something new, something hopeful.

After finally figuring out that she no longer wanted him, Ricky didn't come around anymore. Instead he sent the girls he slept with to find Erycha at school, at the store, wherever, whenever, so that they could tell her about how lucky they were and how dumb a bitch she was. Erycha didn't take any of this seriously: she knew she wasn't dumb and she could care less about being a bitch as long as she wasn't the weak kind.

She plain and simple didn't take the girls as personally as she knew Rick was hoping that she would. Unlike his quotations and his suit, this was a very predictable move on his part. He was male. As young as she was, Erycha already knew that the other half of humanity had their egos wrapped around their dicks. If you denied them sexually and at the level of their ego, they would let you know about it. If these females were Rick's way of moving on she was good with that, just so long as he moved on. He had some truly annoying spiteful bitches hauling his water for him, but she was good with that, too. The girls were nothing to her. All she wanted was to be left to herself. She was best by herself.

It was in fall of her senior year in high school that she saw the blue dancer's dress again. It had been months since any of Ricky's girls had approached her, and then one day walking home from step practice, Erycha saw the pretty little dress again. There were a million little blue dresses in the world, but somehow she just knew that the one the girl walking up Del Rosa Avenue was wearing was the exact same one that Ricky had bought for her and that she had left at his place when she broke up with him.

The girl inside the dress had a red-light, traffic-stopping figure. She overflowed and fell out of the dress in front and even more in back. Her butt was a convex table, the dress a tablecloth barely covering her. She didn't have the dancer's body that the dress seemed meant for, but she had a shapeliness that surpassed the dress. Erycha noticed the cars along Del Rosa slowing as they passed the girl and felt suddenly totally physically inadequate. It had to do with the dress, with the girl, with the fact that Erycha was dressed in sweat pants and a sweat-soaked top and her hair was a wet mess and she smelled like a man and she was walking alone.

Ricky's previous females had been average at best. They were the kind of desperate girls who felt they had nothing but sex to offer. The first one was his G Street jump-off: the girl confronted Erycha outside the high school. She was about six feet tall in her heels so when she walked up to Erycha she literally talked down to her. The spiteful part was that she straight-out told Erycha how even before Erycha was out of the picture she and Ricky liked to have sex in the bed Erycha shared with her man. Then she asked Erycha if she wanted in on a threesome. The second girl stepped to Erycha in the grocery store one day. She was light-skinned, probably mixed with white or Latina, and small like Erycha. She had a mouth on her too, talking about Ricky's size and calling Erycha all kinds of bitches and heifers. They were both small but Erycha was strong and she knew it; knew she could yank the girl by her long hair and slam her into the wine rack if she made her angry enough. When she could maim her so easy, it was hard to feel anything but superior. The third female Erycha barely remembered except that the woman was a little bit older than the others, wore a weave and had what looked like a wedding ring on her finger. She spoke softly, but said most of the same messed-up things. Erycha felt sorry for her soul.

Erycha had as little respect for those females as Ricky did for them. But this girl coming up the street was a little different. More unselfconscious than the others, she walked like someone who wasn't trying to convince herself that the brother she had just slept with still wanted her.

Erycha was the nervous one now. She played her hands through her sweat-drenched hair, tried to make it magically sit up or lie down or fly sideways or anything half-respectable. But, as usual, it was impossible to make wet hair be anything respectable.

As they neared each other, the girl's eyes narrowed on Erycha. She swung her purse in a full looping circle. Erycha could tell something was about to happen. She nodded at the girl. The girl didn't nod back. Erycha kept her eyes on the little purse.

"I like them bangs," the girl offered. "An' that top, too. Gotta get me one 'a them right there." The insults came off her mouth sweet as syrup.

Erycha stopped in the middle of Del Rosa. The girl stopped, too. Erycha waited for something to come to mind, something that she could say in return. But nothing came.

"Yeah," the girl in the blue dress went on, "you don't say much, do you? Makin things all awkward, is that a strategy or somethin?"

Right then, Erycha regretted not having made friends with the younger girls on the step squad who had replaced her graduated friends Quincia and Lindsay. Now she walked home alone from practice. "I just finished step practice," she finally managed. "I'm tired." She still had her eyes on the purse.

"I have a team out in Moreno Valley. I was born an' raised in this filthy ol' town, but I got my ass to Moreno Valley. Ain't nothin worthwhile out here if you tryna put a life together. Jus my dude, he stay out here. An' family. But they all movin down my way. But, yeah, we jus won the all-Inland Empire step competition. Y'all heard bout that?"

Erycha decided from the casual way the girl was holding the purse, she didn't intend to use it as a weapon. She figured she was on safe ground conversationally, too, talking about dance. "I'm not real big into steppin, it's just what I do right now. College, I'ma prob'ly do ballet or modern, somethin more technical, more artistic than step squad."

The girl gripped her crescent-shaped hips. "I don't know nothin related to all that stuff you was jus talkin. I jus know if a chick can really get it, if she can dance, she gon' be good at steppin. If she scared 'a dancin like she still black, if she jus on some white girl shit, then that chick need to sit her ass down, read some poetry or somethin. Authentic or ya never meant it, na'mean."

Erycha noticed how doughy the girl's face was, how the plumpness of her cheeks almost overwhelmed her small eyes. Her make-up sat on her face in thick, inconsistent layers. Erycha started to feel better about her undone hair and sweaty clothing. "Yeah, girl, I know what you mean. But there's more to dance than just stompin the ground an' shakin our yams. Any female with enough ass in her jeans can do that. I'm tryina dance. Dance is an art form."

The girl shrugged and had to readjust herself in the dress. A car riding past honked at her, or at both girls. The dress had a completely different style to it now that this thick girl was wearing it, Erycha decided. Where on Erycha's frame it would have been elegant and just right on a dance floor or at a cookout or to a wedding, now, on this body, the dress spoke sex; sex, simple and plain. The girl could wear it all the same places, but people would see her differently than they would see a girl like Erycha. Erycha saw the girl differently than she saw herself.

"An art form," the girl repeated. "Art form. Like I said, poetry."

Erycha had lived in the hood her whole life. Did you have to dance like you lived? She wanted to say no. There were all kinds of recently immigrated Mexicans and Guatemalans and whatnot right in the depths of the hood who wouldn't know stepping from the Virgin of Guadalupe. There were folks in the hood who couldn't dance at all, let alone bust down. Some of them were even big-hipped black women who didn't hardly have to do anything but wind themselves around a little bit to get men wanting to give them the good news, and still they couldn't even manage that. She went on and on, talking about all these exceptions to the rule. She didn't even speak on the classical colored folk who were into ballet, which was probably only Erycha herself, but, shit, she counted for something too, even if she knew deep down that right now she was mostly into ballet as an argument: something she could bring up out of the darkness to show her difference, her divine spark. Truth be known, she didn't have a studio to practice at and hadn't performed in she couldn't remember how long, for more reasons than she cared to recall. Did you have to dance like you lived? She wanted to say no.

She could see the girl's mind working, trying to come up with some way to come back at her now. The purse swung out in another big, looping, absent-minded motion. Then she did what Erycha did not expect her to do: she conceded.

"Whatever, girl. Go ballet ya'self to death. I could give a damn. I gotta go tend to my grandmamma, pay my granddaughter dues. Cain't keep forgettin to visit the family house. By the way, Ricky movin to Mo Val." With that, the girl brushed past Erycha, and started up Del Rosa's long slow incline.

Erycha didn't care where Ricky went to. But she still watched his new girl stroll off because it was too hard not to. That switching, slow, nowhere to go way her whole body moved when she walked, the way she held her purse like a chain link, letting it wave back and forth in those wide careless loops. Her dress was working overtime now to keep her inside of it. Erycha half-expected some skanky old man draped in furs to drive up next to her and try and pimp her on the spot. But that didn't happen. The girl just walked and walked in the hot afternoon sun, ignoring the honking horns and the money waved from the windows of cars that slowed as they neared her and ignoring the heat of the day. When she had finally disappeared into the gray-white afternoon light, Erycha turned around and made the same demeaning journey going the other way.

High school simplified then. Unburdened of Ricky, Erycha focused her mind on the simplest part of teenage life: she went to class and listened to her teachers detail the lessons and took copious notes. She brought special care to the topics that interested her and studied the rest. School, she found, was incredibly simple compared to life. There were no negotiations, no relationships, no fear of eviction or investigation or violent assault. Just teachers and students and work and grades.

It was especially not difficult to get straight A's at a school where the dropout rate regularly reached 50%. Erycha, knowing this, took full advantage. She impressed teachers simply by being silent. She enhanced her status by standardizing her written grammar and by being one of the few girls at the school who feigned interest in math and science. She told her biology teacher she wanted to research plants and animals for a living. She told her math instructor she wanted to do complicated economics. She told the social science and history teachers that she would like to be a journalist like Ida B. Wells and the English instructor that she wanted to write like Toni Morrison and the P.E. coach that Dominique Dawes was her idol.

Of course, in truth she forgot most everything about the plants and animals and algebra and geometry and social science and history and literature and sports that she studied in her classes. She knew the faculty knew this, too, but the simplicity of school done well was like a fairytale she could tell them and they could tell her and everyone could tell each other in class and wherever else they happened to find each other, like witnesses to an event of which the rest of the world would never know: education is power, the story went. Only the educated are free, some old dead man had said. Yes, the educated would sooner or later someday inherit the earth.

Just teachers and students and work and grades. The whole world would be just that.

Just teachers and students and work and grades.

But when she went to school and aced science tests, Erycha's mind went in two distinct directions, one the official direction of the test, the remembered facts, the teacher, the students, the work, the grade. But the other direction was an under-story of biology as it actually applied to her: how it had made the men around her think that they

were more than they were. How it had made their females worship
that figment of male imagination. How it had given her a body that
wasn't a ballet body because it curved too much for ballet's taut set
positions but that wasn't curvy at all compared to the everyday sisters
she saw in the streets. Math was really a story about money, how it
flowed through everything, in and out of hands, homes, neighborhoods. In her neighborhood, the flow was mostly outgoing: Rent
controls revoked. Home loans and lines of credit never good, gone
bad as rotten meat. Debt collectors and the repo man always bother-
ing people and getting shot at. Fathers who had their monthly wages
garnished by the state as back child-support. Women spending
money they should have saved, just to avoid the shame of welfare,
just so their men could stay in the house when the social worker visited. She thought about how money came back to her neighborhood
not as abstract credit but in paper form, cash money and state-issued
welfare checks and food stamps. In her English class, she read essays
and novels and poems, but her interpretation of the text was always
different than what she wrote down for the teacher. In truth, she
saw only one question in every piece that she read. Every writer
brought her to the same insistent question: what about God? What
was He doing and what was the nature of His judgment? What
was on God's mind every time two people fell in love and made a
child and gave it a life and told it all of the good and showed it all of
the bad there was to see and to do? What was His explanation for
children born in dangerous neighborhoods and kids without parents
to raise them and innocent people killed by stray bullets, and all the
abandoned lives far off from heaven?

For Touissant, high school started simply. Having few friends and few distractions, he focused on his studies and achieved impressive grades. This was the basic course of his freshman and sophomore years, study and success. He was aware that things would eventually get more complicated. He knew that when it came time to decide where to go to college there would be complications. He had seen that process with his sisters and could imagine how fraught it would have been if they had been regular people with doubts and uncertainties. They had none, of course, which was a whole different story. Anyway, high school was simple, or at least the work was.

Touissant didn't so much enjoy school as schoolwork. That which constituted schoolwork, a set of tasks that required skill, effort and solutions, he excelled at. Schoolwork was a part of school, but school, which he disliked, was more than schoolwork. School was boredom manifested as a matrix of stupid kids and stupid cliques and stupid cultures. He barely noticed his teachers and had no concept at all of the people who directed and controlled his teachers, but they were there, too, more shaping of the matrix than the students or the teachers. School was complicated and boring and stupid, and he was as uninterested in it as he was interested in schoolwork. When it came to school, Touissant was a visionary looking forward to the time when high school courses could be completed from a bedroom, via e-mail and teleconference, whatever it would take to get him out of these mind-numbing classrooms where the black jocks and the white nerds walked around like they had hit triples when really they had just been born on third base, due, respectively, to their natural physiques and class privilege. He wanted to meet black nerds and poor white people, but he couldn't find them at his school, probably because of the afflu-ence that characterized the areas the school drew from and the fact that it bussed its athletic talent from the ghettos nearby.

There was another significant group at his school besides the jocks and jerks: the immigrants. Mostly, they had come from Mexico, but some were from Guatemala, Honduras, El Salvador, China, Korea, Vietnam. These folks Touissant had nothing and everything in com-mon with. He knew nothing about where they were from or the dan-gers that had forced them to go through so much just to get to a place he couldn't wait to leave. But, like them, he was not at home. Once in a while, he would make a friend or meet a girl whose family had come from some devastated country full of Communists and rebel militias. Nothing would be different. The conversations, the hang-out sessions, the bullshit, it would all be pretty standard-issue, except that he always felt a little more unsure, a little more uncertain at some inarticulate level, about things that he couldn't even put a name to. It was always difficult to talk about the unknown, especially with strangers.

With the immigrant kids, Touissant settled for the known and the familiar. He felt a need to ground those relationships in easy, acces-sible points of interest. At first, he thought to connect over popular movies. But after noting that among the *L.A. Times'* list of the top ten grossing films of the '90s he had seen only *Titanic* (a garbage film that he was forced to watch after losing several card games to Dea), he knew he lacked the common touch. He decided to try the common grounds of porn, lying about girls from school and weight-lifting. It was with the eses that he began to lift weights. They were short, stocky, with thick necks and deep shoulders and short arms.

Touissant was the direct opposite, tall, thin, loose-limbed. The Mexican kids excelled at the bench press and dead lift, but when it was his turn his long arms would not consent to the elaborate motions that the drills required. Anything that stressed his under-developed core, he decided was not for him.

Touissant's biceps striated into long thin rows of muscle, but his core stayed weak: His chest didn't expand. His shoulders didn't deepen. His body remained thin as mountain air. A matter of genetics, he figured, another reminder of how inherently different he was from the people around him, who were short and stocky and able to put on muscle so easily. Eventually, he stopped exercising with the eses. But he didn't stop lifting weights altogether and, for reasons he didn't think through at the time nor understand later in the athletic aftermath of it all, he began to construct a complex workout regimen for himself. The thing built and built, like additions to a small but growing home. And then he spent a whole summer torturing himself in Highland's burning heat by doing suicidal circuit training, isometric weight work and hundreds of military push-ups and sit-ups that hardened his body in the incredible way that a teenage body can harden. He enjoyed the lack of thought that accompanied the work, the way he didn't have to ask himself why he was running like the devil or to what end his routine was directed. He could just let his brain die for a while and sprint until his body stopped. It was how he hoped sex would be: pure physics. Him and a girl in motion, without questions, without explanations, without past or future. No story surrounding the sex. Nothing but an act. As simple as sprinting. When he ran, he was fucking his body. The lactic acid spread over his muscles and pain exited his body like so many stories that didn't need to be told and for the first time he felt at home in himself.

Touissant went to the first day of football try-outs with his glasses on. He didn't wear them all the time, only for tasks where his myopia hindered him. He didn't want to chance being left blind on the football field.

After he ran the first sprint drill, the coaches decided the glasses were a non-issue.

"4.45," the receiver's coach hummed. "Y'all seein what I'm seein?"

"I've got 4.47," the head coach said. "What about you, Bob?"

"4.44," the one called Bob said in a hushed voice.

Touissant wandered back to the starting line. He could tell that they were impressed. Whatever time they had clocked him at it didn't strike him as very fast for forty yards. He was sure he could run it even faster if they just let him have another chance at it. He hadn't maintained his form nor his speed as well as he could have over the final ten yards. His shoelace had also come untied. Just because his time was already faster than almost everyone else's didn't mean much to him. He had attended two of the school's games the year before and had seen how slow all the players were. He knew he could run faster.

"That's, lemme gauge it, second fastest time on the team," the receiver's coach said, shaking his head. "Yeah. Only Bradley runnin faster. That's beautiful." He kept shaking his head. He was a tall, lean young man with a shiny, expensive watch on his wrist and an even shinier, more expensive rope around his neck. He had probably played college ball, Touissant figured. And from his confident ways, Touissant figured he had more than held his own, a real player not easily impressed. But he was impressed now.

"But we could be clocking him inaccurately," the head coach said, playing the skeptic.

Touissant heard the tinge of disbelief in the voice. He came and stood in front of the starting blocks, ready to run, ready to prove himself. There were others behind him impatient for their turns, but Touissant had a sense of stagecraft: he knew that moments required capturing.

"Damn fast time," the receiver's coach reiterated.

"Damn fast," Bob agreed.

"Could be inaccurate," the head coach muttered.

"I doubt it," the receiver's coach said. "Look at the way he walks, all boundin and shit, that's a sprinter's walk."

"Big calves, little ankles, that's a sprinter's build," Bob agreed.

"Run him again," the head coach ordered.

The receiver's coach ran over to Touissant with his hand out-stretched and snatched his glasses off his face. "I'ma hold these for you, kid. I won't let nothin bad happen to 'em."

Touissant nodded. Then he ran again.

"4.41!" the receiver's coach said.

"4.41!" Bob said.

"Might as well give him his uniform and helmet." The head coach chuckled. "Carmelo," he said, looking to the receiver's coach, "if this kid can run a route he's all yours."

Carmelo nodded happily. He strode over to Touissant, handed his glasses back to him and began talking in slang that Touissant had never heard before and didn't know how to understand. It wasn't street talk. It wasn't Southernisms either. He would've understood that type of stuff. But this slang was something else entirely. He heard the coach say something about flying, or running like flying, or flying patterns; he tried but for the life of him, he couldn't under-stand what the coach was talking about.

Because Touissant didn't even know how to talk to his new coach, let alone how to run a fly pattern, his speed was only of theoretical value. This frustrated Carmelo. The fly pattern was the simplest route a receiver could run. It was also the one most conducive to swift, long-striding athletes like Touissant, especially if they happened to be as slight of build as he was. "Look," the coach said, taking Tou-issant aside mid-way through that first tryout, "it ain't no thing to teach you a fly pattern, feel me? All you gotta do is straight run up that sideline, look over yo' shoulder for that ball. I don't know what yo' grades be like but ain't nobody so stupid they fuck that up. My concern," and now his face grew serious and his gaze more profound, "is that if I gotta teach you fly patterns, then I'ma hav'ta teach you all the routes from the button-hook to the cluster formation. Like, look at this dude Bradley right here, catchin e'rything gets throwed his way. It took that boy a whole year to stop trippin over his own feet. Boy had three left feet! But now look at him, a fuckin gazelle. So it takes time. Half these kids gon' be cut by tomorrow. It wouldn't be worth the time to teach 'em nothin. But you got talent so I'ma work with you. But for now I want you to go over to Special Teams, where you might could contribute right away."

Touissant walked halfway across the field to where the Special Teams unit was practicing. An offensive lineman sat in his crouch and when Coach Bob yelled "Go!" he hiked the ball to the punter, who caught the ball, stepped forward and tried to punt it away before the boy who had by then launched himself like a flying blanket before the punter's foot could block it. There was one lineman, one punter and a line of ten or fifteen boys preparing to launch themselves for the block. Coach Bob gestured for Touissant to stand in that line.

But before he could get his chance to try and block the punt, the drill had to be discontinued when the punter accidentally kicked one of the flying boys in the face and blood coated the practice field like a hundred smashed strawberries. "Broke his nose," the punter said laconically. He bent down and wiped the blood off his shoe.

"No, no," Coach Bob said, "Don't do that, Matt. You're our only punter, we can't have you catching hepatitis or gonorrhea or something. Use a towel." Bob rushed off for a towel.

The punter looked after him in irritation.

The lineman carried the injured boy off the field and dropped him like a corpse on the first lane of the track.

Touissant observed. Special Teams probably was not his calling, he figured, but on the other hand he didn't want to appear weak and quit. He didn't want anyone to look at him sitting on his helmet and say, Oh that's Mr. A+, of course he's scared of getting hurt. But he also wanted to emerge from practice with his face intact.

It was a dilemma. He sat on his helmet on the sidelines and watched the separate units go about their drills and considered his options. As the sky darkened with early evening, the air cooled and the juniors and seniors put on full pads. "Scrimmage!" the head coach yelled. "Defensive and offensive starters only! Everyone else the fuck off the field!"

This didn't require Touissant to move. But he did anyway, taking his helmet down to mid-field and crouching down on it there. It was the best view possible and it also put him close to the coaches where he could hear their head-set communications with the quarterback and their analysis of the other players.

He had already noticed that they talked about the linemen, running backs, receivers, linebackers and defensive backs with the objective distance of scientists analyzing organisms, noting the texture of the beetle's shell, the size of its wings and mandibles, the luminosity of its eyes. Microscope-talk.

Hell yeah, Bradley was gettin better and better. Division I scholarship, easy. Pacific. San Diego State. USC? Now, how's Blake look? Fat slob. What was he doing all summer, eating houses? Fat-ass slob. Count our blessings: a great senior receiver, two bonafide horses at halfback and fullback, and an offensive line of five fat fucks to flatten 'em and protect the quarterback. Put up thirty a game, easy. Good thing, too, because the defense couldn't tackle a crippled bitch on her back. Defensive line is just too slow for the brothers out in L.A. and Long Beach and Oakland. That's the problem, lack of speed everywhere: linebackers are fundamentally sound but can't keep contain, corners are good tacklers but get burned deep, safeties same deal. That's why that one kid was such a breath of fresh air. What's his name again? Mr. 4.41. His first try-out. Got-damn, ridiculous speed. What's his name again? Too bad he doesn't know a thing about football. Probably one of these track stars. Been running track up till

now probably. Teaching him will take patience. What's his fuckin
name now? We can put him in on Special Teams, have him return
kicks for right now. Teach him routes as he goes along, hopefully get
him in as a receiver by mid-season. What's his name, Two-zaint?
Twos-aint? Two-saint? No, it ain't. It's like, Two-cent, something
like that. Too-damn-hard-to-pronounce, that's what it is. Two-cent,
Two-saint. Tupac, maybe. Remember that rapper, the one who got
shot and killed in Vegas over by Circus Circus? Good name, Tupac.
Tupac Freeman. Fast as hell. Just appeared out of nowhere, didn't say
one word to anybody, just showed up. No one seemed like they knew
who the hell he was, just showed up like a miracle . . . Hope no one
slips in that blood. Didn't know a nose held that much blood. How
the fuck your nose got all that blood in it, it's not that big. Hope
Bradley don't slip, break something.

That was how Touissant became Tupac Freeman. He liked the new
name from the first time he heard it. He decided it was no mistake
but only a revision. The change seemed like a natural part of his evo-
lution; it added an element of style and danger where before there
had only been an allusive name. He had always been a nobody on
campus. He was confident that up until now he had made absolutely no impression on anyone. So when people started to notice
him going to and from the training room and his teammates said,
that's Tupac, that's the new kick returner, there wasn't anyone who
knew enough about who he had been before to object.

His real name, Touissant, had been given to him by parents who
believed strongly in symbols and iconography. The strongest symbol
or icon that they could think up was Toussaint L'Ouverture, a man
born into slavery on the island colony of Saint-Domingue. His parents had changed the spelling slightly to maintain their son's individuality, but the point of the name was its iconic association. Freed at
the age of thirty-three, Toussaint L'Ouverture used his wide reading

and study of military tactics to help execute the only successful slave revolution in the history of the world. Toussaint authored the constitution that created the Haitian state and abolished slavery within its borders. Haiti, rooted in revolutionary suicide, rose into two hundred years of hell on earth. Somehow, after not only centuries but across water and much land, the great emancipator's name found its way onto a boy in the Southern California suburbs. Somehow, in the free prosperous land of his birth, Touissant's name was unknown.

He learned not to introduce himself.

He would wait until they said his name.

You're Tupac, they would say, Tupac Freeman, right?

Touissant let these questions stand as if they were answers and eventually they became just that.

That was how he went about changing his identity, ever so carefully, leaving off the old burden of his brain and restricting shell of shyness and the responsibility of his given name. With practice after practice and scrimmage after scrimmage, he turned into the kind of kick returner that bears risk each time the ball touches his hands. With eleven lethal children launching themselves at him, the kick returner keeps his eyes to the sky, watching the flight of the football and not the kids coming for his knees and head; he catches it and releases into the whirlwind. The shortest distance between a kick returner and the end zone being a straight run, he makes an open bet of wrenched-up limbs and broken bones against what his speed entitles him to.

From the moment he announced that he would play football his dad began to regard him differently. His existence took on new, more dynamic meaning all of a sudden. When they drove up to the school's Homecoming game together, his dad spoke on courage: "We've had a lotta athletes in this family. I wasn't one of them. Never played football. I was too into my music. I went the academic route even though I had some pretty fast feet now; still do. But you're putting the two together, the athleticism *and* the academics. That's what makes you unique. You won't need to waste your time passing off a cakewalk like it's worth a three-day conference in Palo Alto."

Touissant didn't know what his dad was talking about, but he liked the attention; he kept driving on toward the Homecoming parade, an undulating, many-colored mercury of insanely happy cheerleaders and painted, costumed cheering kids and banners, neither diminishing nor advancing, just flowing there in the windshield.

"Now, your gramps was a real deal athlete, he just gave it up to go fight for his country. But I've actually seen the newspaper clipping that states he ran a 9.6 hundred-yard dash. A shame he was so ready for war, never got to run with Elvis Peacock and Mack Robinson and those cats. He always told me he got his foot speed from his daddy, Major. You remember his story about Major, right? Running from the war . . . Well, he had a lotta other stories about the man, too, which is kind of strange considering he barely knew him. But according to your gramps, the man could pick 'em up and put 'em down: led some barnstorming baseball league in stolen bases one year. Stole bases against all kinds of major league catchers. Also claimed he played running back in something called the Negro National Football League. You ever heard of the Negro National Football League? Me neither. Anyway, the stories don't need to be true to be true. The Freeman men can run. That's our gift. But when it comes to football, you can't just be fast, you need to be fast with purpose and without fear." Tupac nodded and steered the car around a group of celebrants who'd strayed into the road. "Good driver's eye," his dad complimented him.

"Thanks." He nodded again. He knew he had a good driver's eye. His vision was clear of everything but success, touchdowns and ovations, and for a while he even thought he saw his true purpose in that.

The opposing team won the coin-flip and deferred possession to the second half. Tu fitted the gloves Bradley had lent him over his long thin fingers. Then he opened and closed his hands like pincers, feeling the elastic expand and compress and draw out again as he walked onto the field. He back-peddled slowly toward his own end zone, his eyes fixed on the fleet of red-and-white uniforms before him. There were ten of them, enough for the ten green-and-black uniforms not counting their kicker. They unfolded like paper money across the plane of his myopic vision.

Then the kicker raised a finger to the evening sky, and in a moment the ball was in the air. Tu turned his eyes up to the early night, the first stars, the half-moon, the last of the clouds and sunset. Somewhere in there he saw the brown of the ball looping down from heaven. With an instinct that surpassed adequate vision, he judged the angle of its fall and ran up under it, readying himself. Then he cradled the ball gently and leapt forward.

Forty-five yards later one of the faster green-and-black uniforms angled him out of bounds, tapping his fingers against Tu's right shoulder pad. Two burly arms caught him up as he decelerated along the chalk sideline and lifted him into the air like a trophy. Stars and darkness and stadium lights swirled before his eyes. Suddenly there was noise again and his vision widened to take in the entire scene: the stadium lights were washing the field with their white light, fans were standing and cheering, all eyes were on him. He heard his dad's words echoing back to him, with purpose, without fear.

Conceding an angle and running out of bounds instead of lowering his shoulder into the tackler wasn't exactly fearless, but he had served purpose: the offense would take the ball at mid-field.

Whoever had grabbed him up seemed to realize all this: "Good shit, Tupac. Good shit," Coach Bob sputtered, dropping him back onto his feet.

The referee drifted over and called for the football. Tu took a second to regain his balance, then he flipped him the ball with one hand and took off his helmet with the other. Excitement was rushing through him like electric volts. He breathed out heavily, realizing that he was tired, loving the feeling of fatigue. Then he took his hands off his knees and raised up to look for his dad in the stands.

The defense gave up a lot of points so there were numerous chances to return kickoffs. He produced a long series of impressive run-backs, thirty yards here, fifty there, which eventually even brought his old man out of his seat cheering. He didn't lower his shoulder into anybody or protest the angles defenders took against him, and he didn't score a single touchdown in the first half, but time after time his returns put the offense in wonderful field position. Usually they started their drives nearer the opponents' end zone than their own, and because the team's offense was as good as their defense was bad, they rattled off score after score.

By halftime, it became an open question which school's defense was more porous and which offense more prolific: at halftime the game was tied, 28–28.

In the low tunnel beneath the bleachers, the two teams filed away to their respective locker rooms in parallel lines, only their cheerleaders and coaches walking between to separate them. Tu wondered if this was when fights broke out, if the tunnel was where rivalries were born. Further down the tunnel, he could see his quarterback surrounded by cheerleaders from both teams. Popular guy, Tu thought. But other than the quarterback and his girls the recessional into the locker rooms was a non-event until someone patted his shoulder and said something so softly that he didn't hear her.

He turned and saw a white girl, all bouncy black hair and gleaming black eyes. Her eyes shined in the dark. Her body was a tight silhouette in the minimally lit tunnel. He noticed the dark colors of her uniform and the glitter of the two pom-poms stuck in her skirt behind her back and wondered why she wasn't walking ahead with the other cheerleaders and the star player.

"What's your name?" she asked, extending her hand. "Tu-pac, right?"

"Tupac," he agreed.

"Tu-pac Free-man," she said reverently, her hand roaming along the width of his shoulder pads; the way she breathed his name made it sound like something magical, brilliant and unreal.

"Tupac Freeman," he said.

"Shyanne," Shyanne answered breathlessly.

Their conversation was all stutters and sighs. She told him how cute he was; she said that someway she would manage to slip him her number before the end of the game. Then she trembled on her tiptoes, broke into a smile and reached her arms around his neck. She hugged him to her and he found himself gripping her ass with both hands. "Bye-bye, cutie pie," she whispered in his ear before easing out of his hold and flitting down the tunnel. He looked after her as she disappeared into its darkness.

Then halftime was over and he couldn't remember where it had gone to. A sharp line separated everything before Shyanne from whatever would come next.

I gave her the new name, he kept thinking as he walked back onto the field; I actually told her that was my name! Before, he simply let other people name him. If they wanted to call him Tupac, fine. If they wanted to call him by his actual name he had no problem with that either. But he knew that even in conceding that choice to everybody but himself he had in a way claimed the false name. He might have to surrender to the new identity.

"Freeman back to return!" the PA announcer crowed the next time he stepped onto the field to receive the kickoff. Tupac Freeman, he thought to himself, Tupac Freeman. And he strutted slowly back and forth across his patch of grass. Then he found the ball in amongst the stars and the night, cradled it to his chest and darted his eyes ahead: a huge expanse of open undefended field stretched out before him like destiny itself, and he burst down it toward the end zone. 34–28. Back on the sidelines an anonymous hand passed him a sliver of paper with Shyanne's name and number printed in big unmistakable script. Then the same hand passed him several more paper slivers, each with another girl's name and number. He took them in his soiled hands and stuffed them in his sock. He knew most of them would dissolve down there, dirt and mud, but he didn't have anywhere else to put them. Anyway, he didn't need all those numbers; he realized that he was getting the new-boy treatment now, girls all attracted to the new player, having known the other ones too long to be interested in them anymore.

The attention started to embarrass him, to the point that he decided not to take off his helmet again and didn't listen for the applause at the announcement of his name.

Instead, he went and sat down at the far end of the bench where he had a perfect view of the opponents' end zone and the action transpiring there. The defense was playing much better, pinning the other team back beneath the shadow of their goalpost. Suddenly the disgraceful eleven had become a stone and immovable wall. As the big scoreboard clock ticked away and the defense held, he realized that there would be no more kickoffs coming his way. "Final score 48–28," he called to Bradley, who was stalking the sideline like a pensive lieutenant.

"Maybe. Maybe," Bradley said back. He paused, in contemplation of the appropriate cliché: "Can't let up," he finally said.

Back at school the next day girls too shy to give their names delicately asked if he planned to call.

He called only Shyanne. Hers was the only number that he hadn't put in his sock and let dissolve in the grimy wetness down there. Anyway, he had committed himself to her, and he took that seriously.

"You said to call you," he said over the line.

"You actually did, too," she cooed breathlessly.

"Something to do," he said.

"Uh-huh," she agreed.

"I'm sixteen. My parents just handed down their car to me."

"Uh-huh."

"I could pick you up in it?" he offered, thinking and remembering her perky breasts against the thin cloth of her uniform, and the way she'd let him palm her ass. It would be so much nicer to have a pretty girl in the car instead of the emptiness that he'd already accustomed himself to. The only thing he ever seemed to do with the old Accord was take it through the streets of West Highland and San Bernardino, peer out its dirt-filmed windows at the whores along the boulevard. He imagined their company, what they'd say, what they'd do, their perfume and after-scent they'd leave on the upholstery. Shyanne's school was in San Bernardino, but not in the parts that he traveled through; he found himself attracted to the places everyone else shunned or tried to escape, isolated impoverished places without well-kept football fields or cheerleading white girls. But Shyanne would give him something else to do with the car. "It's no problem for me to come to where you're at," he said.

"Uh-huh," she consented. She had even less to say than he did.

"Is that cool?" he asked her.

"If it's not too much trouble."

"I'm sure it isn't. I live in Highland and you live somewhere in San Bernardino. Fifteen, twenty minutes at most."

"*West* Highland?" she suddenly asked. A tremor of something played through her voice.

"No. East," he said.

"Oh," she said, "Oh."

She was surprised that with a name like Tupac he wasn't from a more rugged neighborhood, but other than that she seemed to like him. They went on dates and grew closer every time she allowed him to palm her breasts or trace the cat's curve of her back, or soliloquize on the similarities between their relationship and Romeo and Juliet's. "Huh?" she said at first when he broke out in full intellectual glory. "What? I mean, I know *Romeo and Juliet*, I saw the movie—but you're a guy, a football player."

"Capulets versus Montagues," he offered. "Star-crossed lovers." He searched her eyes for a spark. "Like us: rival high schools, and all that stuff."

For the good of their relationship, Shyanne took it upon herself to rent the movie and watch it more intently this time. Her eyes were glassy-bright for two days afterwards. "That was sad," she told him over the phone, "We're not sad like that."

"I like Shakespeare." He shrugged.

Like the famous dead Tupac who went to a Performing Arts school in Baltimore, he knew his Shakespeare. Tupac not only knew the plays, he embodied them: he became Hamlet, his soul severed, cut away from his core, multiplying unreal identities at his edges, but somehow still wanting something central, some closeness, some love. And there was the man Tupac Shakur was named for, Tupac Amaru, the Incan warrior who repelled Spanish invaders by using that strange running hiding camouflaging courage called guerilla warfare.

All this, he inherited with his new name.

As the weeks went by and the touchdowns and victories mounted, and Shyanne allowed him closer and closer to her until he found himself spending more time inside than outside her clothes, his contradictions began to clash. The two Tupacs clashed and threatened his surface design, while within or behind the mask of those counter-selves the forgotten hero and the boy named after him shuddered in incapacitation, occasionally demanding back their living body and soul.

He was fighting himself, at surface and at depth. It was too hard for his contradictions to coexist. It was too hard to catch kickoffs and loose his body to the whirlwind without the perfect certainty that the end zone he was running toward had some sort of real meaning, that some sort of reality existed there. But it was also too hard to live in the lie of his name, which itself was a contradiction and a burden. Tupac, one part talent, the other craziness, violence and a stupid fate found in front of Circus Circus. There was no reconciling that division. After sex, he would whisper to Shyanne about Shakespeare's seductive poems, about problem plays and the high tragedies. Lone, broken souls. Lear howling his lucid insanity to the winds, Othello calling all his strength to defeat phantom betrayal, Hamlet on his knees in the church. But she wouldn't always understand, or her patience would sometimes break—and she would stare back at him irritated and moan, "You're a football player, Tupac. You're a football player."

Which was true. He returned kicks for the team and by mid-season he was also running effective fly patterns once or twice each game. The deep pass patterns drew the defense's attention and Bradley invariably ended up wide open on underneath routes, where he could catch the ball on the run and make big gains. This was the substance of his Friday nights: he and Bradley running across spaces of open grass, on toward glory. The defense was holding up well enough that the team's record swelled to a division best 5-1. Now everyone knew Tupac's name.

His parents found it strange that high school football players were taking stage names now, but they were glad to see their child finally adjusting to the culture of public school. They figured the new name expressed something about their boy, his brilliance or his creativity or something, and didn't trouble about it. As long as he was having fun, they had no qualms. But not everyone who now knew Tupac was as forgiving. When Shyanne would tire of Shakespeare talk and roaming hands and they would head out to a movie or a party, they'd inevitably happen past a set of her school's football players. Screw

faces, malicious scowls, threats mouthed in his direction. His con-
flicts being internal, he never paid them any mind: "It's because we're
an interracial couple," he told Shyanne. "People have problems with
that. Just racism, simple and plain."

She laughed, recognizing the joke: in any world outside that of
high school sports that would be a likely explanation. She even knew,
after he warned her, how white girls got talked about in black circles:
they were too whorish for black men to stay away from; they were
thieves stealing good black men, bitches not to be trusted, responsi-
ble for countless incarcerations and murders. Never was the racism
of their accusers made an issue. Racism, he taught her, was one of
those things that was simple and very complicated and hidden in
plain sight all at once.

Conversely, she'd taught him that Friday night football culture
was another world completely, ruled by high school rivalries unrelated to race. The rivalries could be something serious. About once
a year there would be a messy brawl in some extracurricular setting
and kids from the rival sides would end up hauled away in ambulances and police cars.

"Just be careful," Shyanne would say in her simple way; but within
her words was the knowledge that these were boys she knew and
that their beef wasn't with her but with her boyfriend, who was
keeping her from them.

Then one Sunday night Tu was alone, driving idly through the
San Bernardino streets. He had forgotten to keep to the bad part of
town. He had drifted into the wealthy suburban neighborhood of his
rivals. A raised four-wheel-drive truck blasted its horn. He looked
after the sound. It came from the right side. He saw the truck and
four football players from Shyanne's school in their uniforms. The
truck was veering into his lane, slowing and speeding at the Accord's
pace. He didn't think they would try to run him off the road, but

there was a sharp turn up ahead and a small grove of trees that would be disastrous to drive into. He knew he had to evade them quickly, calculated his time: ten seconds at most. He didn't know what to do. He couldn't just keep on toward the curve. He had to make a decision fast. Impulsively, he hit the brakes and sent the car into a skid. He throttled the car into reverse but instead of simply going backward the vehicle veered out of control and off the road. He was looking at the steering wheel and the brakes. He didn't know what tree or wall or signpost the car might be headed toward. He eased off the brake, then back on and the car finally came to rest in what luckily turned out to be a weedy, vacant lot. He looked up the road at the truck, which had slowed but hadn't been able to match the sudden agility or improvisation of the Accord's performance. The truck was just kind of idling down the street now, headed for the sharp curve in the road. The boys' white faces faded away behind a cluster of trees, but as they disappeared down the road and into the night he heard something, someone saying and saying, a distant reminiscent call: *"Touissant!"* The taunt floated back to him. *"Touissant!"* As resonant, clear and perfect as if the boy had named himself.

In the locker room before practice the next day, the quarterback motioned toward Tu. Come over here, he mouthed.

Tu came toward the quarterback's locker.

"Heard you had quite a night last night?" the quarterback inquired quietly.

Tu felt his breath catch in his throat. It was his hope that word of the incident would stay in San Bernardino, that that way his relationship with Shyanne would stay a non-issue. He had almost convinced himself in the morning and moving through his day that the surrounding neighborhoods formed too unfriendly a zone for local gossip to travel. Nobody at school had cut their eyes suspiciously in his direction, or asked a leading question, or accused him of fabricating an identity in order to be accepted. But now things were catching up with him.

"Car racing or something?" the quarterback wondered, when Tu failed to answer his first question. The quarterback's voice remained a virtual whisper but a knowing smile was sneaking across his square-jawed face. "It's high school football. Any time a teammate gets into a scrap with the opposition word gets back to the coaching staff and the team leader."

Tu noticed how the quarterback appointed himself team leader even though his performance was entirely contingent on the blocking of the offensive line, the route-running and catching ability of the receivers, and the threat represented by a competent halfback and fullback. Even in that immediate moment of embarrassment and fear, he still found time to remember how much he disliked young white men in general. "It wasn't a scrap," he finally said, speaking up for himself. His voice came up hoarse and loud and a few heads turned in his direction.

The quarterback shook his head gravely. Tu was tall, but the quarterback was taller and broader across his torso and thicker through his shoulders and chest. The silent calculation of boys at odds was in process: Tu knew that the only way he would be able to escape this situation cleanly would be to shut the quarterback up. The quarterback seemed to know that the only way to get the full story out of Tu about what had happened and about who he really was would be to intimidate him into disclosure. Both stood their ground.

"If it wasn't a scrap," the quarterback said, "what was it?" He was talking louder now, and looking around the locker room nodding at whoever looked his way.

"It wasn't anything important," Tu maintained. He stared the quarterback down to show how seriously unwilling he was to say more.

"If it wasn't important then it must not be a big deal to talk about. What? Were you out partying?" The quarterback's eyes grew colder. "Were you out partying with the opposition?"

Low muttering rippled through the gathering audience to the argument. Tu dropped his head and purged his throat loudly. He wanted to spit. The quarterback talked about the team's rivalry with "the opposition" like he and his teammates were La Résistance fighting back the Nazi occupation one inch at a time in the streets of Paris.

"Were you partying with the opposition?" the quarterback demanded. He stepped into Tu's chest and knocked him back into the nearest locker. Tu swallowed and stumbled back, but stayed on his feet. He readied his hands for a fight. The last fight he had undertaken was against his sister, not against a six-foot-five, two-hundred-fifteen-pound star athlete, and she had punched him to the ground. That was a long time ago, and he was a lot stronger now, but he still didn't want a fight. It just might be his only option. *Ridiculous,* he thought in that hot moment. *Ridiculous,* that he stood accused of team treason, that he stood accused of selling out his own teammates when the only person he had ever sold out was himself.

When the quarterback didn't throw the first punch, Tu decided to continue to speak up for himself. Angry now, he said how he felt: "It wasn't important because the rivalry isn't fucking important. It's just football, man." He looked around the gathered audience. "Get over yourselves."

"I heard that you was with a darkside girl!" somebody, he couldn't see who it was, shouted up.

He kept his eyes on the quarterback just in case the team leader decided to sucker-punch him. "Why do we have to call them the darkside, again?" he asked the entire locker room. "I mean, it's just football." He wanted to give them the head's up that Santa Claus and God were also figments of their collective imagination, anything to fuck-up their group-think. "Goddamnit! What did I do that was so wrong? I can't drive *my* car around *their* neighborhood? I can't date *their* girl? I don't get it. They're just a football team. Shyanne is just a cheerleader. This is stupid."

"Yeah, he's with the darkside," the quarterback said, his voice flat now. He glowered at Tu about as darkly as a kid with blue eyes could glower. "Now it comes out. But I already knew, from talking to people. He broke every rule of the rivalry. He's completely in violation of all our team codes."

The quarterback had finally gotten something right: Tu didn't care about the high school's bizarre codes and rivalries. He hadn't even cared who knew about Shyanne. But maybe even that had been a mistake. He wondered about Shyanne.

The quarterback could turn his head a little this way, a little that, and meet the eyes of everybody on the team. "I'm from *that* part of town. I know what's going on over there. I talk to people."

The quarterback truly was the team leader. He could do whatever he wanted to, including consort with the opposition, and nobody else could do anything they wanted to without his permission. He had figured out how to rally support while minimizing his own commitments and maximizing the commitment and vulnerability of everybody else on his team. The quarterback would probably grow up to lead men into war via satellite, a million miles behind the front lines. Tu realized there was no way to win the argument, if for no other reason than that the quarterback was demanding that he prove a negative. He hadn't betrayed his teammates, but there was no way to prove the truth of something that hadn't happened. He had only betrayed himself and hadn't even thought about how Shyanne could betray him just by being herself, living where she lived, a white girl in the white part of town. There was no way out of the trap he was caught in. Nowhere to run to. It was time to fight.

The locker room doors banged open.

"Hey! Hey!!" Coach Bob's voice rang across the locker room. "You all having a circle jerk in there? Why the fuck are you guys just standing around scratching your nuts. We've got drills to run!"

Later that afternoon during non-contact drills Tu turned his eyes to the sky and searched for the football amongst the clouds, the smog and the sunlight. As he was positioning himself for the fair catch he felt a helmet splitting him at the leg and another shivering his torso, then sudden oblivion.

He never felt the pain, only the subsequent relief of the cast and the soft hospital bed.

To his bewildered parents, Coach Bob explained, "Something happened. I don't know what the hell happened. Mondays are non-contact days. Nobody was wearing pads. I have no idea why we had kids launching themselves around like that. I'd say it was a miscommunication and take the blame for that, but we've been running that drill for seven or eight weeks now. I don't know. Jesus, I mean, I do take the blame: I'm the official guardian on that field so I take the responsibility. But I can't explain what happened to Tupac."

To Shyanne, Coach Bob explained, "Something happened. I don't know what the hell happened. Mondays are non-contact days. Nobody was wearing pads. I have no idea why we had kids launching themselves around like that . . , They say his recovery'll take a couple months. Good he has you around."

Shyanne bought *The Complete Works of William Shakespeare* for $19.99 and left it at his bedside while he slept. When Touissant woke to find it lying there next to his dinner tray he figured that it marked the end of something.

After Touissant's femur had healed enough for him to move around on crutches and he was discharged from the hospital, he returned home. He didn't return to school, though: he was as intellectually proficient as ever without the annoyance of actually having to interact with teachers and classmates. This way, the assignments were e-mailed to him, he completed them and e-mailed back the finished product when he was done. It was the most private schooling he could imagine, and he liked it. Academically, his injuries turned out to be blessings.

But school had always come easy to him. It was the rest of life that posed problems. He told himself he had always known Shyanne was a bitch not to be trusted. But in reality he had foreseen nothing and even now he knew absolutely nothing. All he really had was a bunch of questions and each one struck at the unstable center of his self. Why had he accepted his name change so easily? Why hadn't he been accepted in his earlier identity? And why was everybody associated with the team still calling him Tupac even though the medical records clearly showed that that was not and had never been his real name?

He figured he would never play football again. His teammates didn't trust him, and he didn't trust himself. He didn't know himself. He wasn't the hero, wasn't Tupac or Tupac Amaru or Toussaint L'Ouverture. He wasn't anything in particular. For the first time in his life he saw his future only darkly, a long black drop, a depression that made him wish for tears.

For the rest of the school year and even after, he felt lost. His injury healed, his incapacity ended, but the bad feelings lingered. Some nights the badness was in his head and he could deal with it alright, debate it, come to logical conclusions that made him feel decent about himself and about the world. But other nights it was in his stomach and he felt like an emptied skeleton with only a brain to keep him thinking about the very things that he most wanted to forget. By summertime he found himself in his car nights, with the Buddhist temple always in his rearview mirror, the night black empty San Bernardino streets surrounding him on all sides. Used to looking at things in certain ways, at first the neighborhoods still seemed like one endless slum, desolation along the roads, poverty shadowing the buildings and darkening the little off-shooting barrio side roads, bending low the small hidden homes and leaning apartment buildings, a way of seeing the city that conveniently matched his mood.

But the more he drove, the more he saw, and the more he saw the more he began to learn that the people were not desolate in the least. There was an old man on a bicycle who'd rigged up a metal bar so that all his belongings could hang from it and lie across his shoulders like a mantle of his qualities. No matter how fast he rode, the whole thing held steady. Never trus' no possum-eatin white woman, he sang, never trus' no possum-eatin white woman. A lady with green hair and a tiara spent each night dancing down the near-empty streets to no audience and no applause. She danced faster the emptier the streets got. Specific people going about their highly specific ways. The strong-stance Mexican men crouched on their porches who watched his car come and go and come again with incredibly stubborn unblinking eyes. Their women wandered outside now and again, bantering, laughing, nagging, waving whatever happened to be in their hands. And in the streets, the hollow-eyed sisters of the night guided voicelessly by their plain-dressed corner boys; no pimps, no whores, just children holding the line against their despair, the hustle eternal. With July and August, he turned seventeen and his body began to fill in: fifteen new pounds muscled and deepened his neck, shoulders and arms and his six-foot-two frame no longer looked so tragically light. The physical maturity that playing football was supposed to endow him with came now that he had nothing to do and nowhere to be except those streets.

He spent nights driving all throughout the other half of Highland, through San Bernardino, Colton, Muscoy, Rialto. He was learning now, doing homework that no teacher would dare assign. Some nights the smog never dissipated, it just hung there like a veil between the earth and the moon. He wondered if there had been nights like this in the war in the South Pacific, or in small Southern towns and backwoods one step ahead of authorities; nights when even the moon disappeared and all there was was the earth and the people on it and a boy had to make firm actual sense of life as he found it.

Life, dark life. He wondered if this was where manhood began.

I n the academic year 2000–2001, the Accountability Report Card at Erycha's high school was a slaughterhouse. 2,707 students were enrolled on the campus's killing floor, of which 1,005 were freshmen, 660 were sophomores, 559 were juniors and 483 were seniors. Of those, 20% were African-American, 62% were Hispanic or Latino, 15% were Hispanic-Caucasian or Latino-Caucasian or possibly, though not probably, just Caucasian, and 3.1% were someway ancestrally Asian. Whoever was otherwise unaccounted for the Report Card classified as "Other."

In statistics for "School Safety and Climate for Learning" rates of suspension and expulsion, her high school nearly doubled district averages, 14.4% to 7.3%, and .56% to .3% respectively. In the California Standards Test (CST) 9% of ninth graders, 22% of tenth graders and 18% of eleventh graders scored at or above the Proficient or Advanced level in English Language Arts. Statewide figures hovered between 31–33%, always somewhat higher where the exposure to "whole language" teaching was lower.

In Math, her school tellingly declined to publish the test's findings.

In History/Social Science the scores again fell far short of admirable statewide averages. Delving further, 20% of eleventh grade males, 25% of eleventh grade females, 1% of second-language students, 15% of children receiving free lunch and 39% of economically middling children scored at the Proficient or Advanced level in English Language Arts. 25% of males, 36% of females, 13% of second-language students, 22% of economically disadvantaged children and 41% of more fortunate children achieved proficiency in the Sciences. And in History/Social Science 25% of males, 35% of females, 5% of second-language students, 25% of those receiving free lunch and 45% of those better blessed were graded proficient.

As for racial/ethnic subgroups, in English Language Arts, 14% of African-Americans, 14.5% of Hispanics and Latinos, 47% of Caucasians and 49% of Asians achieved proficiency in Reading and Comprehension. In the Sciences, 6% of African-Americans, 21% of Hispanics and Latinos, 46% of Caucasians and 46.6% of Asians achieved proficiency. And in History/Social Science 10% of African-Americans, 30% of Latinos and Hispanics, 47% of Caucasians and 50% of Asians achieved proficiency.

The School Wide Academic Performance Index (API), which annually measures the academic performance and progress of individual schools in California against a baseline score of 800 points, also looked on her school unfavorably. Her school scored an API of 508. Among racial/ethnic subgroups, African-American children scored 472, Hispanics and Latinos scored at 500, Caucasians at 666, Asians 669 and Filipino, Pacific Islander and Alaskan-American scores went undocumented. Those receiving free lunch, in other words the very poor, constituting 83.5% of the overall student body, scored 495. These scores, predictably, left the school ineligible for the Governor's Performance Award, as well as II/USP program funding.

Depending on the course in question, between 30.3 and 32.2 children filled each class. 73 of the total 109 teachers had full-time credentials, while the rest taught with emergency credentials. There were 5 counselors, 0 librarians, 0 psychologists, 0 social workers, 1 nurse, 0 speech/language/hearing specialists and therapists and 0 resource specialists. A ratio of 541.2 students to each counselor was thus established and sustained, as well as 2,707 students to each nurse established and sustained. And infinite students to librarians, psychologists and so on.

Exceeding the state requirement of 64,800 instructional minutes, Erycha's school offered 64,877 minutes. During those minutes 77.7% of pupils were enrolled in courses required for UC or Cal State admittance. But of the freshmen who had entered high school with Erycha four years prior, only 35% graduated with her. The average SAT I verbal score for seniors at the school was 440, the average math score 427.

Statistics for step squad went unrecorded. Statistics for ballet went unrecorded. Real means for figuring out what these children were actually doing with their lives nobody ever thought to devise, except to fall back on endless formulae.

Neither despite nor because of any of this, Erycha emerged fifth in her academic class, with honors, awards and carefully written recommendation letters to California's upper-tier public universities. Her SAT verbal score was 700, her math score 620, her grade point average 3.91. Erycha was one name. These scores were taken as signs she had escaped the killing floor.

Du Bois and Washington. Washington and Du Bois. *The Souls of Black Folk. Up from Slavery.* The Atlanta Address. The Talented Tenth. Two books. Two authors. And right next to the works of the great black men lay Touissant's October issue of *Black Mack* magazine. He looked from the white woman bending over spectacularly on the magazine cover to Du Bois, to Washington. They were shaking their heads at him from off the page and a century apart.

Before him, too, was a decision that the magazine let him forget but the books forced him to deal with. It was October and already he had applied to six universities, UCLA, UC San Diego, UC Irvine, UC Riverside, Columbia and Xavier. He knew Columbia should be his first choice, then the UCs in descending order of acclaim. Finally, Xavier was less a choice than an inspiration. His high school's Black Student Union had had to cancel their Black College Tour because, with only a minority of the black seniors realistically on track to graduate, it would have been a waste of money and time to bus them across the country to schools that they hadn't worked hard enough to get into. The monies that would have gone to the tour had been redirected into "situational use" and were accessible through written proposal. Touissant proposed the Black Student Union pay his application fee.

Thinking about it now he figured he would consider Xavier only if his other applications were rejected. Even then, he knew his parents would push him to go to a community college in Southern California. Community colleges provided poor schooling, but they figured they couldn't be much worse than the black colleges they'd heard about where college students were assigned a high school curriculum. The community colleges were little more than high schools as well, but they formed a familiar subsystem close to home. The schools in the South seemed a part of some distant older world.

He had also looked to Berkeley. In fact, he was still wondering after that star, deciding whether or not to sacrifice the seventy-dollar application fee, weighing the ego satisfaction that admission to that prestigious university would give versus the knowledge that it would be a hollow accomplishment if he didn't actually want to be there.

The UCs offered so much: Pristine weather. Affordable tuition. High regard. But there was something about Xavier that captured his imagination in a way no California school could.

At first he had thought it was distance and difference that attracted him to the school. But the more he considered his decision and the more he read from the books of black thought that his high school would not teach, the more he felt in Xavier and its surrounding city a homeplace feeling. Somehow, every time he thought of the school it seemed more familiar to him, not like something new or different or exciting, but like a family member he had never seen but always known through stories and letters and intimate mutual acquaintances. His feel for the school and for New Orleans came from nothing read or watched or borrowed. There was an intimacy not desired but deferred and past due in the way that anything necessary eventually requires reckoning.

The real issue went beyond college. The real issue at the bottom of his thoughts had to do with home. Where could he live? This desert city marked by tract homes, lifeless landscapes and an old Buddhist temple, this place where his parents had laid their bucket down was not home. California itself held him at a distance. He remembered his trip to the dentist, one Dr. Emilio Yamamoto, a man of Japanese ancestry, Brazilian birth, an immigrant to America, where he earned his BS from Dartmouth and MD from Texas at Austin and completed residency at USC University Hospital. "California is the only place in America for a person like me," Dr. Yamamoto said. Touissant remembered being puzzled by that statement at first: Dr. Yamamoto had a beautiful wife. His Porsche was new. And he had had to postpone Touissant's latest teeth cleaning because he had been vacationing on Portugal's Madeira archipelago. But that did not mean things had been easy for him. "After Rio, where I couldn't stay for lack of opportunity, after trips back to Kobe, which was not my home the way Africa isn't yours," the doctor's voice took on a wistful quality, "after college in Hanover, after medical school in Austin, I came to California. And I liked it. I still like it." He sighed. "I stay here because it's the first place that reminds me of the world I grew up in, in Brazil. The diversity is special: Japan Town. The Asians and Latinos and Europeans, so many of us immigrants looking for a home, we have been used to making the best of being lost. This is a place for lost people."

It was hard for Touissant to think of his dentist as lost. But he had quite a story. Never being at home in the places he lived, having to travel thousands and thousands of miles simply to find a place like the place of his birth. He had an exilic consciousness, which connected him to so many other people in his chosen home. To be a Japanese Brazilian settling in California was to know some of what it was to be Arab and American or Latino and American or European and American. It was a consciousness Touissant didn't own or envy. He wasn't an immigrant. He wasn't the child of immigrants. His family could claim only America. Ever since an unrecorded Haitian slave escaped into southern Louisiana swampland, the Freemans had had no other nation. For the Freemans, there was no other home below the border, or on a far mother continent. Albert Murray said it most plainly: America was a black country, mammy-made. Touissant was reading *The Omni-Americans* and learning about the unique reconciliation at the historical heart of blackness. The knowledge that black people had both to reject and forgive the nation that had reared black folk in its bottom quarters. For Murray, Black American experience was Southern experience and could best be understood through a soul call that Touissant hadn't heard.

Murray was a man from Mobile, not a Californian. The South was something Touissant would need to learn. California he already knew: the state was a world in itself, all humanity brought together on a long reach of coast. And yet it was also an undignified, bowing-and-scraping culture of Mexican day laborers and maids and blacks gentrified into the desert. There was something cold about this state without any blues, without its voice speaking its complicated condition. He couldn't love California for its silences and its shadows, its transplanted migrants and immigrants afraid of complicating their dreamland with questions about its system of power. What he wanted was to be in love with a world where he could finally really live. But that would be a matter of going home.

Where, finally, was home? He was quickly casting off the idea of Columbia, rejecting the Ivy League before it could reject him. The frigid Atlantic seaboard schools sounded like spaceships or points on a primitive map of the unknown world. Columbia. Yale. Harvard. Dartmouth. Duke. The schools were located in a maze of states and boroughs and district territories so differently organized that they seemed like the jewels of another country. Columbia itself lay on a far island edge of America's opposite coast, as remote and foreign from Southern California as Southern California was from most of the country. His whole existence, of course, was a foreign thing, from his foreign name, to his foreign home, to the fact of his thoughtful nature alive within a world that routinely rejected its history and closed itself to questions about how everything had come to be as it now was. Maybe his home was in foreign places. Maybe, like the doctor, he should just keep going and never stop until he found some otherplace that only cared for the homeless and the lost.

He leafed through *Black Mack* for a few minutes. The magazine was published out of Los Angeles but Touissant recognized none of the settings where the photos were taken. The only part of the city he had real familiarity with was the USC area of South-Central, where he had visited his sisters. Apparently *Black Mack* could do without South-Central. The magazine contained over fifty pages' worth of Caucasian and Asian and quarter-black models with incredible figures, kneeling, bent perpendicular, lain flat. The black male models they were pictured with had distant, distracted eyes, like they were trying to tell whoever would see them that the girls should be better somehow. He remembered his great-granddad with his women strewn across the South. When he thought of the man he always pictured him in full stride on the run from one thing and to the next. But now he saw him walking slowly: the man entered a bedroom, ducking his head under a low doorway. Into a bedroom that was ripe and over-ripe with the funk of flesh aroused, unreleased and repressed. Men who knew what they wanted always talked about females who *felt* better than they looked. The girl lying there was one of those women, all roundness and softness. She was not beautiful, but she was smiling and desirous, and when he came to her he was full of hot half-controlled want. Her skin was chocolate brown in the glare of full candlelight, then she turned yellowbone in the half-glow when he blew the flame low; then her skin took on that sickly-seeming white color tinted olive that married the races in the dark.

He remembered Du Bois: the Negroes, like all races, will be saved by their great men. Du Bois had probably placed too much faith in men, but his was a sincere call nonetheless. Du Bois had lived what he advocated. After college at Fisk and Harvard and in Berlin, he researched and wrote and taught at Atlanta University. Du Bois, Touissant figured, wouldn't dismiss Xavier. But he would also consider Columbia. If Du Bois were Touissant, Du Bois might leave California only to come back when conditions called for it just like he had left Massachusetts only to return when Harvard finally opened its doors to him. Home for him was not fixed but fluid; formed of opportunity, changing values, advancing allegiances. In the end, all those changes led him, at ninety years old, to reject capitalism and America and Europe. His final home was Ghana, his homeplace Africa.

Touissant looked back to the photograph of Du Bois's great rival, Booker T. Washington. His plain, unremarkable face dominated the cover page of the book of his collected writings. Washington's expression seemed determinedly unromantic, almost severe. Touissant contrasted this with the widely reproduced bust of Du Bois: the massive bronzed forehead of the great scholar-activist, the upward-inclined jaw, the total contemplativeness of the eyes, assured, authoritative, even arrogant. The bust reminded Touissant of the impressive busts representing Greek philosophers and of the Presidential heads carved into Mount Rushmore. It was hard to imagine Washington's face on the side of a mountain. In his photograph, Washington sported a threadbare tweed coat. His hair had kinks like sprigs of wilting grass twisting away from the basic cut of the lawn. His forehead was turned down slightly His heavy cheeks were shadowed with concern, His jawline was strong but sad; it seemed more formed of responsibility than skin. His expression said what his address in Atlanta had counseled and what his autobiography advised: Learn a trade. Forgo protest and legal challenge. Remain humble. Do the work. Like his granddad, in a way: Touissant could picture Washington at war in the Pacific, a poor black soldier without a gun ferrying white folks' food and Jap-killing weapons across blood-red water without protection and yet without complaint, not because he deserved this fate and not because he wasn't angry, but out of some churning hunger that had no name.

Empty-stomached Washington had founded a technical school instead of a liberal arts university. But Du Bois was something else, not as hungry and not as basic. Touissant was drawn to Du Bois's complexity. Hope and anger had splintered into a thousand pieces inside that man: the passion that would make of the marginal Niagara Movement the National Association for the Advancement of Colored People had somehow been wedded to the pragmatism of *The Philadelphia Negro*, that Negro problems were the problems of human beings, not to be undone by fantastic theories, ungrounded assumptions, or metaphysical subtleties. His final, tragic rejection of America could only be understood in light of his lifelong love of American ideals.

Touissant was tired. He was tired of his own thoughts and questions and total ignorance. He lay down with Du Bois still on his mind, but in a steadily less and less systematic way. Random facts flitted through his head: after Howard, Harvard graduated more black law school students than any university in the nation. The editor of *Black Mack* was an Atlanta University alum and listed Du Bois among his inspirations. Du Bois was the son of a mixed-race Haitian father who abandoned his wife and children. Touissant's granddad was raised in Tuscaloosa but born in Jackson to the second wife of a man on the run. Touissant's great-granddad was that man and before Jackson there was New Orleans and a woman there, too. The family stories were not facts but lies and dreams thrown together, added to, subtracted from. There was no way of discovering the way things were or where he had come from. There was only re-creation, re-dreaming, re-writing: it was the government and the war chasing the man across the South. It wasn't the war and not his government but a woman and a child; not a woman, not a child, it was an invisible specter that was running after him, pursuing him through niggertowns and dusty work sites strewn along city edges. Touissant

saw a man black as the sun stared at too long and a woman with
skin so white it was almost clear glass. The girl gleamed in the final
sunlight of his darkening mind.

Waking, he found himself staring into Booker T. Washington's
concerned eyes. Harvard? the eyes seemed to ask. Columbia? California? *Cast your buckets down where you are.* The "bucket" was the
necessary work and the "where you are" a segregated and terrorized
Southern homeland. Negroes had rejected Washington in favor
of Du Bois and had left the South, sought advancement through
prestigious universities and high courts and aspirational marching.
But Toussant was looking at Washington now; it was Washington's
words that he couldn't get out of his head.

For Toussant, the "where you are" was not only physical but
mental. Mentally, he lived in a matrix of immediate parentage and
kin and an abstract welter of half-known ancestry and half-known
history and land and money lost through legal theft. Those thefts
were as definitive of the homeplace as the family home or the names
engraved in tombstones or scribbled misspelled in Bibles. The people and things now nameless, unknown, stolen, foreclosed, forgotten,
the speechless invisible absence was a world in itself.

Cast your buckets down where you are. Where am I? A town, he had
to concede, that lived off of a city that lived off of stolen river water.
A place that barely and unnaturally existed. Located at the extreme
edge of the nation, his world was an extracted, stolen one. The black
history of dispossession had its analogue here, in a state that had
stolen from itself and replaced its power from one very old region to
a newer construct. He thought of Langston writing about the lazy
laughing South with blood on its mouth, the child-minded South,
scratching for a Negro's bones, beautiful like a woman and seductive
as a dark-eyed whore. That was here, too, in his dry section of California, amongst not only Negroes but Mexicans; mostly amongst

Mexicans. These men who would love her in the way that all men cast adrift by money and war and restless need would love the womb-home from which they came but for the fact that that mother had turned her back and allowed them to fall from her embrace.

Touissant turned on the upstairs television, flipped from channel to channel until he came to a recorded lecture staged in a drab, non-descript college auditorium: Harvard University Professor Cornel West was speaking at Boalt Hall Law School at California, Berkeley. West's lecture was in its closing stages. The Professor was getting loose now, no longer lecturing but just plain talking about his boy-hood spent in Sacramento, his early struggles with discipline and education. Then about how the non-Marxist socialism and radical Christianity that he preached fit in with Bay Area institutions like the Saint John Coltrane African Orthodox Church in San Francis-co's Fillmore and the social justice mission still present at Berkeley.

Now, he opened the floor for Q & A. A mic was passed through the crowd. After a couple commonplace questions from students dressed in dashikis, the mic made its way to an older gentleman dressed in the tattered fits of a street corner intellectual or adjunct lecturer. The man's words were as plain as his clothes. "Dr. West, why haven't you taught at a black college? An Ivy League University professor like yourself could do so much good by going South to Howard or Morehouse or Fisk. It's what Du Bois did."

More than a few sho' ya rights and um-hmm murmurs circulated through a crowd that had obviously come up the way from Oakland.

Dr. West waited, letting the noise die down. He thanked the man for his question. Then, to Touissant's surprise, he agreed with the man: he had given Harvard *so* many of his best years. The audience broke into laughter for reasons Touissant had yet to grasp. Dr. West went on agreeing with the man's points: the most prolific and signif-icant Black American scholar, he conceded, had not spent his career in the Ivies, but in the Deep South at a historically black university. The breadth and depth of African-American scholarship done by Harvard's black faculty had only been surpassed by the years Du Bois spent working alone. But, he went on, today is not yesterday and new times in African-America call for new ways of negotiating the world. The imperatives of Du Bois's time were different from the challenges now faced by a black privileged class perched at a point of power, holding the line between the elites and the deprived poor. That the class struggle, too, West argued, remained a racial crossroads was unavoidably true. But that crossroads and the decisions it demanded were so different from what had been demanded of Du Bois. It was now imperative that academically, professionally and economically privileged black folk not only go back where the ancestors came from, but go to where power was circulated. Speaking truth to power where power actually lived, in corporate boardrooms and high stakes political negotiations and Ivy League administrative meetings, was also necessary. There was a reason, after all, that such a high percentage of HBCU undergraduates went on to graduate and professional schools in the Ivy League and that reason was pressure for change within the Ivy system. In fact, West's work was part of Du Bois's vision, *the use of education to redistribute power.* As much social good could be done in the conference rooms at Harvard as at a grade school in East Oakland or a homeless shelter in Sacramento.

Touissant turned down the television and let that argument settle: it made good sense, especially for Dr. West. It would probably make much sense for Touissant, too, to attend whatever elite university would have him, move from there to an elite law school, then on to some elite academic or legal post, or editor at *Black Mack.* He could almost see himself moving through the ranks, maybe one day rewarded with an expensive loft in Santa Monica or Manhattan. A good life, if he could get it.

But West's way was only one out of many ways to understand black life in America in the new century. Touissant had also been flirting with Thomas Sowell's *Race and Culture*, reading a section, putting it away, then returning to the simple but strange book. Sowell took the position that the high-ranking liberal arts colleges and universities were mostly misused to create millions of unproductive humanists, legalists, social activists and schoolteachers. Folks with overly refined notions of how the world should be but none of the practical technical skill in mathematics or medicine or engineering or finance that would actually change the world. Minorities were especially prone to mixing sentiment with education and part of the fault for this lay with the major universities. Schools like Berkeley and Columbia accepted talented black students at levels beyond what their preparedness dictated, then routed them into ethnic studies, whereas more slowly paced middle-tier institutions could afford to develop them more slowly so that they could eventually take on more difficult disciplines. Refinements in literature and law ultimately resulted in poetic and political "solutions" to economic problems. This misapplication of talent, Sowell explained, led to blacks misidentifying the source and solution for their deprivation. Writing papers and holding marches would *do* nothing for black people in the twenty-first century but *speak* on their behalf while privileging a select few. Only real skills bettered a community. Rhetoric, flourished over a lecture hall or a courtroom or a political convention, never would. He thought back to Du Bois's dream. The dream of a select few teaching the rest and publishing things and arguing in court: The Talented Tenth, The National Association for the Advancement of Certain People.

Du Bois's dream would die if the romance of it failed to become real.

This was where he came back to Washington. Those eyes that he had woke to. That empty-stomached shadow-faced man. When Washington said to cast buckets down where you are he wasn't only referring to a location but to a way of living that had no time for baseless prestige or beautiful talk. The basics of life and work and learning were all. This was where Washington came back to Du Bois: Negro problems remained human problems; made by people, perpetuated by people, to be solved by people. Du Bois and Washington reminded him of his fighting granddad and running great-granddad, two black men who were apparently different but actually alike. This was where they coincided. This was where everything came together. This was home.

Touissant envisioned himself a year or two on. He could see Ponchatrain from out his window. It was evening now and the lake was a dirty dark soup. Whatever he had foregone in terms of prestige, elite mentorship and the approval of his family he had reconciled long ago. The air was always heavy. On still afternoons and early evenings in New Orleans it seemed like time itself, or the medium along which time, hours, minutes, moments moved, had stopped. This was when he studied, when he wrote, when he thought about his future and reflected on his past. Now, he turned from the window and the water and looked at his apartment house walls, adorned in red, black and green by an idealistic girlfriend. She was born and raised in the same region where she still stayed: the South. Alabama. Her dreams for a black new world that would never be found balance beside a warm knowledge of the life outside school back in Tuscaloosa, all the bookless black life fulfilling itself back there without the help of revolutionary theory. They were sitting back-to-back on his small bed, their spines touching, balancing each other delicately. She cradled a giant textbook. His myriad class notes were sprawled before him, as tangled as the bed sheets. No model magazines in sight. Bounce music from the surrounding apartments and the human traffic from the street below were continual and deafening. Even the apartment's old heater was too loud. It hummed in and out of functionality, its metal expanding as it struggled into action, clink, knock, clink, *bang*. Like a million marbles trickling rhythmically down a glass tunnel, then that occasional gunshot sound when the metal expanded most suddenly. Much of New Orleans was like this, poorer and older and slower and louder and more problematic than the world he had been raised in. But he loved it and he loved her. He knew that one day he would marry her and she would settle him and he would return to his roots by bringing his family to him, to their one true home.

Now he saw himself attending a major university. Could be Columbia. Could be Berkeley. Could be any of many elite institutions. He wasn't at the institution itself at the moment. He was in the city next to the school, Harlem or Oakland or Watts. His car windows were speckled with tear drops of rain, fogged with the warm wetness. He was going to his girl: a chocolate-skinned, duck-bodied, bottom-heavy chick. She lived in a neighborhood full of boarded-up houses, with too many churches where stores should be instead. It was a place much like the small Southern towns he'd visited as a child. Goin to see the folks, Touissant thought. Lots of empty spaces and room to appreciate the way of things. He found himself desiring the absence of things as much as whatever the neighborhood actually held. When he was with her, on the street, on her porch, in her rooms, he took no precautions of any kind and often felt unsure and safe all at once, like a man inside a woman knowing and fearing her fertility but loving her too much to stop.

Now he saw himself with a girl not unlike Shyanne. He was in limbo poised above her. He wondered where he was and knew it wasn't anywhere he knew of, not even Highland. He was deep in his dream now. He was not himself. He was a man all of a sudden and not just a man but a troubled man that he hoped never to become. Poised above her, he could hear the girl mumbling, sweet nothings and more unicorn tears. She was totally oblivious to the war above her. She had no idea that in being with her, he had declared himself a nationalist for a nation of one. That he had placed himself in a void between blacks and whites where no collective would claim him and only his assaulted individuality remained. The white folks were trying to kill him and the black folks wanted him gone, and the girl was too innocent and too much in love to understand any of this. But it was this reality that hovered between them, separating them: a black man could only claim himself and be his own man outside all unions, in exile, nomadically on the run. Even with her, he was by himself. Their desire was doomed at contact. He was leaving her even as his fingers found her and explored her taut and lilting curves beneath the bedsheets. She had this way about her, so light with everything. Her laughter, that he loved; the way she would dance in place in the middle of something else for no reason good or bad, all ease and fun. Now she was careless, and completely willing. The supple arch of her back, its rise and fall, was incredibly inviting. He knew that this moment was all that he could claim other than himself and it only briefly. He lifted her off the sheets and drew her through the troubled space between them and brought her gasping into his mutilated world. She let out a trembling yes and he entered her. This was how the running began, with a pretty girl in a bleak little room; this was how the family line left New Orleans and eventually came to California, this was how the homeplace disappeared and so much fragile first manhood began.

He took Sowell's book and set it down next to the rest of the great books and the stupid magazine. He still hadn't settled on a college. Suddenly he smelled fire. He jumped up and looked out the window: the Buddhist temple was disappearing, spires and roofs and walls, all beneath red-black rising flames. The lanterns along the walkway burst open one after the next, each a ball of exuberant cherry red flame. A shirtless barefoot man with a cross tattooed to his chest stood in the street, arms outstretched, mouth open, face to the sky. People poured from their homes and started screaming about a fire truck that couldn't come fast enough, hadn't come fast enough. Sirens finally sounded in the distance. But it was too late. Touissant knew it was too late: the temple was burning and all that was left was to stare down into the sudden apocalypse of the one and only old true thing in Highland. His own flammable mind burst apocalyptic, fires down from its mountains heading for his scorched exhausted valley.

L eaving the reception desk five minutes before her lunch break and heading down to inspect the homeless hideout, she had the flashlight and the razor.

The real estate office where Erycha received calls was on the second floor while down the exterior staircase there was a derelict warehouse wedged between two storefronts—a shoe repair shop and a sports memorabilia outlet— whose owners had abandoned their businesses without explanation, indefinitely. Both shops were locked and barred up, but the old warehouse between didn't even have a door in its doorway anymore. There were always hopheads and tweakers sneaking in there nights and mornings, and jokers came around and solicited whatever junk they just happened to have on them. This wide variety of nonsense had one result: it scared off most of the real clientele and hampered business. She being the receptionist, it unnaturally fell to Erycha to run off as many of these people as possible.

This time she heard voices from down in the warehouse even before she got there. Light but sharp, addled, irregular: one, two, three, four. She counted four separate voices, three female and one male. The male voice was more regular, more sane-sounding. That reassured her some. She had never actually been confronted, let alone attacked by any of the warehouse squatters or solicitors. They tended to be meek, beaten people running like roaches soon as she flashed the light on them. Or they hesitated, looked at her sadly for a second, then ran. She flicked on the flashlight as she entered the unlit warehouse. She couldn't see anything at first but the usual cobwebs and pieces of overturned furniture, dissembled drawers, and desks. She took a couple more sliding steps inside, moving over weak floorboards that stiffened and gave out like dying bodies beneath her feet. The boards moaned as she moved. That was when she heard, saw, realized. She whirled the flashlight across the darkness before her, washing the warehouse with the yellow eye. She could see the squatters now; there were only three, a man leaning angular in the shadows in a far corner, the other two women sitting before him, prayerful figurines.

"Security!" Erycha yelled. "Security!"

The two women threw up their hands to shield their eyes from the light.

"Move!" Erycha yelled at them. "Move!

They stood holding onto one another and started for the door. Erycha stood out of their way, letting them pass.

The floorboards were crying again, and it was only when they stopped that she realized that the third one was still there. He remained in the corner, motionless. She turned back to him and saw that he was staring her straight in the eyes, trying to read her for intent. Erycha didn't meet his look. She turned the flashlight on the space in front of him, to light his way. "C'mon," she encouraged. "C'mon." She fingered the blade in her pocket. "You gotta leave. Go to the Central City Mission if you need help. This isn't for squatters. You're interferin with J & M business. I'ma call po-lice."

But the man didn't budge the slightest; he just leaned against the far corner-wall and went on staring at her all calm and appraising.

She debated whether to yell upstairs, to threaten reinforcements. "C'mon."

But he didn't come.

"Come-the-fuck-on," she snapped. *"Leave."* Exasperated, she flashed the blade across the space the light illumined, let the threat sparkle in the dark. Now, the motionless man finally stood. He was a deeply dark, almost purple-skinned black man. He was wearing a dress shirt and slacks that were good enough to go to church in. When he moved off the wall and stood up straight and full for her to see, she knew he wouldn't leave.

There was a strange affect in the man's voice, something hard and suddenly new, like vocal coin. "Vanity of vanities," he said, which she had heard and read before, but never in any circumstance that could justify its significance. All is vanity, she thought and almost said aloud. She had no idea it was happening but she surrendered a little right then, not to him, nor to Ecclesiastes, but to a moment in her consciousness that was spreading itself wider and richer than any second on a clock had a right to. She felt it opening and dropping even as he started to apologize and explain his presence.

She dropped the flashlight on the ground and its light went out like a candle blown dead. His words stopped. She bent to pick the flashlight up.

"You should come upstairs," she said on impulse. She stood up with the flashlight and played its solid weight between her hands; she was still looking at him where he stood completely shrouded by the dark once again. She decided not to turn the light back on. The moment pooled outward overlapping what she knew about logic and safety and men and then she was at the reception desk again, sitting where she always sat, and Mazi stood where every client stood on the other side of the coarse wood partition, doing what no client ever did, caring to see her, look at her, speak to her about other worlds. His name, he said, was Mazi. Born in Johannesburg, he told her. There, he had seen poverty and wealth so distant one from the other that it was hard to remember that the two were twins, the actions of one always affecting, even creating the other. His father had moved the family to the States at the first opportunity possible, into a succession of dilapidated, below-code buildings, as well as a few garages and a couple cars. He had learned life in thin passages. By age eighteen he was a man.

He set off on his own, took a job on an international oil tanker for a year, then joined an acting company for a time. Eventually he took the entrance exams and enrolled in university with a perform-ing arts major and an emphasis in percussion. But he neglected graduation, leaving, he said, when he had learned everything his professors could teach him. It was silly, Mazi told her, to measure the worth of his education by a degree or a job or things acquired. He was living hand to mouth and saving the little money he still had toward future plans. He rented a small apartment and, when he needed it, borrowed a car on an hour-to-hour basis from a man who sold used cars out of his backyard. He owned nothing. But he had his words, and, when he saw the women sneaking down into the dark warehouse, he knew he should say something, give something, offer his help. They were crack whores, of course, but that meant little to him.

Mazi spoke on all this with his certain eyes fixed on Erycha and his arms folded over the desk in a way that claimed the space between them. She was surprised that she didn't mind this. It was the first time since Ricky that she felt good about a man moving in on her. She didn't know if her impulse was right. But she talked to him for the rest of the afternoon, and their voices filled the empty offices.

When it came near closing, Erycha expected him to ask for her number. She left long pauses before the beginnings and at the ends of her sentences, giving Mazi time to ask.

"It's so nice of you to let me stay in here, Erycha. In the cool." He gestured out the door at the sun- and heat-bleached world. She nodded a little at that and he said, "You have a quietness, a real quietness. That's a good thing."

"Thanks." She looked up at the wall clock across the room. "Good. Finally gettin close to time. Been here all day." He didn't look to the clock, she noticed. His eyes stayed focused on her. But he did not ask her for her number.

That night, Erycha wondered why Mazi hadn't asked for her phone number. They had had such a good time talking. Why didn't he want to continue it? Did he think her that typical, that uninteresting? She found herself waking and dressing for work in a rough mood. She heard her mother across the way getting dressed for work, stumbling over things in the dark, and she felt the sharp anger that she knew like close kin but hadn't felt in a long time. She had held herself away from men and from feelings for two years now. She had focused herself on schoolwork and prepared for college. The pain and uncertainty that men brought had gone from her life. She even treated her dancing more distantly, as a memory released of any demand. But now that a man that she didn't even know sparked her interest just the slightest something, it was like she hadn't learned a thing. She dressed fast, ran water and her fingers through her hair, and raced out the apartment and down to the bus stop. She wasn't thinking about anything but luck, how it attached itself to her like a bad man and fled her like a good one.

With Mazi it was different, though. He couldn't leave her because he had never been hers to lose. It turned out his interest in her was something different and new, an interest without possessiveness. At twelve o'clock, she heard footsteps coming up the exterior wooden staircase. She recognized him in the sound of the first steady, patient footfall. Everybody else seemed in a rush and impatient compared with him, like they were unsatisfied by their moment in time. Mazi was different and his difference intrigued her. He had appeared, suddenly, out of the boredom, the solitude, and the danger of her days spent behind her desk and down in the darkness looking for trespassers, and now that she'd encountered him she didn't know what to think, or expect, except to hope that his patience and intelligence and simple presence had meaning.

This time he was cradling an armload of books. He was actually near dropping them due to the double-work of carrying the books and opening the door at the same time. She watched him crouch and set the books down and she took the opportunity to spring from her chair, swing around the reception desk and over to the door. She intended to open it for him, but by then his hands were free and he was opening the door. She ended up gliding through the open portal and straight into his waiting arms. He caught her by the shoulders and stopped her short. "So graceful," he said. She wasn't sure if he was speaking in earnest or in sarcasm. She remembered that their conversation had been so focused on him and his life that she had forgotten to mention that she was a dancer.

She looked at him and kept her lips together in a shy way. She didn't say anything, only shrugged. Her dancing, like the rest of her life, was something she had trouble talking about.

———

He stacked the books like a leaning pagoda at the edge of the reception desk. She thought it was funny how they balanced there, a crooked question mark rising up. Then Mazi looked at her straight. "Erycha, do you like to read?"

"Um-hmmm."

"You do? Good. *Cane?*" He picked the top book from the stack and held it out toward her. She took it, shaking her head. Jean Toomer, she read the author's name. Definitely not one that she had come across. She wondered if he had read all these books at Berkeley, if that was how people got so intellectualized up there. She picked through the rest of the titles: *Death and the King's Horseman*, by someone with a hard to pronounce name. Then *The Black Jacobins, Discourse on Colonialism, The Palm-Wine Drinkard and His Dead Palm-Wine Tapster in the Dead's Town, A Question of Power.* She looked back to *Cane,* examined its sultry, dark orange cover art, its lean profile. She could feel Mazi's eyes on her: maybe he thought she was lying, probably thought she didn't read a damn thing.

Opening *Cane,* she read the first lines to herself. She paused uncertainly over the poetry and fought down the urge to look up into his watchful eyes. Her voice rose a little, enough for him to hear her. "When the sun goes down."

"Do you know it?"

She only caught half the question, but the suddenness of his voice pulled her out of reverie, and she looked up at him. But he wasn't looking at her. His eyes were focused on a point past her shoulder. "Know what?" she asked.

"The passage."

"Nah. I don't." She turned back to the title page. "*Cane?* Like in the Bible?"

"Like sugar-cane."

"Sugar-cane?" She knew what sugar-cane was but was more than a little confused by Mazi and his books and the connection, or lack thereof, between these things and her crossed-up urges.

Mazi shrugged at the question and then started rolling his shoulders up and down in a tight circle. She noticed how slight but strong he looked. He was attractive like that, in an unaccountable way: he wasn't big or muscular or V-shaped. His body was long and thin and still, like a rope coiled tight, full of disciplined strength and different potentials. She noticed that the shirt and slacks he had on weren't nearly as nice as what he'd worn the day before, found it appealing that he wasn't even trying to impress her.

She wanted to impress him. "It seems like a beautiful poem," she said lamely.

"Well," Mazi said, "yes. But what's beauty? A dread memorizes Cesaire, we call him crazy. Your professor translates Dante for the hundredth time, we call it the poem unlimited."

She didn't know what to say to that. She had never heard of Cesaire, knew only that Dante had written a book about hell.

"We have a whole unexplored history," Mazi went on, warming to his subject. "The Black Diaspora." He shook his head a little. "It goes ignored. Our artists disappear, our work is stolen. And then they find something. One black thing. To hold high. And tell us that this token is our culture. Who's your favorite author?"

"I don't know," she said.

"Think."

She thought. She remembered how Shakespeare's sonnets had moved her, once, for a good ten minutes. She told him about this.

His eyes lit as he fell into his familiar pose, arms folded over her desk and leaning into the openness that already existed between them. "Proving my point." He smiled. "Proving my point."

That night, at his studio apartment, the conversation turned to dance. When she told him she used to do ballet, Mazi's eyes got big and white, and his mouth fell open in perfect replica of one of those offensive dolls that she'd heard boojie black people kept in their kitchens. It didn't fit her view of him so she felt the need to add: "More like I used to *wanna* be a ballerina, na'mean? Like, kid stuff, childish dreams, a little girl's dream."

"I suppose," Mazi said. "But it does surprise me."

The studio was simple, bed-and-bath, nothing else, the same as most of the places in the Little Africa section of the city. She could tell how little he had by all the emptiness he had managed to fit into such a small place. Whereas her parents' apartment, or even Ricky's spot, was packed to the ceiling with worthless things, Mazi's flat was near barren. He had no furniture, and lengths of random worn cloth were strung across the windows, acting as curtains. She remembered that he was saving what he had, that he even admitted to going without meals sometimes. If he had been a woman, she would've felt different, maybe even said something mean by now. But because he was a man, the emptiness suggested a power unrelated to possession. "It surprises you?" she asked.

"What are your parents like? Did they raise you to revere 'high' culture?" His eyes met hers.

"Nah, they didn't even raise me to revere them." She let out a quick cold laugh, which pealed ridiculously high and thin through the air. She glanced at him, then looked away, embarrassed. It took her a minute to get her manners back. "They interesting, na'mean? I love both them to death, but they get boisterous, dramatic. This whole fire an' ice, love an' hate routine. It's like, my mom's this real emotional lady, always throwin nonsense together to make up new words for when she gets mad, which is too often 'cause she be stressin over each little thing like it's the end-time. She'll swing back an' forth between hatin you an' lovin you, always ready to do somethin dramatic. As for my dad, he brings drama, too, but in a different way, not as outward: he be broodin on problems, lettin it get to him, not even tellin you anything's even wrong. Far as you know, it's all good.

Then he go an' do somethin erratic, start dressin like a pimp, old
gators, feather in his hat, just to rile her, foolishness like that. She
works at the mental hospital. He's staffin at Central City Mission
right now."

Mazi nodded soberly when she was finished. He bit his lower
lip and turned his eyes down. "Was either of them ever in ballet? Is
that why you were so taken with it? Have you ever had any African
dance classes?"

"African dance. Nah."

"Have you ever heard Congolese or Senegalese drumming? To
watch the dancers, to listen to the drums, to hear where polyrhythm
originated. It's my idea of *high* culture, *high black* culture."

She had the hardest time wrapping her mind around what he was
telling her, let alone arranging appropriate responses. Mazi could
begin talking about her parents and end up talking about the Senegalese. One moment, they'd been talking about ballet, then about
culture, then parents, then somehow back to music and dance and
art. A continual improvisation to which she had nothing to contribute: it was all him, all the dance of his mind.

"Would you mind if I brought out my drums, demonstrated for
you?" he asked, standing. Before she could say yes or no he started
over to a half-closed closet door where she could see the edges of
several cardboard boxes tucked away there like secrets. That must be
where his drums are stored, she thought, in those boxes; "Yeah, sure,
play for me," she said after him.

Two earth-colored drums tied the one to the other by a thickly
wound rope, he cradled them to his chest like playful children. She
could see they were heavy by the way his lean back shuddered with
the strain of carrying them. Then he set them down and sat back
down, close to her this time, their shoulders touching. Erycha felt
her blood heat and rise with the nearness. "You'll love this," he

promised. He positioned the drums. That surprised her; he didn't seem like the type to promise things.

She was looking at him, he at his drums. Then he looked up at her, his indescribable eyes so close now, bringing her closer. She wanted to lean into him, kiss him, do more. But she could tell by the stillness that was his gaze that he wanted to tell her something. She waited, thinking, his eyes are like ciphers; that's what gets me about them. It's like they're there, but they're not there. This whole time I been lookin into his eyes like searchin for diamonds or somethin in there. Those eyes. But that's not what draws me to him. What draws me in is the reflection, the shine, the light. Thinking all this, looking at him, wanting to kiss him, she was silent.

From somewhere far off she heard him saying, "Dance if you want. Feel free to dance." He was still gazing at her when she remembered herself. She looked down. His hands were readied over the drums now. Then he began to beat and beat the drums.

For a long while, she wasn't sure whether he was even attracted to her. June passed into July, and, though she was seeing a lot of him, the meetings tended toward the stasis of his apartment and his drumming and his books and his twisting, twining words, which worked beautifully one idea and notion to the next, but strangely without progression. Nights when he had a car, he would drive her home so she wouldn't have to walk through the dark, empty streets to the bus stop or have to depend on her unreliable father to come and pick her up.

He would take her back to his apartment or sometimes to a café in some area she had never been to before, and they would talk for hours, seemingly about everything. Then he would drive her home. That he was willing to spend so much time with her was an encouraging sign. Maybe he really did want her—he even came up the stairs and said hello to her parents once in a while, impressing her mother with his patient listening, his eye-meeting manner and eloquent compliments. He saw where the daughter inherited her attractiveness from, he would say. And that wonderful skin tone! Erycha wasn't sure how her father felt about all this, but his approval was less important than her mother's anyway. Her mother remained in control. While her father childed with age, growing softer and less resilient, her mother changed in the opposite fashion. The baby-fat had finally left her cheeks and there was a fresh hardness to her face and body and personality that spoke to a shorter tolerance. Her emotions, if anything, had grown more volatile with time. She couldn't give up loving her man, but she would fly into rages at the mention of marriage.

Erycha held her parents at a distance now, judging them for what they were. Both still had claim on her emotions, but less so now; both still played on her heart, complicated songs of love, mistrust, and denial, but less so now. She was growing past them. She wanted Mazi. She wanted to fuck Mazi. Now. Nothing short of it. But that wasn't going to be as easy as it should be. Mazi was appealing, but he was also difficult. She found herself confused, impatient. She had never known a man who didn't make his desires known immediately. Did he want her or not? With men, she always knew what they wanted. But with Mazi she never knew anything. His uniqueness attracted her in and held her away.

Blackness, he liked to tell her, was an essential state. Either you were or you weren't, and it had nothing to do with having been born in Africa or Europe or the States or Iceland, for that matter. It didn't

have to do with the darkness or lightness of skin, high yellow, beige
or bone. It was like beauty and sin: you knew it when you saw it,
you knew it when you had it, you knew it when you did it, you knew
it when you were it. Either you were black, or you weren't. It was
birthright and heritage and inheritance dating back to a world now
lost upon earth. In the forgotten world, blacks had constructed soci-
ety itself. The worldwide destruction of black people, even by other
black people, was humanity killing its father, killing its mother and
ultimately killing its deepest understanding of itself.

Listening to him made her consider new things, new possibilities.
She had never heard blackness extolled, let alone explained. Brothers
were always talking about how black they were in the same breath as
they told you how hood, how ghetto they were. They equated blackness with toughness, with thuggishness, with poverty. But Mazi had
reoriented the argument around a whole different set of ideas and
possibilities. His way of telling things and his final conviction *placed*
those corner thugs. He sparked with passion every time he spoke on
his people. The kind of passion that surged, the kind of passion that
attracted. She remembered how she used to stay up nights staring
impatiently out her window at the stars light years away. It would
get to where she could see the stars dancing pirouettes, leaping
heaven high, and her heart would actually beat quicker with it, the
cracks in the ceiling openings onto a world.

Now, listening to Mazi speak, she wondered how she'd mixed herself up so bad, why she'd even tried to align her spine with those thin
shapeless white girls in a tradition that had never been hers in the
first place. She had known all along that her body was incompatible
with ballet. She had always been too shapely. She knew she preferred
dancing freeform and unrestrained to the percussive beat of Mazi's

drums, and she wondered why that was. He told her, predictably, that it was because she was black. That made sense, she supposed. But it also made sense that she was infatuated. He told her that unlike high school, in college there were opportunities to educate herself where before she had only been miseducated, under-educated. She didn't have to take his word for it; she could look forward to taking courses on the Diaspora. She could study African dance. She could take an emphasis in African Studies. Or, she could apply a black worldview to a mainstream field like economics or politics. Her heritage was open to her, Mazi said; she wouldn't have to depend on him or on a European paradigm; she could learn her heritage for herself, its rules of movement.

Slowly, inexorably she was moving away from what had defined her. Ballet was one of those departing things. She even put her do-rags away for good and when she needed to put her hair up she used her old white headwrap. And when July turned to August, when the weather grew hotter and her parents' arguments more persistent and annoying again, she began to think more and more about living elsewhere, in another state or country.

She talked out her thoughts with Mazi one night.

"If they love you," he said, "they will let you leave."

Erycha had no doubt her parents would let her leave. They would be too busy being mad at each other to keep her at home. The real issue was where she would go once she moved out. She looked at Mazi at the opposite end of the rug. His face was not so attractive now but closed and serious instead.

"I been grown," she said.

"Right. True," he agreed. He held her in his stone-serious gaze. "You seem ready for a lot of things."

She felt ready. She felt good and ready. When He has tested me, she recalled the scripture, I shall come forth as gold. She decided that she had passed enough tests, and that if her skin wasn't quite golden, it sure was bronzed enough. Laying herself down somewhere new was probably the best thing she could do at this point in her life. To get away, maybe even very far away from the shouting, from the money arguments, from the total childishness of her parents, all that would be good for her.

He still held her in his gaze, and she still held him in hers. She wanted him, wanted him and wanted her independence, two contradictory desires. "I wanna move away," she said.

He nodded, unsurprised.

"Leave them to their squabbles." She sighed and rolled her tongue along her dry lips. She wanted him.

Mazi nodded again. "Leave them then." He paused. "But don't just hurl yourself into things. I did that, and now look at me. Be intelligent." He tapped at his head Malcolm X-style. Then his voice quickened and went higher as he happened on a new idea: "You know, I've told you about my used-car man. He will sell you a good car for, I believe, less than a thousand dollars. Do you want me to put you in contact with him?"

She paused over that, unsure. She hadn't expected him to change the subject. "OK," she said after a moment. "It's a good car, you sure?"

"It's good," he said.

She thought about the money she had saved. She wanted to be sure about the price. "Less than one grand?" She waited. "One grand?"

"Grand? Oh, I see, right, less than that, yes." He broke into a broad smile. "You Aframericans with your fortress of slang."

Erycha broke into her own little smile. If she was using slang words, so was he. She had never heard anyone call black people *Aframericans* before. It sounded new. It sounded like the description of an altogether new people. She wanted to ask him what he meant by that word, but he wanted to talk about the car. "I'll see about the car," she said.

"It's another step toward your independence. You should sound more confident about it."

She didn't want to talk; she felt confident about one thing, that she wanted him. She leapt or fell into Mazi, kissing him as she collapsed his body into the unfurnished carpet. It was a good thing the place was so barren, that there was almost nothing but the two of them. If there had been tables and chairs, the violence of her need might have hurt him then.

Afterward, he slid from underneath her slick body and said, "Remember about the man and the car?"

"Car?" she asked, peering between her breasts at him.

"Yes, a man and a car. I know a man. He will sell you a good car. Less than a thousand dollars. I will put you two in contact." He said all this very matter-of-factly, as if the sex hadn't affected him much.

She tried not to notice. As for the car, she nodded. "We can do that."

Forty-eight hours had passed since they'd had sex, most of which she had spent with him, yet he hadn't even hugged her since. She wondered what was wrong and searched his eyes for an answer. He seemed a little reluctant to meet her gaze now, which made her remember the way he used to stare at her with such calm appraisal. His eyes seemed cautious now, the way she imagined her own, moving this way, then that, not staying still for long.

———

Mazi took her to his friend's dealership. Old Japanese cars and worn American trucks and depreciated motorcycles with their prices chalked along the hubcaps sat idle in the Arab's backyard. By her count there were at least fifteen vehicles sharing space in the small, densely packed yard, but most were priced well above a thousand dollars. The Arab directed her to the very back of the yard where a keyed, dented, decayed Datsun sat on blocks beneath an incompatible palm tree. Its red paint had chipped along the doors, and the bumper looked like it had been forged from rust. The steering wheel, she could tell just from eyeballing it, was unaligned, and the palm tree was raining whatever died on palm trees and fell to earth onto the hood and roof.

"This thing run?" Erycha asked, staring at it.

The Arab nodded with the same assuredness that Mazi always used with her. She looked behind her at Mazi, who began nodding as well. Then he started to caress her back with his strong, practiced fingers.

"It runs," the Arab said.

"But it cost eight-hundred fifty dollars," Erycha countered.

"Yes." The Arab nodded again. "Do you have that much?"

He cut his eyes at her, and she found herself glaring back at him in the August sunshine; they stood there exchanging unprofessional glares for a long minute. Her underarms moistened. She thought about old movies she'd never actually seen, how this was the part where, probably, somebody got shot. "Yeah," she conceded, "I got that."

"Then, buy?" the Arab suggested.

She looked back at Mazi for guidance. She felt uncertain again. "Buy?" she asked.

"Buy?" Mazi looked to his friend.

"Buy," his friend said.

"Buy," Mazi said.

"Buy." She finally agreed.

———

She could trust him now. Their bond had tightened. She would look into eyes that reluctantly reflected her body and the darkness encircling her and decide night after night that, yes, she could trust him. Sometimes they had sex, and other times, most times, they just talked. The talking alone was enough, despite those eyes, which fell away and drew her close all at once, forcing her to choose how to see him. She always decided to be entranced, night after night. The promise of cinnamon and sex glinted there like dark little gems. It grew total, and she knew that she could release herself into its depths. Watching him move between empty rooms, from sparse meals, to the dense thought processes of his books and the hollowness of his drums, she didn't notice the moonlight so much anymore. And when he would move into her, kiss her, take her, she wouldn't notice the way its pale white light colored their limbs like lightning across black sky. And in the after-sex moment he'd explain and explain, explain and explain, Blackness is this, Blackness is that.

Half-hearing him, she'd fall into his eyes, go down and down. When he was done talking, she would let him take her home, neglecting to notice his insistence on that point, and in the mornings she would wake and hear feet stumbling over things in the first light and wouldn't notice the sun so much.

"I love you."

"You do?"

"Can I?"

"Of course, you're free to. I would never dissuade you."

"What's dissuade mean?"

"Much like persuade; the negative form of persuasion."

"That's not the passionate response I's hopin for."

"Well, I'm not your perfect dream man. I'm only me."

"Fair enough. But I'm still in love with you."

"Erycha."

"What?"

"I've always meant to ask you, a strange question, can I touch your cheek? Is it a birthmark? It's shaped like lightning, you know?"

"I know, it's a birthmark. Tell you the truth, I ain't, haven't thought about it in years. I still love you, Mazi."

"Like black lightning, quite startling."

Eventually, she knew they'd have to discuss their relationship and expectations more concretely.

She raised the subject only to be stonewalled by Mazi's vague, non committal remarks. He was saving for the future, he'd say, but between things at the moment. Why couldn't she just proceed with her life and let him do the same with his? he'd ask when she pressed the matter too much. Then his eyes might move a little too much or go still, and she would be left confused in the breach. She wasn't sure what to think of their future and wouldn't be sure until they talked it out, but he never wanted to talk about it, which was his prerogative, she supposed; but she couldn't read his ambitions in his mind any more than in his eyes. If anything, his eyes read reluctance: they didn't stare at her the same as before when all their relationship had consisted of was philosophical abstractions; they were more energetic and roaming now. When she discussed anything that touched upon the future, his eyes would start to move. Maybe, probably, he simply didn't know what he would do or where his life was headed; but on the other hand, maybe he did know, maybe he was just holding back in the same way he'd held back from sex until she came forward. Maybe all he needed was her urging. Or maybe it was something altogether different that she didn't even know to think of. She wanted to know.

———

She asked him about the future again and again.

When he finally agreed to sit down and discuss the future in blunt terms, it was nearly September. She asked him if he planned to stay or to leave. "I never known a man who loved a woman enough to be faithful to her," she said. "Especially not no black man." She worked her hands through her headwrap and let her wild unbraided hairdo flow out.

"That's that old racist thinking again." He tapped his head like Malcolm. "Your conditioning is so deep."

"It's not racist; it's the truth."

"It's not true." He held his Malcolm pose.

"Prove it."

"Black men don't need to prove anything. Black people don't need to prove anything. I don't need to prove anything."

She shook her head. She disagreed. All of life was show and prove. Everything she had ever done or seen or had happen to her was a test.

"What do you want?" Mazi asked. "What do you want, Erycha?"

"You," she answered flatly. "Besides that, I need to be out my parents' place. They don't know how to live together like grown folk. They argue 24/7. I cain't be in college with that in my ear at all hours."

"I agree." Mazi sighed. "Riverside will be more difficult than your high school in the slums. You'll need a reliably quiet space to concentrate."

"Well." She shrugged.

"Quarreling like that amongst grown people," he said. "It's unfortunate."

"Whole world's unfortunate. Most of it, anyway."

"I agree."

It was, at least, a beginning. It was, at least, an initiation into focused dialogue.

"I need to live somewhere else," she would reiterate, when they were together. "I cain't live alone, don't have the money for it. I'ma need to stay with someone."

"I agree," he would say. "I agree."

"I need to live somewhere else," she would say. She would play with her tightly wrapped hair. "I'ma need to stay with someone."

"I disagree," he said, the last time the subject came up. He tapped at his forehead. "You don't need a provider or protector any more than the African women who demanded and won the right not to be buried alive with their dead husbands."

Then everything fell apart. August was almost over. She didn't think she could stand another month in the Del Rosa apartment. She couldn't stand not knowing his future plans. She told him this, and then she asked to live with him.

He looked at her calmly, appraisingly, in that way he had when they had first met and he had transfixed her. "You can have my apartment in September, when I leave."

Something, she thought, had been lost in translation. "What you tryina say?" she asked helpfully.

"What I said," he said.

"Nah, you said 'when you leave'; but what did you mean?" She closed her eyes and breathed down through her chest, feeling the brief coolness radiate down her insides. "What did you mean?"

"Erycha." He looked at her calmly. "We speak English in Johannesburg, too."

"Don't play."

"I am not playing. I have done a lot of things. I came to this country on my own. I went hungry here, I went to college here. I know myself and the things I say."

But his meaning still didn't quite register with her. She started in about alternate living arrangements, negotiating the issue. "There's the townhouses right across the street from the college, but them places cost seven-hundred an' up. Then there's some cheaper places a little further down, right where the city gets rough. Or, I could keep in Highland, San Ber'dino, where it's really cheap, but it'a be a commute that way. But it's hard to pass on $450 a month."

He tossed her a ball of blankets to cover herself with.

She caught them up against her chest but just held them there. She couldn't look at him all of a sudden.

"Erycha," he said. "Erycha."

"What?"

"Erycha, I thought you wanted to move into my apartment. That would save you the trouble of having to search for someplace suitable and save you some money."

I want to move into your apartment with you still in it, she thought. What did he mean, leaving? He hadn't discussed leaving, his leaving, not once, not one solitary word. She didn't understand. "You're leaving?"

He nodded slowly, yes.

"Why you just mentionin this now?" she said back.

"Because," he began, "I was saving and trying to plan and not sure what I wanted next. Now I know. But tomorrow is not September. I won't be leaving tomorrow."

That qualification didn't ease the sense of sudden dislocation. If anything, she was feeling worse. She fell back into the bed and drowned herself down under the waves of pillows and sheets. She could feel his hands roving over the sheets, searching for her with careful fingers.

"Erycha," he was saying, "Erycha; I understand you are upset. I understand. But you do not need me the way you think you do."

—————

When he finished, she moved into him and lay somewhere around his feet, his legs, like a child having built a tunnel out of her bed-sheets, grown exhausted now. From where she lay, she couldn't see a thing except tunnels of darkness running away in all directions and the occasional spear of light that found its way in. She had never known a black man who loved his woman enough not to leave her. She heard his gentle, faintly accented laughter.

"What's so funny?" she asked, after hearing it for a minute.

"Nothing. Nothing. It is not funny."

"Then why you laughin?"

"Better than, how should I put it?"

"Put it like, 'I ain't leavin.' Put it like that."

"I can't do that."

"You can do anything."

"No, I can't."

She picked out a tunnel of darkness that seemed to lead down his leg, down and down to a small black hole where the bedsheet ended and his foot probably began. Even blackness, it seemed, had limits. "You cain't?" she asked.

"No," he said.

"Where you goin, Mazi?"

"To Oakland. Then Atlanta. Then further on."

"Why those places?" she asked. She was not listening when he answered. She was close to crying, but down beneath the bedsheets she knew it wouldn't make any difference: crying only helped if the man could see you.

She thought about those eyes now. Night-climbing eyes. Eyes that hinted at depths of dark love and moved women: they were trickster-eyes, really, reflecting and persuading their watchers into a love of their own reflections. It was not that he was good or bad, or trying to hurt her, but simply that he had: she shuddered. A sudden laceration. Then she went stiff in the bed, and his gentle hands fell across her back, caressing her, rubbing reality into the wounds.

She tried to come to terms with his leaving. She stopped sleeping with him. She stopped reading his books. As September neared, she stayed home more often. She tried to focus her mind elsewhere. Watching the changes in her parents, she learned from them. They were barely even middle-aged, but she could already see definite changes in them: the growing entitlement in her mother, the fading light in her father. They were getting older, she suddenly realized. And with that knowledge, change in all its forms became more apparent.

Fall came early that year, appearing one morning not in the form of clouds or sunshine that backed off just a little but in something else. She sensed September everywhere she went, in each street-fallen leaf and the smell of turning death that hung in the air. She was trying her best to let Mazi go, but the dream of him passed hard. She found herself tearing up for no reason, or drifting into back-looking anger over him where she should only be looking forward to college and her new studies and her new life.

That fresh start still seemed far off, though college would begin in a matter of weeks. What seemed close and real was what she'd always known, the boy she had lived with, the man she had known, her parents, ballet. These losses were her knowledge. She couldn't just leave a person, any person; she was learning that now. She couldn't just kill off her feelings like scurrying ants underfoot. Feelings had a way of surviving. For years she had figured it was just her mother's weakness, women's weakness in general, her father's weakness, men's weakness in general that kept them both in a chaotic relationship that didn't make good sense no matter how hard she looked at it. But now she saw more than weakness; actually, it did make sense that people stayed together despite all the nonsense they caused each other. She still felt herself turning back to and away from and back to the people she had known, full of hard shock that she was so much in love with everyone.

Erycha helped her mother, who was turning true Jamaican after work now: her latest hustle was cooking up plantains for the folks around the way. She could call them plantains and sell them to the black people; she could call them dodo and sell them to the immigrants from Nigeria and Sierra Leone, call them platanos and sell them to the Mexicans.

Don't use the green fruit that's the color of my pearls when you slice it, she taught Erycha. Them pearls in my dreams, girl. Ain't no one slippin here. An' don't use the black fruit that's softer 'n oatmeal. Take the yellow fruit. The half-ripe ones that ain't gon break nobody's window, but that stay firm to the touch. Warm water you wash them in, then cut off their ends. Cut through the skin like this, yes, Erycha, all the way through the fruit. Peel that thing open: that's that creamish yellow color that lets you know that the starch has turned to sugar so the fruit will be sweet to eat. Slice it thick. Thick circles. These Mexican folk probably want somethin sprinkled on theirs, whatever's hot spicy or salty in your cupboards might do. But as long as black folks still exist, somebody's gonna want their food sweet and not too salted or hot onto death. So keep most of them plantains plain, that only makes sense in this building full of simple Negroes. Separate the jazzed-up ones from the plain ones. Two pans. Olive oil now. Fry them bad bitches. Pay attention to your work just like you would anything else you happen to be fryin: let them all brown a little, golden-brown, not charcoal-black. Out the pan, drain the oil just like we do with chicken. We need to eat healthy 'round here; remember, we got diabetes and heart disease and all kind of devilment at work in our bloodline.

Side work like this had helped them move from out of that first Del Rosa Gardens apartment with only the one real bedroom and the improvisation of bedsheet curtains and an air mattress to this second-floor Del Rosa two-bedroom home.

She liked working the afternoons with her mother because she didn't have to think about Mazi. She just needed to learn her way around a plantain, pure and simple. After each batch was cooked and ready, she took the trays one by one and set them in the open windowsills. It was late summer now, and the air flowing inside felt like a blow-dryer blasting on high held to her face. "Plantains! Platanos! Plantains! Platanos! African bananas, whatever you want me to call 'em."

She put away her headwrap and started to wear her do-rags again.

She still talked to Mazi, at night, after everything was cooked and sold and cleaned and put away and taken to bed.
I want you, she said in her dreams.
I want you, too, he said, in each dream.

———

She was a bad dreamer, tending more toward nightmares.

The night before he left, she imagined his plane or car crashing on its way to Oakland and woke with a terrible guilt, knowing the dream was born from fear and anger. She needed to get free of both impulses. She talked to God and knew she couldn't wish a single bad thing on Mazi; and she stayed up, stayed awake all night as a protection against and punishment for dreaming. Then in the morning she drove the few blocks to his place.

"I'ma move in," she said, when he edged the door open.

He seemed acceptant on that point and even a little glad for her having come. He stepped out of her way and invited her into the apartment.

"Uh-uh," she said, pausing outside the doorway that she would eventually have to enter, but not this second.

"Please," he asked, "Please. Come in. Have you eaten breakfast?"

She shook her head. She stood still outside the doorway.

He reached out his hand to her, and when he touched her she felt further than ever from him.

"Plantains! Platanos!"

The last batch was nearly all sold, which didn't surprise Erycha, considering how cheap they sold the things. What did surprise her, always, without fail, was that they actually made money at it. A man with the El Salvadoran flag imprinted on his shirt ended up paying for the last platanos. Walking back into the kitchen, Erycha watched her mother count out the earnings on the counter-top. She added the El Salvadoran's money to the pile of dollar bills, then asked, "Do I get any of that?"

"Family money, girl."

Erycha knew it would have to happen like this, quick-fast, no proper lead-up, just said plain. "Yeah, family money all good, but I'm movin out next month, I need my own."

Her mother didn't look up and didn't stop sifting the bills through her fingers. It was evident now to Erycha that money was trust.

"It's not like I been on strike demandin market-rate all these years." She laughed shakily, remembering how when she was a child it had been divine privilege to hand her mother a hot comb, clippers, a brush.

"Now you know this ain't about no few dollar bills, Erycha." Erycha wasn't sure about that: there were days her mother seemed half-ready to die for a dollar. "This is about you not gettin caught up. Look at me: done been caught up ever since I seen that boy leavin out Allen Temple." The money kept moving through her hands. She had lost count and wasn't trying to regain it. "You know the story." Erycha nodded. She remembered being a quiet child good at listening. "An' you never have forgiven me that error, so why would you wanna go shack up with some boy, then end up walkin in the same path as I have?" She turned her face up and looked steadily at Erycha. The new leanness was something, especially with the beaded sweat from the labor of cooking still on her skin. Her face was a fine-cut and polished stone left out in the rain.

"I don't see how you were wrong," Erycha said a little suddenly. She brought her hand up to her mouth and took a moment. "I don't see how you were in error even back in the day, at the Temple, in the beginning, or however it began. It don't matter how it began. You did the right thing when it came to Dad. You had to follow him."

She watched as her mother chewed at something that Erycha figured probably didn't exist. She watched her jaw work in tight internal circles. "I had you; that's why I followed him."

They were learning to trust each other all over again.

"The thing is, Erycha, you'll learn this sooner or later: whatever the story behind the story is, in the end it's gonna be the same. If you leave a man or if he goes off without you, he takes somethin from you. It's just the way it is. Ain't right, but it's true. A lil piece 'a you breaks off an' either he took it from you, takes it with him when he goes, or who knows what, but you don't get it back. So you can either go with him an' stay whole on the inside an' accept whatever comes y'all way, or you break a lil bit. Break enough, you be broke."

Erycha listened, then told her mother about Mazi, about how she loved him, about how he left her. "Should I have gone with him?" she wanted to know.

"Nah." A police siren mumbled like a furtive, nervous child outside. "Nah. I think that woulda been a bad idea. You have college. I didn't have that. You don't have no kid to raise. I had you. It was different. I had to. But you, I always wanted you to be strong enough to break. I wanted you to be a woman that had her own, inside herself. Like I was talkin about, we break, but some women they break on the outside but still be whole on the inside. Know what I'm sayin?"

Erycha nodded yes.

By the time she took over Mazi's apartment, there was little left of him in the space. He left her a month's rent in an envelope tucked in a notebook. Besides the money and the empty notebook, he had left nothing. Even the subtle evidence of a person and his possessions was gone.

Maybe his minimalism had rubbed off on her because she brought only a few supplies at first, a change of clothes, a do-rag, toothbrush, toothpaste, a towel, and soap to shower with, a book of her own, and the key he'd given her to unlock the apartment door. All she wanted was to spend one night there and feel what it was to go to sleep alone. It struck her that she had been alone all her life, but had spent so much time sleeping next to Mazi and Ricky, or only a thin wall away from her parents, that she had never realized how truly alone she was. There had been so much movement, noise, life and death all around her that she had confused it with closeness. But now she knew she was alone. She knew there was no one else like her, that her uniqueness was not partial or alterable by the presence of a boy-friend or a mother, but absolute. She saw a black snowflake falling, falling, falling through a soft white mist of white snow and white snowflakes; and the black snowflake was so singular and strange it could only be a hallucinated moment in her mind.

She went and found a soft clean spot on the floor. She tried to read the account of Josephine Baker's life and career that she had checked out from the public library. But she found herself unable to get past the story in the introduction: Baker walking her cheetah along the Champs-Elysées. Now that was black power. That was the baddest girl breathin. Now, put Queen Josephine down South in some ghetto slum, take away her cheetah, she could stay as fine and talented as she pleased, girl wouldn't get two glances. But she had gone to Paris, found her a cheetah and done big things. Ol' girl knew where she had to go and what she had to do to isolate and empower herself.

Erycha thought about her own isolation and wondered where her empowerment lived. She read a little further, finished the introduction. Then she went back and read over the cheetah-walking story again. It was the act of a poor girl in a rich world. The kind of crazy thing that desperate, neglected people did all the time, the kind of thing you could see some version of sooner or later in just about any ghetto space. But Josephine wasn't in the ghetto. She wasn't around people who were used to wilding. She was in Paris shaking up very comfortable, complacent Parisian folks. She had been smart to get away from black people and isolate herself in an alien world. Smart to turn her sudden uniqueness into power. Smart girl. Obviously.

Desperate girls were common as hot days in the desert. Same for the poor and neglected. But Josephine had made herself rare as snow. That was why her life had lived on beyond her body. Rare girl. Obviously.

Erycha laid herself down and waited for the sky to get dark. After a while she noticed how tense her body remained, how far from sleep she remained. Doesn't make much sense to close my eyes, she thought. Cain't sleep, might as well get up. Time to get up. Look around.

She went from room to room, actually exploring the apartment for the first time. She wandered it inch by inch, looking for things that would be memorable, that would catch her attention. But Mazi had lived so sparse a life inside these walls that the apartment had barely recorded him. Where normal people stained carpets, left pictures drawn in permanent marker on walls, broke out irreparable holes in windows and doors, soiled everything with themselves, he just disappeared.

She went and searched in the cupboards and drawers of the bedroom, then the bathroom, then the kitchen, but everything had been cleared out. In the refrigerator she found a Tupperware container with a few pieces of leftover tofu still in it. What black man fuckin eats tofu? She shook her head. She was thinking about him, seeing him again: Mazi in the abandoned warehouse, Mazi at the reception desk, Mazi with his drums, Mazi with her in bed, caressing her back and moving over her with true desire.

When she woke, she couldn't remember falling asleep. She saw the moon hanging up there, a hollow head. In her first life, it was always wonderful to lie down and look at the moon. That was when she was still a dancer and a stepper: her body had two choices back then, constant motion or constant pain. Coming home, the only thing she ever wanted was to lie down and note the slow pain working its way through each of her muscles, the avenues and side streets that pain would take just to get from her head to her toes. It would require willpower and concentration to complete her homework, but after that was done she would just lie there and occupy herself in seeing and feeling, the sky and the pain. But now the pain she felt had moved beyond the physical. She wanted to believe that he was too bright too beautiful too unique, that those were the reasons he left. But a rising bitterness worked over her like a processional pain: she reconceived him and now she placed him with the other brothers she came across in the streets. His uniqueness had always been obvious, but now it seemed superficial, too. Down deeper, she was starting to see something else, something common: men always play their women short. Always. An' this one, he cut me loose easy, real easy. That low Negro. Shoulda seen it comin, girl; shoulda seen it.

She felt her stomach coiling snakelike about itself. She raised her shirt and saw where her ribs, always noticeable along her slim sides, were visible in front profile too. Shit if I ain't one skinny-ass chick, she thought. Gettin too skinny. She thought about the free food baskets at the Mission. She was very hungry but she knew as soon as the thought occurred to her that it was no option.

She saw the black snowflake again. Now it was flying through a world of black snow. The world was so thick with it, so overwhelmed in it, the snow seemed endless. But even in amidst all that black snow, she could still see the snowflake. It stood out black and beautiful, an improbable design unreconciled to its world.

She went and got her matches, lit the stove burners with the matches. She let the small flames lick up toward her lips, singe her a little, just enough to hurt, before she blew the matches out, each withering like a fallen truth. Leaned against the stove, she warmed her body one cold limb at a time.

The Beginning

————

He woke with an impressive erection. It seemed to salute him from the South. He wondered what he should do with it, noted the spent condom lying on the bed; noted the lines and rings of dried red wine running along his stomach and down his legs. He looked over his shoulder at the nightstand: a half-empty wine bottle stood next to a box of condoms. The box was open and condoms still in their wrappers decorated the nightstand. He wondered if he had dreamt last night into existence and was waking somehow both within and beyond the dream. He looked across his body to the other side of the bed: she was still there, Ocie, her serene, naked form even more enticing in the morning than his night-memory of her. She'd turned away from him, at an angle where he could see the intricacies of the tattoo that ran from the nape of her neck down along the length of her torso, a procession of black snowflakes or crisscrossing fleur-de-lys or broken arrows. He remembered now noticing the design while he was taking her from behind; at the time her hair kept flying all over the place, getting in his line of sight, and it was too dark anyway to make out what the tattoo actually portrayed. But he remembered being struck by the chaos of it, liking the way the lines ran at such sharp angles like limbs flying apart and reuniting all at once. Now he was looking at it with real care, differentiating its fine points, reading it like a puzzle: at her neck, the design was floral, a bed of unfolding flowers, but with the lines drawn sharp so that it looked like the flowers were blossoming suddenly or unfurling in a final skeletal moment before death. Working its way along her shoulders, the little flowers were drawn upside down and rightside up and sideways and in places they actually looked more like snow-flakes or arrows than flowers, and in other places it was more obvious that the tattoo was just the state symbol reproduced again and again, dozens of fleur-de-lys at numerous different angles. It had seemed chaotic in the dark; now it was not chaotic and not tacky like he might expect it to look but beautiful there engraved upon her soft cream skin, almost too fine to be true.

It was hard to judge just how fast asleep she remained. He knew that when she had fallen asleep, after sex, she had slept hard. They had fucked passionately and long. He was so spent he thought he might sleep all day. But now he was up and he wanted her again. Wanted to place her on all fours, or up against the hotel wall. Her hair was long and red and full of wild looping curls that ran every which way. Her back was a perfect arch, a line flowing away from him, her ass that same undulant line flowing back toward him. She was almost too good to be true. Her curves put Shyanne's curves to shame. He even thought about the black dance student, Erycha Evans, with whom he'd attended the orientation banquet in River-side: Ocie's waist was as slim as the black dancer's, but Ocie filled in above and below, thick and rich as the soil that held his newly cho-sen city. He edged closer to her, where he could see across her body, the unsubtle lift of her breasts, the way her stomach, by contrast, barely moved when she breathed. There was so much about her that he found lovely.

He remembered being with Shyanne. At the time, being with her had seemed like a dream, too good to be true, too. He still remem-bered lying next to Shyanne and noting the difference in their skin pressed against each other: a white girl, her skin always reddening in the places where their skin touched; him syrup-dark brown, almost black along his back, hands and forearms. He remembered how her blue veins stood out and wondered how somebody who lived in such a brutally hot place could manage to stay so light-skinned. He recalled someone telling him that Italians in the north are blond and light-skinned, but the Italians who had come to America were the poor, the farmers, and that they are always dark-skinned and black-haired. This had made sense to Touissant, while it had always seemed strange that a girl from San Bernardino, California, could avoid a tan so perfectly. San Bernardino was almost as far south as New Orleans, after all. But Shyanne's complexion hadn't carried the weather the way this girl's skin did; or it carried it differently, spoke to the dry sterile heat of the desert where this girl's complexion was a confluence, a mess of white and black and Indian brown, all mired and living in the dirty rich swamp of her.

He wanted to know what he was seeing and feeling and remembering was real. He wanted to have her again, right now: he pressed himself against her, his cock swelling. He almost went inside her raw, he wanted her that bad. She had no reaction. She just kept breathing evenly, her stomach barely moving, her globe-like breasts rising and falling at the same even tempo. He looked into her face and saw that she was still deeply asleep. He thought about waking her, but didn't.

Naked and erect, he rose and went and found his glasses and walked to the window. He pulled back the curtains and let the light flow in: the summer sun had risen and was shining with eye-watering brilliance down upon the city. He could see folks below, along Canal Street, with their do-rags and fedoras and the sweat still pooled like fetid glade waters on their black skin. He was in New Orleans for the first time in his life and he was in love. He was in love with the city, with the humidity, with the sweat and the festering murkiness of late summer in the South. The feel and the sight and the smell of all these new things was almost too vivid and new, almost too much to be true. He saw a woman in the hotel down the way: she was as naked as he; she was walking about her room doing chores, folding towels, replacing objects. Her curves moved with her but slightly behind. She had no consciousness of an audience.

Naked in the open window, he felt invisible and free. Damn: for the first time, he felt unwatched and it was a beautiful thing to just be here in this created moment doing his own thing. Damn: he thought about his great-granddad's evolving story of escape from Louisiana. A black man on the run. Now he was returning to New Orleans and wasn't running from anyone or anything. The old man had been on the run from his country, but now Touissant could see that he wasn't on the run in the way everybody said he was. It was a different type of escape. Taking literally the myth of a free country, Major slept with a white-complexioned woman and thus floated into a no-man's-nation between white and black. He had to leave New Orleans. He was a nationalist sure enough by the time he met the mother of his child, in Jackson, a too-loving and acceptant woman whom he also ran from, on general principle, only to send for their child and her once he had finally settled in Alabama with a widow who needed him as idiosyncratically as he needed every woman he'd ever known. Then, with two women and one son his unacknowledged nation had grown to four outcast people. They were running free, if nothing else. The family line stayed on the move in subsequent generations, outcasts on the run, all the way to the South Pacific, then back to Chicago and out again to California's far corners. They earned money and impressive education and social access through the back doors of their world. Now Touissant found himself headed in the other direction, going back South, away from that refugee history of isolation and placelessness. And he wasn't running from anything, but instead returning through the front door: into New Orleans, to a hotel overlooking Canal Street, to a little room with a cream-complexioned girl. Now he felt that whole fraught family history opening before him. He was returning to all of it, living it now, learning it fresh. The night in Riverside at that orientation, *that* was when he realized New Orleans was inevitable: Kai Jefferson came to the table where he was sitting with Erycha. Touissant and Erycha had already told each other so many lies and had each figured out each other's lies so thoroughly that there was nothing they could say to each other that would mean anything. They were talking and dreaming at the same time and not listening to each other at all.

Kai Jefferson. The girl introduced herself as if they hadn't already met.

She asked his name.

She must be horrible in history class, Touissant thought.

Touissant Freeman, he answered.

She tried to repeat the name: Two-cent.

Touissant repeated the two-syllable construction slowly: Two-saunt. He spelled it out: T-o-u-i-s-s-a-n-t. He wondered again at his parents' confused reasoning when they decided to spell his name differently from the man he was named after: they claimed they wanted to preserve his individuality by spelling the name differently from its traditional construction. Once someone is named after an icon, placed within a pantheon, how individual can they become? Not very; he answered his own question.

Kai reintroduced herself to Erycha like they had never met. Then she asked, "What does it mean?" She was looking at Touissant again. "Your name?" she clarified.

"My name." He glanced at her Minority Student Union shirt and wristband and notebook. He didn't know why he had expected that the Minority Student Union rep would know her black history. He cut his eyes over to Erycha: she wasn't daydreaming now. She was full-black but she stared at him just as unknowingly as Kai did. She was waiting for his answer, too. Neither girl had ever heard the name. They had no idea of the true Toussaint, Toussaint L'Ouver-ture, the student, the warrior, the emancipator. He told them about his namesake and about Dessalines's burning the land and crazy Henri Christophe with his mountain citadel and his paranoia and his tainted love of nation. It was an incredible and tragic story, the greatest history ever hidden. He'd told it many times, usually while pronouncing, spelling and explaining his name, but this time the more he talked, the more he wished he were named after an unknown slave buried in the cane fields, or a forgotten witch doctor drowned in memory, or a sellout coward from the revolution who was better off forgotten. Having to explain his name only made him feel more out of place at the banquet, at the college, in the city. He remembered how he used to be annoyed when white people would mispronounce his name and then asked him what it meant. Now Erycha and Kai were showing him that what he felt was not rooted in race. It had to do with home.

He began counting down the minutes until the orientation ended and he could fly out of California. He still had two college visits to make: first, Xavier in New Orleans, then a return trip to Columbia. Because it was a small black school tucked away in an old mosquito-ridden swamp, he had left Xavier for last. He had expected his visits to the prestigious schools to be more decisive than they'd been. He'd expected the trips to stir him in ways they hadn't. It was time for New Orleans.

His parents were surprised when he told them that he hadn't made up his mind, that he still needed to see Xavier, but they weren't against him visiting. Maybe he would learn something about medical school while he was out there, they said.

Ocie Duneier was only an undergraduate but she already knew she wanted to go to the pharmacy school at Xavier. From New Orleans originally and planning to stay as long as she could, she said she took the job conducting the orientation tours because she knew the school and the city too well not to get something out of it. "Might never leave, if I'm not careful." She laughed, talking about Xavier, maybe, he wasn't quite following. "Definitely was not plannin to get with no one," she said as she gave him directions to her hotel and told him to come by about midnight. "I saw you. You looked good. When we started talkin, you was, like, wide open: you wanted to know things. It was somethin bout you, I cain't call it. Maybe it was that name had me like that. I cain't even call it. I don't know why I'm talkin to you like this. Lord knows. But come see bout me tonight."

He looked at her, wanting her to repeat herself to make sure he hadn't misheard or imagined those words. He didn't even answer her question. Too good to be true, he was thinking to himself. Too good. But after the orientation and a little before midnight, he took her directions and came to the hotel. She'd paid for the room herself. It was small and cheap. But it was clean, and the bar downstairs served alcohol all day and night and did not check identification.

They sat on the hotel bed and drank. It was already too good to be true, this moment in time. But he didn't care. He wanted her totally. Halfway through his second glass, he brushed her locks out of the way and tucked his finger under the strap of the dress she was still wearing. It was a thin white dress, the kind that became translucent in the daytime from all the wet heat hanging in the air. Just watching her that day, seeing her ass through her dress bouncing while she walked, her breasts pressed up against the dress, moisture pooling around her nipples, he had imagined being with her. He had wanted her from the first moment he saw her.

The dress only had the one strap. On the opposite side, it was backless, and her hair ran down like a red waterfall, the only thing clothing her exposed shoulder and the naked feline curve of her back. He began to take down the lone strap, but then she pressed her lips against his hand. At first he thought she was kissing him, but then he felt the slight impress of her teeth, a soft bite. He drew his fingers back a little, in real surprise. Maybe that was when the wine spilled all over the bedsheets. She smiled and laughed at herself. Then, with impressive flexibility, she tucked her teeth underneath the strap and brought it away from her shoulder. Letting it fall, she eased out of her dress. She fell back against the headboard, rocking the bed. And she looked at him, soft, demure, waiting.

He took her up against the headboard, first with his eyes riveted on her, collapsing into her gorgeous body again and again. More than a few times, she had to draw him away from her, ask and tell him to keep going, because he was so satisfied with the beauty of her, of being inside her. The lights were turned off at some point. It was only sometime later that, in the darkness, his intensity returned: he turned her around. Her wild hair was in his teeth. He took her hands and clutched them to the headboard and that was when he saw her complicated, violent art, written upon her neck and along her shoulders. He remembered what it had felt like when he was an athlete, plunging into her, making her orgasm and tremble and go limp and come back again in love with the sheer challenge of their movement together.

He came on her and, laughing, she said something so deeply accented he had no idea what she had said. She rolled over on top of him, mixing the sweat and the wine and the cum on their skin and in the sheets. Too good to be true, he thought, but so good. He would need to cancel the trip to New York. No point in going now that his decision was made: Xavier. Released from doubt, he fell into the hard sleep that carried him to the morning's new world.

Touissant was still looking out the window, down Canal Street. His new world demanded a new story: he could smell the French Quarter in all its nasty might, strong unmistakable smells. Vomit. Piss. Pussy. It was the same Quarter the escaped Haitian ancestor must have come to after serving the rich mulattoes who could afford to escape so luxuriously from the rebellion in Port-au-Prince. After the docks and Place de Nègres, he would have found himself here, looking out at the same free and shackled space. No longer a slave, at this portal into a new world, every shade of humanity suddenly come vivid. The lover he eventually found on Canal Street was a cre-

ole who wanted for herself the darkest man proud of his color that
she could find. It was she who gave the family its name: Freeman.
Their daughter was Sabine. They lived as free blacks in a slave state.
A century later, the family still lived confined to the Negro hovels
of Central City, free within a cage. Touissant's great-granddad was
the first Freeman in a hundred years to walk the city like everything
within it was his for the having. He found a moneyed octoroon girl
who went around town as a white lady but who was actually mixed
with every race under a Louisiana sun and beautiful as daybreak. She
frightened all the sane men black and white in town and, knowing
him, his people warned against this rich, careless girl with the wild
spools of red hair and no common sense. But they did not know her.
This was a girl who deserved obsession. She knew how to take a man
body and mind and lead him off from whatever he had been before
knowledge of her, fascinate and seduce him and have him fighting
for her like she was his life. He was in love with her and she was
desirous of him. Meanwhile, a few wealthy white men decided that
even though, or perhaps because, they knew they couldn't handle her,
what they truly could not deal with was a black man involved with
anything lighter than a field nigger in summer. All warnings were
useless. Then even the black folks decided to keep their distance.
They dropped him from work crews and treated him as if he had
no name in the street. Eventually, they simply sold him out, labeled
him a radical Negro nationalist. By this point, he had stopped caring and now let himself be seen with his woman on her balconies
and leaving her gates in the mornings after their time together. It
was only as those forces more powerful than cautious black people
became involved that the risk of standing in the break between two
new worlds finally became too much for her to risk. She told him
violent men were laying for him and that she sensed her own death
in the still air, around quiet corners. His last night in New Orleans
in the Garden District villa where the girl was kept, he left a note
on a high mantel between her gem-lined brooches and her Rimbaud

explaining to whoever wanted his head, *We are in love & would elope but for it would get her killed as well as me & so despite of God who is a nigger from the fields commanding us to love each other you people will get your wish because I am gone.*

The way Touissant figured it, there was nothing to do after that letter but run for dear life.

Down on Canal, he saw the fleet of Asian girls from the night's orientation. They were very thin, with porcelain-delicate faces and incredible certainty as to their future education and careers and way of life. They were the kind of girls that, where he was from, everyone envied, everyone wanted. But he was becoming attracted in a completely different direction. Ocie was more than just a desirable willing girl to thrash around with in bed; she took him down inside of herself into a space both dark and lit, and once descended she stilled him and in the break that was her body she synthesized him, united him, even as they rocked away above in the physical world.

Touissant let the odors rise pungently through his sinuses. He felt himself ebbing and looked down at what was left of his erection. Hell. Out the window, a homeless man self-harnessed to three shopping carts filled with scrap metal struggled up Canal like a centaur. He was well behind the Asian girls.

"Can you believe our school is only a few minutes away? This a university town." Ocie laughed from behind his back. "Smells like folks."

She was standing there, right behind him. He wondered how she'd managed to get up and come across the room without him hearing her. He turned from the window and looked at her wonderingly. He wanted to ask how long she'd been standing behind him waiting for him to see her. She was looking straight into him, her eyes running through him. He thought again that maybe this whole trip and the evening with her and the morning now was more than reality and too good to be true. Maybe it was all in his head and his body was asleep somewhere else.

But the look she was giving him was hard and real as every black woman he'd ever known. The irony was, he didn't know her at all. She might be soft, or hard, or a lot of other things he knew nothing about. He would need to separate the figment that he knew her as from whoever she really was. In his mind, she stood where he stood between social worlds, but here she was standing not between societies but in front of him, in this hotel, in this moment. Tattoos dashed haphazardly across her brown skin, long dreadlocks fell in black vines before her eyes and high, gently curved cheekbones, and her big soft lips pouted in their nature, without trying to. She was a real girl, not a dream. And yet he didn't know her any more than he knew his family's real but unrecoverable history. But unlike that history, which was only stories now, the reality of it lost, he could still learn her and know her. He wanted to know her and her city and the totally unknown but recordable recoverable world.

Now he realized that she was no longer naked. When had she dressed? Just how dreamy-unaware was he? Touissant shook his head, confused, and looked around at his own passionately scattered clothes: since she was dressed already, maybe it was time he put his own fig leaves on. Maybe then they could go out into the world together.

Even outgoing, flirtatious Sanjay, who had invited her to movies and parties at least five times in the first few weeks of school, kept his distance. The Omega fraternity brothers who lounged on the benches catty-corner at the intersection between the long walkway running from the university bookstore all the way to the English Library and the canopied area outside the school commons did not hand her their flyers or try to chat her up. The iguana peeked up at them from the small blue blanket where Erycha held it and they stared back at it and at her like something in the universe was suddenly amiss. When she arrived at Dance Professor Krivoshopka's office to turn in the paper she had worked over so hard that the professor had complimented her on her thoroughness before she'd actually read it, the exchange was brief, distracted and awkward. Professor Krivoshopka kept stealing glances at Erycha's iguana, which Erycha had let loose from the folds of the blanket and placed on the office floor as soon as she entered. It was somewhere between its childhood and its maturity and was still, to Erycha's eye, rather small, even with all its scales and reptilian green and yellow patterns. It moved as slowly along the office floor as a sea turtle upon the ocean bottom.

"Those things eat flower petals, do they not?" the professor asked. She held Erycha's term paper in one hand, but seemed ready to toss it aside any second and go and defend the bouquet of roses that sat in a pretty vase in her windowsill, a bow wrapped around their long tall stems.

Their student–instructor relationship had gotten off to a bad start a few weeks back and had steadily worsened. For the term paper, Krivoshopka had suggested that Erycha write about *Creole Giselle*. The class was Introduction to Theory and Technique. *Creole Giselle*, or even regular old *Giselle*, could have been included in the course materials, but neither had, that Erycha could see. She asked Krivoshopka what it occurred to her to ask: if the whole class would be assigned the topic.

Krivoshopka had looked at her like an iguana had suddenly appeared balanced upon Erycha's head. That was when the idea occurred to her.

"Iguanas do eat flower petals," Erycha affirmed, "but this one's just a baby. Plus, I think she's scared of you."

The professor alternated her gaze between the term paper and the animal.

"Iguanas," Erycha offered, by way of assurance, "tend to be timid and cautious in unfamiliar environments."

"Hopefully," the professor said, without the slightest trust in that assessment. She swept past Erycha, placing her essay upon a free-standing stack of books and then quickly made for the windowsill.

The university was not the Champs-Elysées and her iguana was no cheetah, but her created spectacle was achieving what Erycha figured was her desired effect. Then she reflected that she wasn't exactly sure what her desires were. She wasn't sure what she wanted out of the iguana except that after moving into Mazi's place all by herself she'd found herself lonelier than she had expected she'd feel, and the iguana was quieter than any dog and more consistent than any cat. It rested almost all hours of the day and when it did travel between rooms, it did so slowly and silently. She wasn't sure what she wanted out of Sanjay or the fraternity brothers either, or from Professor Krivoshopka and the Theory and Technique course. She didn't really know what she wanted from her college experience. As she walked back across the campus with the iguana wriggling in the blanket, peering at passersby, she imagined it symbolized something; but she knew, even as she imagined differently, that life was short on symbols. The iguana was not a symbol any more than she herself was. It was just an animal, like everything else living, breathing, eating and sleeping, no more symbolic than she was symbolic, or than Mazi or Ricky were symbols of anything. Things were just alive, and figured out what they wanted as they went along.

She came to her car and placed the iguana in the passenger's seat, where she could keep an eye on it. She put the key in the ignition and the old Datsun swayed like a bucket over-full with gurgling water. She imagined the Datsun's engine and valves and oil and water simply spilling out right there in the university parking lot for all to see. She imagined cleaning up the mess on her hands and knees, a maid tasked with unfamiliar objects and circumstances. Once the car steadied itself, though, it did not spill. She drove away slowly, out of Riverside and north toward Highland and San Bernardino.

As she drove down Barton Road, favoring the streets over the freeway, she began to notice the landscape in a way she hadn't before. Now, everything had its accumulated history, its purpose and a story behind it. She could see a vacant lot that she had never noticed before and see, implied by its vacancy, the life and death of the establishments that had been built and demolished there, as well as the hopes and wishes of those who had brought it into being and taken it away. She could see in things the future, too. When she saw a mess of dry scrub she thought about the fire that would one day kindle from that collection of twigs and desiccated weeds and destroy whatever found itself in the fire's path. Nothing existed simply anymore. Everything was wrapped in past and future. Dance was the same way, which was what her term paper for Krivoshopka's class had attempted to explain: she could not, she had written, engage dance without the complications of the culture that surrounded it, not to mention the culture that surrounded her. Moreover, that the culture of dance, be it ballet or modern or anything in between, save for step squad, was so different from the culture that surrounded her only complicated things all the more. The point of the paper was that she could not simply dance the way she had when she was a child and her parents would argue and she would use their inattention to dance away as far as her body and imagination could take her. She had risen or fallen into an entirely more complicated consciousness wherein movement was a mental, historical, risk-laden venture.

But where is there room for innocence? Krivoshopka would ask. Dance is a human element, as much as the chemicals are made of elements. Where is there room purely for dance and purely for joy?

Erycha would have no answer to that question.

Her mother was no friendlier to the iguana than Professor Krivoshopka had been, but at least she was used to it. She didn't balk when Erycha let it slither around the living room. She didn't watch it out the corner of her eye as the iguana made its way to a window and stared at the foliage outside. The first time she'd brought the iguana over, Erycha assured her mother that it wasn't going to try to claw through the glass pane, and that when it looked through the window it was no different than a dog poised before a TV screen or partition of clear glass contemplating some object of its desire. Erycha refrained from adding that at least she hadn't brought over a cheetah, now *that* might be more trouble. That last part left out, the assurance was enough. Now, she handed Erycha the portion of the plantain money meant for Erycha's dad. "I think he's down at the Mission. You got time to do this?"

Erycha knew her mother already had the answer to that question in her very arrival. "Yeah. Enough."

"Well, just don't blame me if you have to go huntin around a lil bit to find him. You know how he is."

Erycha knew quite well how he was. He'd been working at the Mission off and on in various temporary roles since before she could remember. All the times she'd gone there looking for him, he'd never once been easy to find. He was always busy behind some closed door listening to someone who needed to talk, or fixing a pipe; or he was hidden in plain sight beneath a table resecuring its legs; or he was visible in glimpses through the swinging door into the Mission kitchen where he sometimes cleaned dishes. And other times he simply wasn't there. Always there was something he knew how to do, whether it was fix something that needed the repair, or disappear. She took the three $5 bills her mother held out in her hand.

The Datsun shifted beneath her as she drove to the Mission. She counted the potholes between her parents' place and G Street: fifteen potholes. She hit three, not noticing them until they were under her wheels. The iguana's belly and jowls pulsed with each violent movement. She also counted two dead birds, three mutilated squirrels, and some other animal that she couldn't identify out the corner of her eye as the car doddered along. She counted the sideways stop signs, the fallen junk from the day-laborer vans lying undisposed of in the street and the tire tread fallen in huge black spools like so much dead black skin.

Eventually, she came to the Mission, parked the car. Here, for what it was worth, stood her first memory of fear: Sunday mornings when she was a child, she and her mother would walk along G Street shoulder-to-shoulder with the padres and the large Mexican families three and four generations deep crowding the sidewalk and spilling onto the black asphalt street. Erycha could still remember the first time, how her mother had stopped both of them in their tracks (because she was holding Erycha's hand and guiding her movement). After a moment, that grip loosened and Erycha could remember her mother sighing and then mumbling, "Well, I'll be."

Erycha stared at the graffiti, its fine lines and fearful details. Her shoulders seized and her breath caught in between her throat and a word.

The graffiti was incredible. Three men were depicted. The first man splayed crucified, the wreath of thorns ringing his bloody forehead, his distended ribs defined against his chest, his body riddled with bullet holes and leaking syringes driven into his wrists, his skin Chicano brown. At his sides, a sacrificial girl wound her exploited body around a second cross, her tattered white dress withering from her; and a boy in an orange prison jumpsuit, his face gang-tattooed, his shoulders fallen, was pictured rigged upon the final of the three crosses. The sky that backgrounded the crosses was a writhing red blue fire and above the fire stood a steeple cross. A tablet affixed to the wall of the church entranceway read

THESE CROSSES REPRESENT THE BURDENS
SHARED BY OUR COMMUNITY. THEY WERE CONCEIVED
& PAINTED BY THE CHILDREN OF THE MISSION.

Over the years, Erycha learned not to be scared of the raw iconography that fronted the Mission. Now she let the iguana eye the mural for a moment, then she entered the Lord's doors, which stayed unlocked and open into night, when the overflow of men from the Mission's homeless shelter massed in the rugged splintering wooden church pews until the capacity limitations were reached.

It was Wednesday now, early afternoon. The place was so empty she could hear her heels grinding at old floorboards that moaned back at her. She passed through the church and into the main hall of the Mission. Down this corridor, each door announced its purpose within its walls with a large placard nailed above the door frame: The G Street Clinic; Adolescent Healthcare Program; Immigrant Cen-

ter; Adult Center; St. Martin's Place; Free Community Breakfast &
Dinner Program; After-School Children's Zone; Orphanage; College Volunteer-Training Program; The Men's Shelter. She knew her
father had worked as staff in most every part of the Mission's small
but extensive campus. But she wasn't sure where he was working now.

She didn't want to spend all afternoon looking for him, but things
were never simple with her dad. There was always some catch, some
problem or excuse for why his duties either were resolved too slowly
or didn't get done at all. Working at the Mission, he had mended
furniture and painted walls and cleaned rooms and filed papers, had
seen after HIV+ persons and homeless men. But that didn't make
him reliable.

"My dad?" Erycha asked, letting the G Street Clinic double doors
swing closed behind her. "Y'all seen Morris today?"

"No se," the overweight receptionist answered from across her
desk. "Aye, you guys, anybody see Morris?" She called behind her.
Then she noticed the iguana and paused. She stared at it, and it hid
from her, diving into the blanket folds. None of the staff said anything. Apparently, there were no answers for Erycha's question.

"Lo siento," the receptionist offered, "sorry."

Erycha felt a twinge in her stomach, a brief hunger pain.

At the door leading to the Adolescent Healthcare Program wing
of campus, a hanging placard noted that a study by a research group
found San Bernardino to be "the least kid-friendly city in America."
She thought about how Ricky used to send lil one to the Mission to
get his teeth checked at the Healthcare Program and, other times,
when funds were low, how he sent the boy to get the meals that were
served in baskets one door down, one wing over, at the Free Community Breakfast & Dinner Program. Sometimes Erycha would

notice that Ricky brought home a basket with a fresh fish dinner inside it, or healthy deep-colored organic vegetables, or good lean cuts of chicken and pork, categories of food that clearly weren't on the menu at McDonald's or sold at FoodMax, and she would wonder if he was visiting the Mission his own self. But it wasn't her place to ask questions that might make him feel lesser-than.

Central City had always been there, in the background of her life. When she checked for her father at the After-School Children's Zone, she walked in and saw the little stage and the rusted metal chairs rowed neatly before the stage, and she remembered that this was where she first saw local step squads dance and first learned that black people didn't care a thing for ballet. This was where she met Rick, where he caught her attention with his dumb little raps. She remembered how he fed off that attention, how he started to feel like he was something more than a poor kid in a poor city that no one anywhere even knew existed.

She didn't even try the Immigrant Center, where you needed to speak Spanish to be helpful, or St. Martin's, where folks with HIV got counseling and their check-ups and antiretrovirals. She remembered her father telling her that he did work at Martin's for a minute, how he spent patient time listening to the HIV+ street prostitutes talk about their lives. He might be there, but she wasn't up to looking in.

She came to the Men's Shelter. She glanced at the placard over the door, which she had memorized some time ago.

THE MISSION HAS COMMITTED TO THE
FORGOTTEN MEN OF THIS CITY:
WE WORK TO RESURRECT THEM ON
EARTH AND IN OUR TIME.

She knew he was here. She had figured from the start that this was probably where she'd find him. By the way he talked about the Shelter, she could tell he liked playing cards with the homeless old heads and talking shit with the impoverished vocational school students much more than any of the other work he was called to at the Mission. Erycha remembered the winter when the Mission management had nearly decided to close the Shelter because they couldn't afford to heat its several rooms and partitions. The mood her father fell into was bad: a lot of rambling about the Pacific Gas & Electric kingdom and the cost of living and how cheap life would get on the streets in the wintertime.

She walked inside and saw him. He was huddled amongst a group of men overlooking like hovering helicopters the craps game that they guarded and contested at the same time. She heard the familiar talk, the numbers called and hands hitting the floor each time the dice did. Erycha felt something hot and resentful go up her spine and radiate out along her limbs. She wanted to turn around and walk out of the Mission right that minute. Give the $15 to the first homeless person I see, she thought, which'll take three seconds, tops. Then leave and go about my business. Hell, I'm hungry; I should spend this money on some sustenance.

She felt the money, sharp-edged and crinkled, in her back pocket.

"Erycha."

She glared without meaning to.

"E-girl. You here so soon." Her dad strolled happily toward her. Fresh from the craps game, his shoulders were set back the way men set their shoulders when they feel good and confident. "Thought y'all might be sellin them plantains still."

"Nah. I was over at the college. Had to turn in a paper. She just asked me to come get this money to bring it to you." She reached in her back pocket.

"How's that comin, by the way?"

"How's what comin?" She paused and looked at him questioningly.

Fifteen dollars, she knew, wasn't going to change the world. Maybe she should just give in and move on. She was wrestling that decision back and forth in her head, letting it toss her across a two-cornered space, but now he was changing the subject—

"School," he said abruptly. "Your studies. How's your classes? I know you takin English, computer science, po-litical science an' dance, right?"

She smiled despite herself. She hadn't thought that he knew much more about her studies than that they existed, that they happened to be happening. That he actually had memorized her class-load gave her pause.

"How's all that goin?" He rephrased the question.

She told him the particulars of her English 1B, Introduction to Computer Science, and Political Science 10: Pre-Columbian History of the Americas courses. She told him what her grade reports stated, the assignments that she had completed and was working on, the names and defining characteristics of her professors. The English and computer science classes were staffed by graduate students only a few years older than herself. The politics class was taught by an eccentric scholar who had spent the past year in the Andes and passed out cocoa leaves before class. Then she came to her dance course. She didn't know what to say. She saw by the light in his eyes he was about to ask her about it specifically. Give him credit, girl; he does listen and he does care and he is good to me, still and all.

"I know you was lookin forward to that dance class, though. With that Russian instructor. She been showin you what she know?"

Erycha nodded. "But we're not dancin so much," she finally managed. "We write, mostly."

"Write? In dance class?"

"In college, it's always some term paper."

"I know it's a lotta writin in college, but damn. How you even s'posed to write about dance?"

"Good question. I don't really know. What I'm tryin to tell her is that, well, it's complicated. I don't really know how to write about dance, but I'm comin to think it's all I can do." She looked into her father's eyes. He didn't understand but at least she could trust that he would listen and maybe try to sort through it later after the talk and after his game, when he went home and it was quiet late at night. "That's not how it was meant to be, nahright. Dance is action, not thought; not somethin to be thought about, or talked about, or written about—all that stuff just makes it impure—except that for me, an' I think for anyone comin from where I do, we gotta talk it out first, get right with it in some way that makes sense to us. How we came to college just to dance with these rich white girls an' love things that never existed in the one world we knew before we started to dance." Erycha supposed when her dad heard the word "dance" he was thinking more along the lines of James Brown or Usher than anything Krivoshopka would teach. Assumptions sealed her off wherever she moved. And the otherness that confined her came in now, a tidal flow forming around her waves of pressure and restriction. "It was never pure for me."

"But how you gon' have fun wit it if all you get to do is write an' rack yo' brain on it?"

That, Erycha conceded without saying so, was another good question for which she had no answer. Her dad, in all his time on earth, more than twice her years, had never had to cross the lines that she had had to. She might as well be speaking to Krivoshopka. Neither of them had ever had to face the fact that something no matter how beautiful could become countlessly complex, a million shards and partial truths shattered on the ground.

This was the most focused and serious she could remember being with him. He was so careless with everything in life, Erycha had never thought to talk to him about the thoughts that stirred her mind and complicated her passions. Even now, though she knew he had disengaged from his friends and was listening to her, it still seemed strange. She didn't really know how to share herself with him. She hesitated over the next thing she wanted to say to help him understand what she meant when she said that dance was never pure and was trapped within all the writing and the talking and the thinking about it. Her eyes started to wander worse than a runaway child. She tried to meet his gaze, only to find she was looking all around the Shelter. She felt a space opening between the two of them, a gap that had no distance or shape or feel, just space. She saw him hesitating and she hesitated, too. She was on the edge of an unknown, afraid to look over.

Then the iguana sprang against her chest, the hard ridges of its head moving like a file across her breast. It didn't hurt, but it startled her.

"What the—." Her dad sprang back.

Erycha laughed, not knowing what else to do. The iguana kept twitching its head this way and that. She relaxed her hold on the blanket and after a moment, the animal became more still, though its enormous eyes continued to take ranging inventory of the large shelter space.

"Jesus, girl. You ain't tell me you was bringin that thing in here." He only slowly regained his composure, one limb at a time. He planted his feet and stuck his hands in his pockets. "Bad nuff it be gettin free reign in our home an' nary a peep from Evelyn. Why you gotta bring that thing down here?" He sniffed in harsh disapproval. "In a blanket, no less."

"Because," Erycha said, remembering a phrase that had never worked on her back in the day. Now it was a placeholder for a thought that was coming to her, but too slowly for her to articulate it the way that she wanted to. What she was thinking then, but couldn't yet tell her dad, was that she had finally realized what her attachment to the weird little animal was—its otherness. Even after the idea was fully formed in her head, it would be years before she could meld into her life as something more than an idea in the air or words on a page. For now, the iguana was something else, a different and isolated creature.

Her dad laughed. "Remember when I tried to get over on you with that line? Because—*Because what?* Because ain't no answer, girl. That one don't even work on lil kids, let alone a grown man!"

"You tried it. Why cain't I?" she challenged playfully.

They both laughed.

"Now, can I get you to gimme that money, girl?"

She handed over the three crumpled bills. Her mind was chasing after the eloquence that could express that moment of recognition when the iguana had lifted its head. "You know if you don't win, she will be mad at you. I will be, too."

"I'm not *even playin* wit these cats, E," he insisted.

Erycha realized that this was hardly a pledge not to gamble, only not to lose. As backward as it seemed, she knew that this dance was part of her as well, part of the strange routine that she was accustomed to. She found herself lilting and then giving in; there was no changing her dad's ways or the ways of her given community any more than she would ever change. She was both a part of it, and wholly separate. She was passionate and cold-hearted, acceptant and recalcitrant, a severe judge and a consenting child. She saw the contradictions of which she was composed and didn't know what to do or say. She remembered, or felt again, what had come over her that first night she spent alone at the apartment that had been Mazi's, but now was hers. Then, it had been a slow progress, now it was a fast but familiar feeling: she had been very hungry and hadn't been able to think about anything else but food for whole periods of time. Then something at her core, which she couldn't extract from her being, softened. Then, even faster, whatever it was went radiating out across her limbs with warm relaxation. The hunger was still there, its press more abstract but no less real and present. She was in the second night.

"I should go," she told him.

"You always welcome to stay," he said.

Walking up the campus's main corridor, the multiple wings of the Mission's design flanked her path like so many sad but real, undeniable possibilities. The iguana fell still as a sleeping child in Erycha's arms and against her chest. It disappeared within the blanket, hiding her otherness as well as its own, for the moment at least. Her hungry insides rippled in a sharp acid ballet. A hunger pain more demanding and persuasive than the earlier twinges she'd felt. She remembered the third night in the apartment by herself. She had thought through her options then just as she was doing now. There were taquerias all up and down G Street. Food was forever abundant. But both then and now she had ceded the money that she had had to the family pot. She considered returning to campus, but knew if she went there she would have to ask someone for their meal card, probably have to flirt with Sanjay or some other random boy. Her stomach turned a little sour.

In the apartment that night her mind and body had tired of hunger and had fallen peaceful and still in a deprivation something like dying. Now an old opposition within her fell and died, and it came to her, an acceptance where before she wouldn't have tolerated this to even enter her mind, like allowing herself this one particular concession to circumstance would have broken her someway she couldn't even put words to; it was something that even when lil one and Ricky and in a lean moment even Mazi gave in and put their hand out, she would shake her head and turn away and look at a wall or go into another room; something even though it was just a small simple little letting go, she had sworn on her mother's name to God she would never do: through the doors of the Free Community Breakfast & Dinner Program, Erycha went asking for a basket.

Acknowledgments

Peace and blessings to the entire Heyday family, especially the wonderful Sylvia Lindsteadt, Gayle Wattawa and Malcolm Margolin. I also want to bless up Jeanne Wakatsuki-Houston for establishing the James D. Houston Award in honor of her husband and as a vehicle for publishing unestablished writers like myself. Your efforts, combined with those of Heyday, are remarkable. As for my little novel, the conferral of this award upon it is the great honor of my professional life.

My teachers have helped me more than I can describe. Susan Straight is the greatest teacher I have ever known, and I am immeasurably grateful for her endless energy, passion, commitment and critique. Victor LaValle, whom I studied under at Mills College, thankfully purged this story's worst pages. Gloria Loomis's suggestions also aided in the reclamation of this manuscript: thanks to both of you for seeing its potential and urging me to improve it.

I want also to note the work of Rudy Lewis at nathanielturner .com, Ken Robidoux at *Connotation Press* and C. Leigh McInnis with *Black Magnolias* literary journal for seeing enough value in the unfinished forms of some of these chapters to publish my work. Thanks also to Andrew Tonkovich for advice proffered on this and other manuscripts of mine. This novel has been a long time in the making. Melanie, thank you for reading when this was but unformed clay. EJ, Laleh and Nayomi, thanks to each of you. I look forward to lifelong literary friendships with each of you. Hilary, thanks especially for the experiences in modern dance that you opened me to.

Taj and Ayori and April Marie Smith, I feel that in some way Erycha's journey is yours. Thank you, thank you, thank you.

Much gratitude to Faron Roberts and Phenix Books, the only black bookstore between Vegas and L.A., an E Street institution; I am so fortunate that Phenix existed when I was seventeen and searching. And let me, lastly, acknowledge two good brothers now passed on: Dr. Lindon Barrett of UCs Irvine and Riverside, and Reggie Lockett, the poet laureate of West Oakland. They wrote. They taught. They are remembered.

About the Author

Keenan Norris teaches English and African-American Literature and helps conduct the Affirm program at Evergreen Valley College. His work has appeared in the *Santa Monica, Green Mountains* and *Evansville Reviews, Connotation Press, Inlandia: A Literary Journey through California's Inland Empire* and *BOOM: A Journal of California.* He is also the editor of Scarecrow Press's upcoming collection of critical essays, *Street Lit.* He lives in the San Francisco Bay Area.

James D. Houston Award Fund

Heyday wishes to thank the following individuals, foundations, and corporations for their generous support of the James D. Houston Award.

Anonymous; Barbara Adair; Dugan Aguilar; Linda Allen; James J. Baechle; Tandy Beal and Jonathan Scoville; M. Melanie Beene; Ralph Benson; Edwin Bernbaum; Claire Biancalana; Rita and Thomas Bottoms; Roberta Bristol; Julianne Burton-Carvajal; Gail Canyon Sam; Bessie Chin; Lawrence Coates; Kathleen Croughan; Peter Dahl; H. Dwight Damon; Sylvia De Trinidad; John and Harriet Deck; Sandra Dijkstra; George and Kathleen Diskant; Amy Doherty; Laurel Douglass; Paul and Charlene Douglass; Glenn J. Farris; Liudmila Finney; Judith Flanders; Rebecca Foster; R. Dennis Fritzinger; Maria Gitin; Jan Goggans; Hilary Goldstine; Jane Gregorius; Alice Guild; Charles Haas; Joell Hallowell; Masaru and Marcia Hashimoto; Gerald and Jan Haslam; Hawaii Sons, Inc.; The Brian and Patricia A. Herman Fund at Community Foundation Santa Cruz County; Jack Hicks; Carla Hills; Donna Hoenig-Couch; George Hong; G. Scott Hong Charitable Trust; D. Tomi Kobara; Arnold Kotler; Michael Kowalewski; Joe M. Lamb; Elinor Langer; Jacqeline and Homer Lohr; Laura Louis; Susan Maresco; Judy McAfee and John Mikols; Mary McGrath; Virginia and David McGuire; Joyce Milligan; Clare Morris; Scott Morrison; Nam Hee Mun; Victoria Myers; James and Carlin Naify; Thad Nodine and Shelby Graham; Regina Ockelmann; Rodney A. Ohtani; Charlotte Painter; Theresa Park; Gerri Pedesky; Daniel and Judith Phillips; Kathleen Marie Pouls; Madeleine Provost; James Quay, in memory of Jeff Lustig; Richard Reinhardt; James and Janet Reynolds; Fred Setterberg and Ann Van Steenberg; Victoria Shoemaker; Susan Snyder and Richard Neidhardt; Robin Somers; Tom Sourisseau Jr.; Byron and Lee Stookey; Craig Strang and Persis Karim; Barbara Tannenbaum; John C. Thorland; Andrew Tonkovich; Kerry Tremain; Gail Tsukiyama; Eugene Unger; Daniel Urbach; Louis Warren; M.C. Winkley; Jane Yamashiro; Andrea Yee; Stan Yogi and David Carroll; and Ruth S. Young.

HEYDAY

into California

About Heyday

Heyday is an independent, nonprofit publisher and unique cultural institution. We promote widespread awareness and celebration of California's many cultures, landscapes, and boundary-breaking ideas. Through our well-crafted books, public events, and innovative outreach programs we are building a vibrant community of readers, writers, and thinkers.

Thank You

It takes the collective effort of many to create a thriving literary culture. We are thankful to all the thoughtful people we have the privilege to engage with. Cheers to our writers, artists, editors, storytellers, designers, printers, bookstores, critics, cultural organizations, readers, and book lovers everywhere!

We are especially grateful for the generous funding we've received for our publications and programs during the past year from foundations and hundreds of individual donors. Major supporters include:

Anonymous (3); Acorn Naturalists; Alliance for California Traditional Arts; Arkay Foundation; Judy Avery; James J. Baechle; Paul Bancroft III; BayTree Fund; S. D. Bechtel, Jr. Foundation; Barbara Jean and Fred Berensmeier; Berkeley Civic Arts Program and Civic Arts Commission; Joan Berman; Buena Vista Rancheria/Jesse Flyingcloud Pope Foundation; John Briscoe; Lewis and Sheana Butler; California Civil Liberties Public Education Program; Cal Humanities; California Indian Heritage Center Foundation; California State Library; California State Parks Foundation; Keith Campbell Foundation; Candelaria Fund; John and Nancy Cassidy Family Foundation, through Silicon Valley Community Foundation; The Center for California Studies; Charles Edwin Chase; Graham Chisholm; The Christensen Fund; Jon Christensen; Community Futures Collective; Compton Foundation; Creative Work Fund;

Lawrence Crooks; Nik Dehejia; Frances Dinkelspiel and Gary Wayne; The Durfee Foundation; Earth Island Institute; Eaton Kenyon Fund of the Sacramento Region Community Foundation; Euclid Fund at the East Bay Community Foundation; Foothill Resources, Ltd.; Furthur Foundation; The Fred Gellert Family Foundation; Fulfillco; The Wallace Alexander Gerbode Foundation; Nicola W. Gordon; Wanda Lee Graves and Stephen Duscha; David Guy; The Walter and Elise Haas Fund; Coke and James Hallowell; Stephen Hearst; Historic Resources Group; Sandra and Charles Hobson; G. Scott Hong Charitable Trust; Donna Ewald Huggins; Humboldt Area Foundation; James Irvine Foundation; Claudia Jurmain; Kendeda Fund; Marty and Pamela Krasney; Guy Lampard and Suzanne Badenhoop; Christine Leefeldt, in celebration of Ernest Callenbach and Malcolm Margolin's friendship; LEF Foundation; Thomas Lockard; Thomas J. Long Foundation; Judith and Brad Lowry-Croul; Kermit Lynch Wine Merchant; Michael McCone; Nion McEvoy and Leslie Berriman; Michael Mitrani; Moore Family Foundation; Michael J. Moratto, in memory of Ernest L. Cassel; Richard Nagler; National Endowment for the Arts; National Wildlife Federation; Native Cultures Fund; The Nature Conservancy; Nightingale Family Foundation; Northern California Water Association; Pacific Legacy, Inc.; The David and Lucile Packard Foundation; Patagonia, Inc.; PhotoWings; Alan Rosenus; The San Francisco Foundation; San Manuel Band of Mission Indians; Greg Sarris; Savory Thymes; Sonoma Land Trust; Stone Soup Fresno; Roselyne Chroman Swig; Swinerton Family Fund; Thendara Foundation; Sedge Thomson and Sylvia Brownrigg; TomKat Charitable Trust; The Roger J. and Madeleine Traynor Foundation; Lisa Van Cleef and Mark Gunson; Patricia Wakida; Whole Systems Foundation; Wild by Nature, Inc.; John Wiley & Sons, Inc.; Peter Booth Wiley and Valerie Barth; Bobby Winston; Dean Witter Foundation; The Work-in-Progress Fund of Tides Foundation; and Yocha Dehe Community Fund.

Getting Involved
To learn more about our publications, events, membership club, and other ways you can participate, please visit www.heydaybooks.com.